I ... writing authentic ...
I ... ..n my first novel, a historical, when I was sixteen, but
lif... ...erailed me a bit when I started suffering with Ankylosing
Sp... ...dylitis, so I didn't complete a novel until after I was
thirty when I put it on my to do before I'm forty list. Now
I love getting caught up in the lives and traumas of my
cha... ...ters, and I'm so thrilled to be giving my characters life
in ... ...rs' imaginations, especially when readers tell me
th... read the characters just as I've tried to portray them.

Y... follow me on Twitter @JaneLark.

The Lost Love of a Soldier

JANE LARK

A division of HarperCollins*Publishers*
www.harpercollins.co.uk

HarperImpulse an imprint of
HarperCollins*Publishers* Ltd
77–85 Fulham Palace Road
Hammersmith, London W6 8JB

www.harpercollins.co.uk

A Paperback Original 2014

First published in Great Britain in ebook format by HarperImpulse 2014

Cover images © Shutterstock.com

Jane Lark asserts the moral right
to be identified as the author of this work

A catalogue record for this book is
available from the British Library

ISBN: 9780008105761

This novel is entirely a work of fiction.
The names, characters and incidents portrayed in it are
the work of the author's imagination. Any resemblance to
actual persons, living or dead, events or localities is
entirely coincidental.

Automatically produced by Atomik ePublisher from Easypress

This is an unusual story for me. I chose to write the prequel to The Illicit Love of a Courtesan - The Lost Love of a Soldier - because the readers who love the series asked for a prequel. But when I decided to write this, I realised I had to follow elements of a real story.

I'd made the decision when I wrote The Illicit Love of a Courtesan to use the title of a real regiment who fought in the battle of Waterloo. I chose the 52nd (Oxfordshire) Regiment of Foot. So when I began this story my first task was to research the 52nd, to find out how they came to be there, and what part they played in the battle. The 52nd returned from The Peninsular War to Britain, in the summer of 1814, two hundred years ago to the year of this novel, and therefore this became the window of opportunity for my fictional characters, Paul and Ellen, to meet.

I dedicate this story to all those who serve in the military, and the families who support them.

Jane Lark

Chapter One

"Lady Eleanor…" A gentle almost-knock struck the door as Ellen's maid whispered through it, as if she feared someone hearing her, even though she knocked on the servants' entrance to Ellen's bedchamber.

Ellen's father, the Duke of Pembroke, would not be near the servants' stairway.

"Pippa?"

The handle turned. The door opened.

"My Lady, a letter." Pippa held it out as she came in. "It is from the Captain."

"From Paul?" Ellen swept across the room, her heart clenching as she moved. Paul was the reason the whole house had slipped into tiptoeing and whispering. He'd caused her father's recent rage, and now everyone was terrified of causing offence and becoming the next focus for her father's anger.

If it was rude to snatch it from Pippa's hand, then love had made Ellen rude.

Her fingers shook as she broke open the blank seal and unfolded the paper.

My love.

Holding the letter in one hand, the fingertips of her other touched his words.

My love… He'd only said those words for the first time a week ago, and yet she'd hoped to hear them for weeks, perhaps for months. *Paul.* An image of him dressed in his uniform crept into her head, his scarlet coat with its bright brass buttons hugging the contours of his chest. She loved the way he smiled so easily, and the way it glowed in his blue eyes. But he was a man of strength and vibrancy; life and emotion burned in his eyes too, and power cut into his features.

He was a breathing statue of Adonis; his beauty more like art than reality.

Her gaze dropped back to his words.

I'm sorry. Your father has said, no, and by now I am sure you know it. I tried Ellen, but he would not hear me out. He said I am not good enough for you. He would not even consider me. He will not have his daughter become the wife of a mere captain, no matter that I am the son of an earl. He wishes you to be a duchess. He will never consider a sixth son who must earn his living. He actually had the audacity to tell me even if I had been my brother and the heir, he would not agree to our match.

But I refuse to give you up, and I must leave for America soon. My love. I want you with me. Will you come with me without his acceptance? Will you run away with me? We can leave at night and head for Gretna; elope. You know how much I feel for you. You know I cannot bear to let you go. Remember my love burns brighter than the sun for you. You are my life, Ellen. Come. Send word via your maid if you will. My heart shall ache until I can look into your topaz eyes again.

All my love, forever and ever yours,
Paul

Tears dripped onto the paper, blurring the words. She loved him too. They'd met in June. He'd come for a house party with his father, the Earl of Craster, and his brothers. His family had come to talk politics, but Paul had only come to entertain himself.

Ellen looked up from his letter, wiping away her tears. "I will write back, Pippa. You will take the letter for me?" The maid hovered near the door watching.

When Paul had come here, even though Ellen was not officially out and allowed to socialise in high-society, her father had agreed to her joining the party.

She'd been sixteen then.

She'd eaten with the men during the day and entertained them in the evening, playing the pianoforte and singing while they stood or sat in groups and talked. But in those weeks Paul had singled her out. He'd sat next to her for several meals, and turned the music sheets for her when she'd played; his thigh brushing against hers as they'd shared a narrow stool.

She'd known her father's intention had been for her to draw the interest of the Duke of Argyle, but she didn't want to marry an old man. Paul had talked to her and made her laugh, whispering as she played, while the other men talked politics and struck bargains about the room.

They'd communicated through the servants since the beginning of August.

Paul had befriended a groom while he'd stayed here and the man took letters back and forth, passing them through Pippa.

Ellen's conscience whispered as she turned to open her writing desk, which stood on a small table before the window.

The very first time she'd seen Paul, before they'd even been introduced, something had pulled her gaze to him.

Perhaps it was his scarlet coat which made him stand out among her father's political friends, or his dark blond hair, which swept sideways across his brow, as though his fingers had combed through it. Or his blue eyes which had looked back at her. Or the dimple which dented his cheek when he'd smiled before looking away.

When they were introduced, her stomach had somersaulted, and when he'd kissed the back of her fingers her knees had weakened. It was as if she'd known him a lifetime as he'd held her gaze.

She'd told her sister, Penny, she wished to marry the soldier, not the old Duke.

She should not have written to Paul though, not without permission… Thrusting the guilt aside, she put his letter down to start her own, sitting before a blank sheet of paper.

Paul.

My father has shut me in my room. I am to stay here until I agree to marry the Duke of Argyle. You would not believe how cruel he was about you. I know he is a Duke, but I have three sisters who may marry who he wishes. I choose to marry a captain. Yes, I will elope with you. Only tell me when! Send word as quickly as you can. I do not wish to stay here another hour even.

I cannot wait to see you. Come and fetch me.

Love, love and more love.

Yours and yours always,

Ellen

Ellen blotted her words, then sealed the letter, dropping a little melted wax onto the folded paper. Then she blew on it to cool it, and waved it in the air. She finished by kissing the still warm wax, before she gave the letter to Pippa.

"Be careful, do not let anyone see you pass it to Eric."

"I shan't, my Lady. Did you wish me to bring you something to eat? I can fetch something from cook."

"No, do not take the risk, Pippa. If my father's steward or the housekeeper discovered it you would lose your post and I will never forgive myself. I can manage. It is just a little hunger." *It shall not be for long…*

"Then is there anything else, my Lady?"

"Nothing, Pippa. Go."

The maid bobbed a curtsy, then left, the servants' door closing behind her.

Ellen walked over to a chair by the fire and looked into the flames. Her fingers curled into fists as she held on to her excitement.

It was Christmas in a week, mid-winter.

She picked up the handkerchief she was embroidering for her youngest sister, Sylvia, and sat down, then took out the needle intending to sew again, but her hand dropped as anxiety twisted and spun in her stomach. She'd felt muddled for weeks – quivery inside. She'd been confused ever since Paul had left in the summer.

Before he'd gone he'd slipped a note into a book he'd read aloud to her. It had said simply, *may I write to you?* She'd nodded, her heart blooming with relief that his leaving would not be an end to their friendship.

His first letter had come by mail, but her father checked the post and when he'd spotted a letter to her he'd read it and returned it to Paul, telling him not to write. There had been nothing condemning in it, no words of love, only facts and stories, but still she'd endured a severe interview, and her father hadn't even known she'd given Paul permission to write.

Paul's second letter, telling her about his first, had come via Eric and Pippa. It had still been merely talk, but he'd said he'd taken lodgings nearby for a week or two so he might establish a way to communicate with her. Her heart beat rapidly even at the memory of that first letter. She'd thought, surely if a man would go to such lengths, then his feelings were more than mere friendship.

A week later she'd ridden out with Penny and Eric, and met Paul briefly. They'd walked through the woods at the edge of her father's land, near his tall red-bricked folly, and they'd all laughed. Laughter was a rare thing in her family. Only when she was with her sisters, somewhere private, did they ever find moments to laugh.

Paul had gone to London after that, but he'd continued writing. He'd mailed his letters to Eric, who'd carried them to Pippa. For weeks they'd been conversational, but in November their tone had changed. He'd spoken of the summer, and said pretty things about the colour of her eyes and hair, and the fullness of her lips.

A week ago he'd written to say he'd hired a room at a local inn and asked to meet her. She'd ridden out with Eric, and not even told Penny, fearing her father's reaction.

She'd known what she'd wished Paul to say. Over the months since the summer she'd fallen in love with him.

Numerous hours had been wasted ever since she'd met him, lying on Penny's bed, or her own, whispering about Paul. When Penny had met Paul, he'd smiled his charming smile and bowed in his regimental way. Penny had been enchanted, and Ellen had loved him even more for being nice to her sister.

Rebecca and Sylvia were too young to be confidents, yet she did love all her sisters, but now, if she went with Paul, she'd have to leave them behind. Loss shot through her heart like an arrow passing through it.

A tear escaped. She wiped it away.

When they'd met a week ago, Paul had taken her hands and said he loved her, that there was no other woman he wanted, or would want. He'd been ordered to go to America and wanted her with him. He'd asked for her agreement to speak to her father. She'd given it, her heart swelling and bursting with joy.

If she'd stopped to think, she would have known her father would never consider a captain of the 52nd Regiment of foot.

She did not want to marry anyone else, though, and if she wished to marry Paul, she had to leave. That was her father's fault.

Paul was one and twenty, but she was seventeen – old enough to know her own heart but not to marry without the consent of her father, unless they went to Scotland.

~

"Captain, there is a letter waiting for you at the desk," a maid said.

Captain Paul Harding crossed the bare boards of the inn's entrance hall to collect it, his gaze running over the wooden racks.

"My letter?" The clerk turned to pick it out from a pile.

"Thank you." Paul turned away and headed to the taproom, his boots brushing over the beer scented sawdust spread across the floor. Looking at the maid who served there, he said. "May I have an ale?" The girl nodded and moved to pour it. After accepting the full tankard, he occupied an empty table in the corner of the room, ignoring the general conversation of the local labouring men.

His heart clenched at the sight of the familiar flow of letters forming his name.

Ellen had written them. Lady Eleanor Pembroke.

He'd fallen hard for this girl in the summer when he'd never fallen for a woman before. But Ellen was uncommonly beautiful. Her hair was raven black, and her skin like porcelain, while her eyes, which shone bright as she spoke, were the palest most striking blue he'd ever seen in a woman. She'd captured his attention in the summer, like a siren.

Perhaps he'd been at war too long and now he just wished for peace and beauty to surround him, to shut out the bitter memories and images of blood and corpses strewn across fields. Who knew? But he'd not wanted to leave this girl behind in August, and now he had to go back to war he did not wish to leave her in England. He craved this girl, as he'd craved water after hours of fighting, dry mouthed, thirsty and heart-sore.

She was young. But if he waited someone else would snap her up by the time he returned. To keep such a beauty, he had to take her with him. The girl could keep him sane, when all about him was brutality and madness.

He'd spent the last three years watching the few men who had their wives travelling with them, following the drum. It was not a pleasure filled life, but at night they'd had each other, before and after a battle.

His choice had been the comfort of a camp whore or the camaraderie of jaded war beleaguered men.

Not that he did not like his men; they'd survived too much

13

together. But there were times a man wanted a woman, and there were times only one woman would do.

He wanted solace, someone to take to bed and escape war with – someone who would help him shut out the visions of the death he'd left behind.

Of course more fool his heart – picking the daughter of a duke.

He'd held little expectation Pembroke would welcome his proposal, but Paul had known he had to try to do things properly.

God. His father would go mad when he heard of this. It would set Pembroke against him for years, when his father sought a political alliance. But self-sacrifice be damned. He'd given his life to society. Now he'd discovered something he wanted more than others' good opinion. Ellen.

He'd had little to do with his father though anyway, since he'd gone to war. His father had paid for his commission, and then his duty had been done. He'd ensured his sixth son had an independent living.

At first Paul had kept in contact with them, but war was not a thing to write of, he'd grown distant from his family now. In the summer when he'd been with them at Pembroke's, he'd had little conversation to share with them. He was not interested in politics, and they would not have been interested in his tales of survival and death.

He cracked open the seal on her letter and read it quickly, drinking his ale as he did. She'd said, *yes.* Not that he'd doubted she would, he'd known since the summer the girl was attached to him. But before he'd felt guilty. Now he did not. Argyle? God, her father was a bastard. Paul would be rescuing her from a life of hell.

Her father, and his, could go hang. This girl was meant for him, and he was right for her. He needed her too much.

He couldn't remember the point attraction had become love. At some point between catching her staring at him across the room the first day he'd arrived at Pembroke Place and hearing her sing as he sat beside her turning the pages of her music, while her thigh brushed against his through a thin layer of muslin, her cotton petticoats and his pantaloons.

Any day soon this girl would be his, and she may have to learn how to endure the hardship of an army camp, but regardless he would make sure she never regretted eloping. Determination to make her happy gripped in his gut, and determination to love the girl so she'd never feel she lacked a thing.

Setting his empty tankard sharply back on the beer stained table, he rose and returned to the clerk's desk. "When may I hire a yellow bounder? I need a fast carriage."

"I can find out for you, Captain. Are you dining? If so I'll see what is free while you eat."

"Yes, I'll dine." Paul turned away and returned to the taproom. Not that he was hungry. His stomach had been tied up in knots for more than a week. Ever since he'd received his orders to sail and decided to come back and get Ellen he'd hardly been able to eat a bloody thing. He wanted this woman too much.

She'd stayed in his head since he'd left in August. She'd hovered in his dreams at night and walked with him in daydreams in the sunlit hours. She'd enchanted him, and he'd found her unfledged and ready for flight.

Thank God he'd come to entertain himself when his father and brothers had visited Pembroke's. He could so easily have stayed away and gone to London.

But his father and hers were going to be mad as hell.

He asked for another tankard of ale and ordered the pork dish. He'd eaten enough bloody rabbit for a whole century during the Peninsular War. He would not touch the rabbit pie. It reminded him too much of the biting pain when hunger gripped inside you and you still had to march or fight. Yet he barely touched the meal, his hunger now was for a certain pale-blue-eyed, black-haired beauty.

Finding Ellen had been like finding treasure on the battle torn fields in his head. His sanity clung to her, something beautiful to

15

remind him that everything was not ugly. She was someone to fight for. Someone to survive for…

The clerk arrived. "The day after tomorrow. Would that suit, sir?"

"Yes." The sooner the better. Tomorrow would be torment. Now he'd made up his mind, and Ellen had agreed, he simply wished to go. But if there was no choice. "That will suit."

"Thank you, Captain." The man bowed.

~

Ellen's stomach growled with hunger for the umpteenth time as she lay on her bed. She'd been confined to her room for four days, but this would be the last day… She was leaving. The thought clutched tightly in her heart. No one knew. In ten hours Paul would come to meet her.

She'd not even told Pippa, she was too terrified her father would hear it from someone if she said the words aloud.

Every detail of their escape, in Paul's words, was safely tucked inside her bodice near her heart, pressing against her breast.

"Eleanor."

Heavens.

"Eleanor!" The sound seeped through her bedchamber door; a deep heavy pitch that made her instantly wish to comply. Obedience had carved its mark into her soul – and yet she was about to disobey. Where on earth would her courage come from?

"Father?" The key turned in the lock on the outside and Ellen scurried off the bed.

When the door opened she stood by the bedpost, her hands gripped before her waist, her back rigid and chin high, but her eyes downturned. It felt as though she was one of Paul's soldiers on parade when she faced her father. She did not feel like his flesh and blood.

"Your Grace." She lowered in a deep curtsy sinking as far as

16

she was able, in the hope he would think her penitent and be kinder. She did not look up to meet his gaze in case it roused his anger. But she needn't even look at her father to know when he was displeased; displeasure hung in the air around him without him saying a word. Yet he never showed his anger physically, apart from barking orders and offering condemning dismissals.

Those cutting words and his exclusion were enough punishment though. He never looked at her as if he cared, never smiled…

What I am planning will horrify him…

Her father's fingers encouraged her to rise, with a beckoning gesture.

"Papa." She lifted her gaze to his.

Paul's words, promising faithfulness, love and protection, pressed against her bosom as she took a deeper breath. A blush crept across her skin. She feared even the blush might give her away.

Compared to her father, Paul was water to stone, something moving and living.

Vibrancy and approachability – warmth – emanated from Paul.

Her father hid beneath coldness and disdain. If there was any warmth in his soul she'd never been able to see it. He most often communicated in a series of bitter glares rather than words.

Yet Paul had experienced awful things. Death. Illness. He had cause to be bitter. He'd seen friends die, and killed others for the sake of freedom in Europe. He never spoke of it though, even when she'd asked. He always spoke of good things. But she supposed his months in England were months to forget the Peninsular War.

"Well? Have you thought about your behaviour, Eleanor?"

Paul's letter was warm against her heated breast. Yes, she had thought, and she had made a choice – to leave. "Yes, Papa."

Until this summer she'd thought her father was unaware of his daughters, they'd grown up in the hands of servants, with a daily visit from her mother. But last year she'd reached a marriageable age, and now he saw her – but only as a bargaining tool. He wished her to marry to secure a political alliance.

"And are you sorry?"

Ellen's gaze dropped to his shoes. She felt no regret. "Yes, Papa."

"You will take Argyle?"

Ellen took a breath longing for courage. She did not feel able to lie to that extent.

"Eleanor?"

Looking up, she faced his stern condemning glare. His expression was as unreadable as marble. "I cannot, Papa. I do not wish to marry His Grace." Her father had a way of making other people seem small and insignificant – incapable. "Papa?" *Do you love me? Will you miss me?*

"You do not have a choice, Eleanor. You will do your duty."

His gaze held her at a distance, blunt and cold.

Hers reached out, begging for a sign of his affection. "I cannot, Papa. He is so old, and–"

"You are being wilful and defiant, Eleanor. You will do as I say and that is an end to it."

The words inside her pressed to escape catching up in a ball in her throat as she longed to plead, to make him accept Paul, but her father did not like emotion. As children they'd always been taken from his presence whenever there were tears, or shouts or laughter. But today, today she could not quite hold herself back. "Papa, please… What would be so wrong with Paul? I love him and he loves me…"

He gave no obvious sign his anger had escalated, yet she knew. It was in the stiffness of his body, in the cut of his silver eyes as they glared at her. He was like her in appearance – or rather she was like him. She had his eyes and his jet black hair and pale skin. But she was nothing like him in nature, and she did not wish to be. What possessed a man to be so cold? He would be handsome if he smiled but he never smiled, merely glowered and growled.

"Do not be ridiculous, Eleanor. Love? What is love?" *Something you do not feel, Papa.* "You are talking nonsense. There is nothing in it. You are the daughter of a duke. You have a duty and

18

responsibility, and that is what you must think of in a marriage. It seems you are unrepentant then, and you've learned no lesson at all. You will spend the next full day on your knees. Study the bible, ask for forgiveness and pray for guidance. You will learn, Eleanor. Your mother has been too lenient, letting you dream of such fanciful things. I'll return tomorrow."

I'll be gone tomorrow. She could continue to argue, she could beg and try to cajole, but her father would never change his mind; he had never done a single thing out of kindness.

Eleanor lowered in another curtsy. "As you say, Papa."

"As I say indeed, Eleanor. It will be so. You will marry Argyle. I shall write to him today." *You may write, Papa, but I shall never marry him.*

"Kneel at your bed, child." She turned and did so, she'd never disobeyed him and even now her heartbeat thundered at the thought of doing so in a few hours. Where would she find the courage? From Paul. Her father would be so angry.

As Ellen lifted her skirt and knelt, her father turned to the door and called to a footman. "Bring the bible from the chapel, my daughter needs time to search her soul."

No she did not. She had found what her soul looked for. She'd found Paul.

~

"Ellen?" A quiet knock struck her bedchamber door.

"Penny?" Ellen stood. It was dusk, her family had probably just eaten dinner, and their father would be sitting alone at the table drinking his port.

The handle of her door turned but it would not open. Papa had the key.

"Mama said I must not speak to you, Papa has forbidden it, so of course *she* will not come, yet I had to know you are well. Are you hungry? Do you wish me to send you something to eat?

Has he beaten you?"

Ellen rose from her kneeling position; she should not move, and yet she could not shout across the room in case someone heard and told tales on them. Then Penny would be in trouble too.

Ellen pressed her fingers against the door, leaning to whisper through it. "I know, and I know Mama cannot defend me, she must obey Papa. I do not want him to be angry with her or you. You should go, Penny…"

"Why?"

"Paul made an offer. Papa refused it. He is angry because I encouraged Paul. Do not become caught up in this or Papa will confine you to your room too."

"Paul? Captain Harding? Oh Ellen. I like him."

Resting her forehead against the wood, Ellen smiled. "As do I, but Papa does not. He wishes me to accept the Duke of Argyle."

"Ellen… I shall come through the servants' way and speak with you. You cannot marry that old man. He is awful."

"No. Papa would be furious. Do not take the risk. I can manage, I am merely a little cold and hungry," *and I will be gone soon…*

"But you will not agree to marry that old man. I saw him in the summer and—"

"Of course not." An urge to share the truth and speak of her elopement shot through Ellen's heart, another arrow of love passing through it, but it would be wrong to involve Penny. Penny was fifteen, she would not be able to hide her knowledge if their father questioned her, and Ellen would not have Penny hurt.

"I miss you. Rebecca and Sylvia do nothing but play silly games. Life is so dull without you."

Penny's words tugged as if a cord was tethered to the arrow through Ellen's heart, and Penny pulled it.

But Ellen could not stay. She wanted to be with Paul.

Her hands trembled as her palms pressed against the wood and she leant closer, feeling the presence of her sister on the other side in every fibre of her body…

This life, this house, was all Ellen had known. She'd never travelled beyond the local towns.

Paul had travelled the world. He'd told her what life as an army officer's wife would be. Hard. She was not to expect luxury. But she would be loved and cared for and adored by him. She longed for it. Her heart ached for it. But voices in her head whispered, *be afraid…*

"You will manage without me Penny."

"I know I shall. It will only be for a few days Papa cannot keep you locked away forever."

"Yes, only for a few days…" *Years.* A desire to speak the truth to Penny fought to break the words from Ellen's lips. But if her father discovered Penny had been told he'd hurt her. "You'd better go. I'd never forgive myself if you're caught."

"As soon as Papa allows you to come out, find me and tell me everything. Promise?"

"Promise."

"Good-bye."

"Good-bye." Tears flooded Ellen's eyes as she heard her sister go. Leaving Penny behind without explanation, would cause Penny pain, but it tore at Ellen's heart too.

~

The room had become bitterly cold. Her father had forbidden anyone to tend the fire. It had burned out hours ago. Ellen's knees ached from kneeling, yet still she'd not risen, even though no one watched her. Her father's will had been forced upon her for so many years it was her instinct to obey. Yet she'd break that tether at midnight.

She read through the Ten Commandments for the thousandth time. "*Thou shalt honour thy father and mother.*"

Was she about to sin then, because she was going to run away and betray them? Her mother would be heartbroken – *she* knew how to love. She was even loyal to Ellen's father, respecting their marriage vows despite his coldness towards them all.

Ellen could not do the same. She could not stay here. She wanted a life with Paul – even if it was sinful and selfish.

It had been dark for hours, and every time the clock in the hall struck she'd counted the chimes. It was past ten.

Pippa had brought her some bread and cheese at eight, wrapped in a cloth, but Ellen had sent her away with a need to obey her father, at least in that. It was a penance for the moment she would break free and shatter any feelings he had.

Excitement and anxiety warred with guilt and sorrow; sadness weighing down her soul. She did not want to leave her sisters and her mother.

But the sadness was out balanced by the gladness and expectation which hovered in her other half. She was going to Paul. Running towards love. Yet what else? All she knew was *his* love bore more weight than her mother's or her sisters'. It owned her heart and made it pulse – not simply made it feel tender.

The clock began to strike again, the sound echoing. One, two…

Ellen knew how many times it would chime.

Leaving the bible open, she rose, even now unable to fully disobey and close it.

Her feet were numb and her knees stiff, the payment for what she was about to do.

Everyone in the house retired early to avoid wasting candles. They rose with the sun and retired with it. They would all be in bed.

The chilly air made her shiver, or perhaps it was the overwhelming mix of excitement and fear. She still could not believe she was doing this. She took a leather sewing bag from a cupboard and began empting it of embroidery threads and ribbons. The clock outside chimed nine… ten… eleven…

Ellen's eyes adjusted to the shadows cast by the moonlight pouring through the open curtains, she looked about the room.

One hour.

She picked out undergarments and three of her muslin dresses. Then she fetched her hairbrush and the mirror her mother had bought her when she'd reached six and ten. That had been over a year ago, but she could remember the day as if it were yesterday. She'd been here in her room, and Pippa had been brushing her hair out before bed with her usual one hundred strokes. Her mother had come in to say goodnight and she'd carried a beautiful wooden box containing the set.

When she'd given it to Ellen, she'd said it was to mark Ellen becoming a woman. She'd kissed Ellen's cheek and wished her happiness.

That is what she was running to – happiness. But she couldn't fit the beautiful box in her bag, so she left that behind and just packed the brush and mirror.

She sifted through her gloves and picked four pairs, and she picked a dozen ribbons to change the look of her dresses, and some lace.

She had no ball gowns, she'd never been to a ball, although she'd watched one through a door that had been left ajar when her father had held one here. She did pack two of her evening gowns though. But there were many things she had to leave behind, bonnets, shoes, dresses, her lovely room with its pretty paper painted with birds – her sisters – her mother.

Pain caught in her bosom, sharp and tight, like the press of a little knife slipping into her flesh. How would she live without them, and yet how would she live without Paul? And if she chose to stay, what if Papa would not bend and he forced her to take the Duke of Argyle? No, she was doing the right thing.

She stopped and looked about the room. She could take nothing else. But she wished she'd thought to cut a lock of her mother's and Penny's hair at some point in her life to keep as a reminder.

She wiped a tear away before closing the bag and securing the buckle. Then she took her riding habit from where it lay in a drawer and began changing. The thick velvet made it too hard

23

to fit in the bag and it would keep her warm as they travelled.

It was a fabric her mother had urged her to buy, a burgundy red, as deep a colour as port. She was lucky that it fastened at the front so she could dress in it without Pippa's help.

When it was on, she looked in her long mirror which stood against the wall in the corner of her room, and saw a woman. Not a child anymore. A woman about to desert her family. Sighing rather than face the guilt which crept in, overlaying her excitement, she turned away to collect her bonnet, cloak and a pair of kid leather gloves. She would have taken her muff, but she feared carrying too much. Lastly she put on her half boots, and laced them neatly.

Then she looked into the mirror again, at the Duke's daughter. She would not be that now. She would be an officer's wife. She would no longer live in luxury but in simplicity. It was what she chose. It was what she wanted.

Her gaze spun about the room, looking at everything one last time. "Goodbye, Mama," she whispered into the darkness. "Goodbye Penny…" Her voice caught as tears burned her eyes. "Goodbye Sylvia and Rebecca. I will pray for you, I will pray for your happiness and good fortune." She paused for a moment as though she half expected them, or the house, to reply. But no sound came. She picked up her bag and went to the servants' door, then out into the narrow hall. It was little more than a person wide and pitch black. She hurried down the spiralling steps which would take her to the service area and the stables; the fingertips of her free hand skimming across the cold plaster on the wall to guide her way, while her heart pounded out a rhythm that made her light-headed.

Chapter Two

"Ellen?" Paul whispered her name into the night as he heard the rustle of frost bound leaves on the ground. His breath rose in a mist into the cold winter air. He was on the Duke of Pembroke's land. He'd not dared encourage her to take a horse, so he'd come close enough that she might walk from the house and find him.

He waited at the end of an avenue of yews, out of sight of the house, in a place she could easily see him. His horse whickered, sensing something, or someone. "Ellen?" he whispered again.

Still no answer.

He stayed quiet. Listening. Wondering if she'd been caught as she left the house. He hoped not. If she'd been caught her father would give her no freedom. Short of leading a military assault on Pembroke's home, he would not be able to get her out then.

The horse shook its head, rattling its bit, and snorted steamy breath into the cold air. The chill of the winter night seeped through his clothes. There would be a hard frost. He hoped she'd dressed in something warm.

He'd have to buy more clothes for her before they sailed. She would need garments to keep her warm in the sea breezes she'd face on their journey to America.

There was another sound.

"Ellen?"

"Paul?"

How did this woman manage to make his heart beat so erratically whenever he saw her? He could run into battle and not be so affected.

She looked even more beautiful in the dark. Ethereal.

A band of silver light reached through the scudding clouds and caught her face.

He let go of the horse's bridle and instinctively moved forward. He'd never held her. In the summer there had been no moments alone, she'd been strictly chaperoned and even when she'd come to meet him she'd brought the groom and her sister. When they'd met a fortnight ago, she'd still brought a groom. For the first time they were alone. "Ellen." He stepped forward and embraced her. In answer her arm came about his waist. It was the most precious feeling of his life. He would always remember this day. She was slender and delicate in his arms.

She slipped free, but he caught her nape and pulled her mouth to his, gently pressing his lips against hers. It was her first kiss, he knew; he could tell by the way her body stiffened when he'd pulled her close. He let her go, a tenderness he'd never known before catching in his chest.

"Come." He took the leather bag she carried. "Will you ride before me, or would you rather sit behind my saddle and grip my waist?"

"Would it be easier if I ride behind you?" Her voice ran with uncertainty. She was giving up everything to come with him.

"Do what feels comfortable for you, Ellen."

She nodded, not looking into his eyes. "I would prefer to ride pillion."

"Then you shall." He warmed his voice, hoping to ease her discomfort.

Turning to the horse he slipped one foot in the stirrup, then pulled himself up. "Did you have any difficulty leaving the house?"

"No, the servants' hall was quiet, and the grooms had all retired."

26

He rested her bag across his thighs, then held a hand out to her. "Set your foot on mine and take my hand. I'll pull you up." He watched her lift the skirt of her dark habit and then the weight of her small foot pressed on his, as her gloved fingers gripped his. She was light, but the grip of her hand and the pressure of her foot made that something clasp tight in his chest, and the emotion stayed clenched as her fingers embraced his waist over his greatcoat.

He shifted in the saddle, his groin tightening too. A few more days. Just days. He had been waiting months. As he turned the horse, Ellen's cheek pressed against his shoulder.

"Did you tell anyone you were leaving? Your sister? Or your maid?"

"No, I did not want them to have to face Papa knowing the truth. He would be able to see they'd lied, and then who knows what he might do." Paul urged the mare into a trot as Ellen continued. "He made me spend the day on my knees reading the Commandments because I refused to marry the Duke of Argyle."

"Today?" He wished to look back at her but he could not.

Her father had been diabolical to Paul, sneering as though he was nothing when he'd done the decent thing and offered for her. He could not imagine the way Pembroke treated the girls.

He had to get Ellen to Gretna before her father caught them, so she never had to come back and face his retribution.

He stirred the mare into a canter. Ellen gripped his waist more firmly.

"Yes today," she said, leaning to his ear. "He came to my room this morning, to ask if I was repentant."

If she was repentant? She'd done nothing wrong, as far as her father was aware. He'd not told her father they'd been communicating since the summer. He'd expected to be refused, and he'd not wished their pathway of communication closed. All she had been guilty of, as far as her father knew, was that her presence and her company in the summer had attracted a man her father deemed unworthy. She bore no guilt for being beautiful and charming.

27

God, how had Pembroke brought up this untouched, unscarred girl? "Did you tell him you repented?"

She laughed; a low soft sound he hadn't heard before. "No."

He smiled. It had taken him so long to make his offer because he'd wanted to feel sure she could cope as his wife, that she had the strength to follow the drum. She had it. She had a core of iron. She would survive. He would make sure she did; though he didn't doubt his way of life was going to come as a shock to her. He'd tried to warn her in letters, preparing her, but he could tell from her responses it was all whimsical rather than real. It would become real.

He stopped the horse suddenly, and strained to look over his shoulder, as it restlessly side stepped. "You're sure of this, Ellen? I mean, if you are not, I can take you back."

In answer, her fingers slid further about his midriff and gripped him harder. There was a pain in his chest and his groin again. "I am sure."

I am sure too.

"Then let us hurry." He kicked his heels and set the horse off at a canter, his mind on the treacherous tracks they were likely to encounter on their journey north. This was a race now.

The ground was hardened by frost, and slippery. The horse's breath and theirs rose as steam in the air.

They had a few hours lead, but–

"Papa, said I was to have nothing to eat either, at least he played into our hands. I told Pippa not to bring me any food."

Then perhaps their head start would be twelve hours to a day, but even so it was the wrong time of year for haste. He hoped the cold weather and frost would hold, better that than rain and mud bound routes when carts, horses and men became bogged down. His head had already begun ordering the flight like a bloody military campaign.

"The coach is waiting for us at the inn. It will be ready. I've hired a yellow bounder."

"A coach and four?"

He smiled at the tone of excitement in her voice. "Yes. You sound as if you fancy driving them?"

She laughed again, that low heart-wrenching beautiful sound. "No, I wouldn't have a clue, but I have never ridden in a fast carriage. It sounds exhilarating."

Exhilarating? This girl was so wonderfully innocent. But that was another thing that had drawn him to her, her naivety, it was such a contrast to his own knowledge of the world; she knew nothing of the horrors he'd lived through, though he was only a little older than her. She was here to wash his soul clean of war and brutality.

They had to pass through a gate, but he did not dismount, he merely leaned down to open it, and then they were in the woods, where the frost had not yet settled.

Here the darkness reigned. It left him reliant on the eyes of the horse as they kept low to avoid tree branches, and he had to slow and keep the horse at a trot.

When they reached the clearing at the bottom of the ridge on which her father's tall folly stood, he took a moment to regain his bearings and then set off through the trees again.

Due to the darkness it took half an hour to reach the inn. When she dismounted, his mind counted the minutes passing, aware of her empty bedchamber and the people asleep back at Pembroke's palatial mansion. At some hour tomorrow they would discover her gone. His heart beat in a steady firm rhythm as he gripped her hand and she slid from the horse.

While she waited on the ground, her arms nervously clasping across her chest, he dropped her bag on to the cobbled yard then slipped his feet from the stirrups, swung his leg over the saddle, and dismounted.

The ice had not yet settled in the enclosed courtyard, but the street beyond was white with cold. He patted the mare's cheek as it snorted, and whispered a thank you, then looked at the small,

29

yellow painted carriage, and the animals which waited impatiently shaking out their manes and snorting misty breath into the night air.

A groom took the bridle of the hired mare he'd ridden to fetch Ellen and another collected Ellen's bag to place it in the boot of their carriage.

"Come." He held out his hand to Ellen and she took it, in complete trust. He was a lucky man.

The inn's grooms hurried ahead to open the door.

It was strange, holding a woman's hand. When he'd walked with a woman before, she'd only ever lain her hand on his arm. This was more intimate. She belonged to him. He was responsible for her now; even if it was not yet official.

Paul handed her into the carriage. She climbed the single step then slipped inside. Once her hand left his, he reached into his pocket for a small bag of coins. He looked at the groom beside him and then to the other two who stood in the yard. "For your silence." He passed it to one to share out among the rest. He could ill afford it and it would be no guarantee, yet he did not want Pembroke warned. He hadn't said who she was, but she had the distinctive Pembroke colouring and beauty, with her dark hair and very pale blue eyes. She would not be forgotten.

"Thank you, Captain." The man pulled his forelock and the others bowed their heads as Paul glanced at the postilion rider and the man on the box.

They had two men to keep them going through the night, so one could sleep while the other rode a lead horse.

With a nod Paul climbed into the carriage. The moment he closed the carriage door, they were away. It lurched forward and even before they left the silent village, shrouded in its blanket of darkness, the postilion rider had upped the pace into a gallop, not at all heedful of the frosty track as the carriage bounced over the hardened muddy ruts. "We must make haste," he'd told the drivers three dozen times before he'd gone to fetch Ellen. It seemed they'd heard his words.

"We are going to be mightily bruised by the time we reach Gretna," Paul said.

There was that wonderful laugh again which stirred something incredibly masculine in his soul – an instinct to gather her up and protect her. He lifted his arm. She slotted beneath it, pressing close to his side. And there was that ache in his chest and his groin again. *Ellen.* He could see her face clearly in the lamplight which glowed within the carriage. Beautiful. Perfect. Flawless.

His arm around her, and her warmth clutched against him, he began explaining. "It should take us about three days, I think; maybe less if we are lucky with the roads and the weather. Then after Gretna we shall travel to Portsmouth. From there we will sail with my regiment. I'll purchase the things you'll need as a soldier's wife in Portsmouth. You shan't be able to carry much, there is a need to travel light, but we can spare you more than a single bag of clothing."

He couldn't see her smile, but it was in the press of her hand against his greatcoat over his chest and the stir of her cheek against his shoulder.

He would love this woman for the rest of his life. He knew it. "Come now. Let us take off our outdoor things and use the blankets, then you may sleep a little, if the road is not too rutted." He moved, letting her rise, and she set her feet on the hot bricks the inn had put on the floor and took off her bonnet, cloak and gloves. He took off his gloves too and gripped her hand as she moved back beside him spreading the blanket over them.

It was even more intimate than before, holding her naked hand, skin against skin – their first physical contact without the boundary of clothing. "Ellen, you need not fear me. I shall not press you. We will be travelling day and night. I shall not ask you to do anything with me until we are man and wife. If you change your mind…" He would not want to let her go, but if she wished to return to her father then he would–

31

"I will not change my mind. I wish to marry you." The answer rang with vehemence as she sat up and glanced at him, her pale blue eyes bright and determined. Yes, she had a core of iron. She would survive. "I love you."

Those words… He smiled. They'd only shared them for the first time a fortnight ago. It had been the first time he'd spoken them to any woman, and the first time he'd heard a woman say them to him. But the feeling was true, it was in his blood and bones. "I love you, also, Ellen. And I shall make you happy and keep you safe. I swear it."

~

When Ellen woke, her head rested in Paul's lap, and the weight of his hand lay on her shoulder. She sat up, blushing. "Sorry."

He was awake. He'd been looking out the window but now he looked at her and smiled – that gentle, warm smile she'd become used to in the summer. "It is of no matter, Ellen. You were tired."

She smiled too. "Yes. Did you sleep?"

"A little."

"Where are we?"

"Close to High Wycombe."

It had been foolish to ask. She had no idea where High Wycombe was, or how far that meant they'd travelled.

His smile opened and his eyes glowed. "We are the other side of London, eight or nine hours away from your father's estate." It was as though he'd read her mind, or perhaps her expression.

Her stomach growled, and she pressed her hand over it, blushing again.

A humorous sound came from his throat. "Are you hungry?"

Yes. She was starved. She nodded, her smile quivering. She'd felt a closeness between her and Paul, which had begun in the summer and gathered through their letters, but now awkwardness hung between them because she knew very little of him in the flesh, only his written words.

"We will stop at the next inn. But we cannot stop for long. We need to make sure we keep ahead if your father follows."

A knot tied in her stomach as Paul leaned forward to open a slim hatch and shout up to the man on the box. "We wish to stop at the next coaching inn!"

If her father followed she would be in trouble. He'd never forgive her for this. But she was not sure he would follow; there were her sisters. He'd never shown any sign he cared for her. Perhaps he'd decide to wait until Penny came of age, and let Penny take her place.

Guilt rushed in. What if Penny had to endure the fate Ellen had run from? It would be Ellen's fault. But she could not regret this – because she was not running from – she was running to. She would never choose to give Paul up.

Paul sat back in the seat, and his fingers lifted and tucked a lock of her hair behind her ear. It had fallen from the pins.

She smiled, sitting back, and began trying to re-pin it without a mirror.

His fingers touched beneath her chin. "You need not pin it, you look beautiful if a little tussled by a bumpy carriage ride." She laughed, but she still re-pinned it, and touched it to feel if it was in place.

The carriage jolted over a deep rut as it turned off the road, sending her off balance and toppling her backward. In a moment he'd caught her upper arm in a firm grip holding her steady. She smiled, warmth and emotion running through her blood. He'd take care of her now. Moisture clouded her vision.

"Are you well? Happy?"

She smiled, swallowing back the emotion in her throat. "Yes." She leaned forward and hugged him, aware her breasts brushed against his chest through their layers of clothing. This was only the second time she'd been held by him, by any man. He kissed her temple a moment before she pulled away and her heartbeat thumped.

The carriage slowed, and through the window Ellen saw a row of thatched cottages, then they were turning into a courtyard.

"Come, let us get you some refreshment." Before the carriage had even stopped, Paul opened the door, and when it did he knocked down the step and lifted a hand to help her out.

When they returned to the carriage less than half an hour later, refreshed and more awake, Ellen let Paul hand her in as he'd handed her out. She did not feel guilty about making him stop because the drivers had changed the horses while they'd eaten.

The carriage lurched as they pulled off into a canter.

The ground was still frozen which meant the lanes were passable, but the frozen ruts cast by previous carriages in the mud strewn tracks made the journey bumpy.

The day was freezing, but new hot bricks had been placed inside at the inn, and Paul drew the blankets around them.

"Come here, let me hold you, then you will not be so thrown about by the rough track."

She smiled, sliding to sit against him. Her thigh pressed against his and his arm lifted so she might slot beneath it. He was warm and solid. Dependable.

She rested her head against his shoulder but his palm touched her cheek and his head turned and he kissed her, gently at first as she tilted her neck to better receive it. But then he kissed her more ardently as he parted his lips and brushed the seam of hers with the tip of his tongue, in a silent command that implied – *open your mouth*. She did, and then... *Heavens.* His tongue slipped into her mouth searching and exploring. *Paul.*

Her hands instinctively clung at his shoulders as she answered, her tongue weaving about his. She couldn't breathe. He'd lit a flame which melted wax within her. Heat and pain dripped from it into her blood.

He kissed her for a long while, his hands either side of her waist, a gentle, secure pressure.

Then a hand came up to the back of her head, steadying her

as for a moment his tongue pressed deeper into her mouth before he broke the kiss.

Her stomach somersaulted as she looked into his blue eyes; the colour of the winter sky outside the carriage. His lips tilted in a half smile, a dimple denting his cheek. Heat flared under her skin. She'd not known kissing could be like that. Images spun through her head. What would come next?

Chapter Three

They'd spent a day and another night in the carriage. Paul ached from too many hours of confinement, so they'd stopped again to break their fast and for him to stretch a little. Now they'd eaten, he'd left Ellen to refresh herself and walked about the yard of the Bull's Head in Leamington Spa. He did not dare take a proper walk and venture out onto the High Street in case Ellen followed. An officer and a dark haired beauty might be remembered. So he kept to the confined space at the inn, walking a circular route a dozen times.

Anxiety raced through his blood. His senses were as heightened as they would be before a battle. But he'd no idea where the enemy was. The Duke of Pembroke could still be in Kent, or he could be a few hours behind them, riding at a gallop, eating up the ground, pursuing them as they lingered here. Paul hated stopping and yet they had to eat, and… Well, they could not simply stay constantly in the carriage.

Bored with walking in a circle he stopped at the stable and moved to a stall where a horse whickered from within; one of those they'd just relinquished from their traces, to be returned to the Black Horse at Bicester, the inn they'd stopped at before nightfall.

"You have a connection with horses, and you ride well. I remember from the summer. Why did you not join a mounted regiment? I would have thought you'd be in the cavalry instead of a regiment of foot soldiers." Ellen stood beside him.

Her fingers touched his arm as his reached out and patted the mare's neck then stroked its cheek.

"Because I could not have borne to watch a horse that I'd brought to battle, die. I made my choice to fight. My horse would not have had the same luxury." He patted the animal once more, denying the images of battles crowding into his head. He did not want to remember. He turned to her and immediately all the memories of war and brutality faded.

She did not answer; perhaps he'd said something too morbid.

Her pale blue eyes held questions. Maybe she had seen the memories in his eyes. He did not wish her to see – with her he wanted to forget those memories. Yet he was taking her to a battleground, albeit not to fight.

Perhaps it was wrong of him.

But he could not regret it. In their hours in the carriage, the attachment she'd planted in his heart in the summer had emerged like a shoot from a seed, germinating and growing to full flower. Ellen Pembroke was the woman his soul chose; he could not leave her behind. Love clutched about his heart, a vine wrapping around it. "I love you." The words slipped from his mouth without thought.

She was young, she knew nothing about brutality. He did not wish her to, but she would learn.

He was young too, but the experiences of war, and now having her to protect, made him feel much older than he was.

She smiled. "And I you, Paul."

"Come, we had better go. There is no knowing how much ground your father has gained on us, if he is following." He gripped her elbow, gently, and turned them both.

When they were back in the carriage he kissed her, desire and need roaring in his blood. He could not wait until they were out of this damned carriage and in a bed. But he did not press her for anything more. She was innocent, and they were unwed, he could wait until the moment came. For now he just revelled in her kisses and her tender, beautiful responses as shallow sighs slipped across her lips and her tongue tentatively entwined with his, while the weight of her arms rested on his shoulders.

This girl was a treasure. He was going to protect her and love her all his life. He would not allow the brutality of war to touch her.

~

Ellen woke. Shouts echoed outside the carriage. The vehicle hit a rut, tipping and throwing her into the corner. She gripped the strap above her head fearing the carriage might roll, but it righted itself. Outside another shout rang out, then gunfire. She jolted forward as the carriage suddenly rocked to the side again then slowed.

Paul had been asleep too, but now, wide awake, he moved and turned the damper, to put out the lantern. The light died instantly.

She watched, still half asleep. "Paul?"

"Stay quiet, stay in the carriage and stay down." The sharp order cut her as he pulled the curtain back from the window and looked out when the carriage came to an abrupt halt.

"I said get down," Paul whispered harshly, bending down himself, but he was not trying to hide, he pulled something out from beneath the seat. A pistol and a sword. She caught a glimpse of the metal in the moonlight.

Ellen slid off the seat and landed on the cold bricks on the carriage floor. She started to shiver. "What is it?"

"Highwaymen. Do not say a word. Act as though there is no one in here. I'm going out." He pulled the curtain closed again.

"Paul…" She grabbed his arm, to stop him, but he shrugged her off as he opened the carriage door. The door banged shut behind him.

Her heart thundered. This was a nightmare. She would wake in a moment. But the cold air and the hard bricks beneath her bottom felt real.

Outside Paul shouted, his voice low in timbre and threatening. Her heartbeat rang in her ears, loud and deafening. A gun went off. Then another.

Oh. She could not stay in here. "Paul!" Scrabbling off the floor she reached for the door handle and clicked it open. She heard more shouting and almost fell out onto the frost bound earth. Her feet landed on the ground as her hand still gripped the handle, wrenching her arm as she slipped but stayed upright.

Paul was a silhouette cast by the moonlight and the frost covered earth. He faced away from her, a sword held in one hand, the tip pointing towards the ground. Something dark dripped from it. His other hand still held the pistol. A wisp of smoke rose from the barrel and the cold air carried the bitter smell of gunpowder. He dropped to one knee as she watched. She was unable to speak; shock had solidified every muscle in her body. There was a figure on the ground. A man.

Paul rested his hand which bore the gun, on the man's chest, while his sword slipped from his fingers and fell on the grass.

He reached to the man's throat and pressed it for a moment, then searched through the man's coat.

"What are we going to do with him, Captain?" one of the drivers shouted, climbing down from the box.

The statement brought Ellen back to her senses. This was no dream. "God help me." she whispered.

Paul rose sharply and turned to face her. "Get back in the carriage, Ellen. You do not want to see this."

But she had seen it.

Her hand let go of the door handle and she walked forward.

"Ellen, go back." Paul's words were barked. But she couldn't stop herself.

"Who is he?" The man on the ground hadn't moved.

"A highwayman, chancing his luck. Go back in, Ellen. Please. Let me sort this."

The man on the ground had still not moved. A macabre desire

to see pulled her towards him.

"Ellen," Paul snapped as she got closer, in another warning. But her body refused to be warned. She kept walking, and it only took a few more steps. The man lay there, as white as the frost stained grass beneath him. Except the grass beside his head was not white but dark, marred by something fluid that glistened in the moonlight… and half his forehead had been blown open.

Ellen turned away and cast up what little she'd eaten when they'd stopped for supper. Paul's hand touched her back. "Ellen, I told you not to look."

She was sick again.

He pressed his handkerchief into her palm as she fought to catch her breath. "Ellen." Paul's voice was quiet, as though he was afraid of her reaction.

After a few minutes, she straightened, the world about her turning to dust. "You killed him."

"I had to–"

"Could you not have merely wounded him?"

"It was self-defence, madam. The Captain had no choice. The highwayman had his pistol aimed at the Captain's head. If he'd not sliced the man's leg open to get him off that horse–"

"Would that not have been enough?" Ellen's words echoed back on the night air.

Paul raised a hand, his fingers reaching for her. "Ellen, come." She backed away. "That man would have raped and murdered you without a thought. I had no choice."

"I'm glad, you did it, Captain. The bastard hit me."

"Hit you?" Paul turned away, facing one of the men who drove the carriage.

The man walked towards them, clutching his upper arm.

He looked as pale as the dead man.

"Bullet's gone clean through my arm, Captain. I was riding postilion. He wanted to stop the horses."

"Sit on the backboard, before you fall down," Paul said. Then he glanced at her. "Ellen, tear a strip off your petticoats."

She bent to do it. Any moment she would wake up in her bed at home, and this whole journey would be a dream.

She could not tear the cotton.

"Wait." Paul walked back for his sword. She straightened as he wiped it clean in the grass.

Her gaze caught on the dead man. Paul seemed so unemotional. He rose and turned to her.

Ignoring her observation, he squatted, gripped her hem and sliced into it with the sword's edge. After he'd done it, he dropped the sword and tore a strip with his hands. She stood still. Frozen.

When he straightened, he said, "Ellen, can you tie this about the man's arm?"

Her fingers shook.

"Here." He gripped one of her hands and pulled her towards the postilion rider who sat at the back of the carriage. "Do not worry about taking his coat off, just tie it over the top, just above the wound, as tightly as you can to stop the bleeding. Do you understand?"

She nodded and began as the man watched her in silence, in pain, looking faint as blood dripped from his limp hand onto the ground.

Paul walked away. She heard him talking to the driver behind her. They were moving the body. Her fingers shook so much she struggled to tie the cotton off, but she managed.

Cold seeping deep into her flesh, she shivered, her teeth chattering.

"Ellen, get in the carriage." Paul's words were an order. Not knowing what else to do, she did. It was just as cold within, and dark, and lonely.

After a moment he opened the door. "I am going to ride on the box to the nearest inn. We will sort everything out there." There was a dark stain on his grey pantaloons. Blood.

She nodded; she'd left everything she knew behind her. This

41

was a world of unknowns. She'd never imagined anything like this.

The carriage lurched into motion. She heard Paul talking on the box above her, but not his words.

Images of the man lying on the grass and Paul standing over him cluttered Ellen's mind. Her senses waited for something to happen as the carriage rolled slowly on towards the next inn, their pace restricted by the wounded man who sat on the box beside Paul.

Every sound reverberated through her body. She could still smell the gunpowder as if it was in the carriage. She shivered, gripping her arms as she swallowed, trying to clear her dry throat. Then she gritted her teeth to stop them chattering.

The next inn was in the middle of nowhere at the edge of the road. The golden light of an oil lantern bleached out the moonlight when they turned into the courtyard, but the carriage was still dark inside, since Paul had put out the lamp.

Ellen looked through the window, her fingers shaking as she put on her cloak and bonnet.

Yawning men appeared from the stalls, grooms ready to change their horses.

She saw Paul jump down from the box and say something, and a man's eyes opened wide, staring at Paul. Then the man ran into the inn.

Paul turned to the carriage, opened the door and knocked down the step, not meeting her gaze until he offered his hand to her. The hand that had recently killed a man. But then it must have killed many men during the Peninsular War. Her fingers shook as she took it.

"Ellen," he whispered, "I've told them you are my wife. I've asked for a private parlour for you to wait in while I sort this mess out. Do you wish me to order a warm drink for you, chocolate? You look in shock."

She nodded. She was in shock.

His fingers holding hers, he lead her across the courtyard, and she tried not to think of the dead man whose body lay sprawled over the back of the carriage, on top of Paul's trunk.

But she did think of the injured man as she heard him climb down behind her. There was a word spoken, "Surgeon." Then a single rider left the courtyard.

Paul had killed the man to protect them.

This was the ugly world he knew, she'd only known the sanctuary of her father's property.

"Ellen, wait here," he commanded when she was seated in the parlour. But he did not then walk away; he squatted down and rubbed her gloved hands as he held them together, as if warming them. Then he said more gently. "I will be back in a while, as soon as I can."

She nodded.

He had not returned when her warm chocolate arrived. She sat in silence, sipping it – drowning. How would she cope on the edge of a battlefield? Paul was not who she'd thought he was, the man who overflowed with vibrancy, who smiled and laughed easily.

She had neither taken her bonnet nor her cloak off, and the fire in the hearth blazed, but she was cold.

When Paul arrived an hour later – an hour which she'd endured in the form of a statue, sitting in the chair staring at the cup of chocolate gripped in her hands.

He shut the door behind him; the action sent her nerves reeling. She was unused to being in a room alone with a man, and yet they'd spent days confined in the carriage. But now she knew she'd spent those days with a man who could kill brutally and close his heart off to it.

An expression of pain passed across his face as she looked up, he'd seen her flinch.

He no longer wore his blood stained clothes and he'd put on his greatcoat.

"Have I made you dislike me?" The words held anguish. He looked younger. His age. "I am sorry, you–"

She stood, setting her cup down.

43

How could she balance the man she loved against the soldier who could kill? There was a lethal warrior living inside the gentle man she'd met in a drawing room.

He was not gentle.

But she did not dislike him. Her heart loved him. She'd known he was a soldier, she'd just not understood what that meant. Now she was terrified of the choice she'd made.

She went to him, sobbing, and her arms embraced his midriff; doing what she'd longed to do for an hour – hold him and cry – and pretend that what had happened, hadn't happened.

His hand slid her bonnet back so it hung from her neck, then he kissed her cheek and her forehead, holding her. "I've spoken to the magistrate. The villain was known here. There will be no prosecution against me, and the driver who is injured is being replaced. The injured man will stay here until he is well enough to travel back. I have given him money for his lodgings."

Ellen nodded against his chest, not knowing what else to do.

His palm lay on her hair, a gentle weight of reassurance.

How could he touch her with such gentleness yet do what he'd just done?

"You've had a taste of death tonight, Ellen. Has it made you wish to turn back? I will take you back if it's changed your mind."

Had it changed her mind?

She could not remain with her family if she'd stayed at home. Her father would force her into marriage with another man, and what then? She would have to endure ugliness anyway, perhaps ugliness worse than the death of a thief who chose to kill or be killed.

But Paul had killed a man…

She pulled away, although her hands still gripped Paul's greatcoat either side of his waist in fists. "Was killing him the only way?" Maybe she showed her naivety by asking. But she was a little afraid of him.

His eyes studied her in the flickering orange light of the tallow candles which burned in the room. "Not the only way, no. I could have brought him down from his horse and shot him in the shoulder or the arm. But it is my instinct, Ellen. In battle, a soldier cannot risk simply wounding a man. Otherwise, as you fight on, a dozen men could be aiming a pistol at your back and.... you were in the carriage... and I did not know if there were more men in the woods."

She could not judge the colour of his eyes in the candlelight, but she could see regret and pain. He had killed, but he did not wish to kill. He was not a murderer. Sorrow caught in his gaze, as if ghosts walked about him.

She pressed herself against him, holding him. This time it was not to receive comfort but to give it.

"Ellen?" His hand ran over her hair. "Do you want me to take you back?"

"No." She did not want to go back, but she did not know how to go forward.

~

Ellen's answer was warmth seeping through the clothing covering his chest, into his heart. It would have hurt to let her go. But he would have done it, if she'd wished it. Thank God, she did not. He'd promised himself barely hours ago to protect her from the brutality of this world, and he'd not even reached Gretna before he'd failed. "You are strong, Ellen. You are going to have to face unpleasant things if you follow the drum with me. But you will survive."

She sobbed and more tears dampened his collar in answer. He held her tighter for a moment. But then he set her away. If her father was behind them, they'd lost hours... "We need to leave, Ellen. Are you ready?"

Her gaze met his, flooded with the uncertainty he'd dispelled before this incident. She was brave and strong, and she loved him, he knew it, but he could see she was also a little afraid of him now.

A sigh left his throat. He could do nothing. He had been trained to kill, and he had killed. He was a soldier; it was his instinct to fight and protect.

He pushed his thoughts aside, along with the memories of dead, dying and wounded men. They had to reach the border before her father reached them. *If* he'd followed.

Within a quarter hour they were in the carriage with freshly heated bricks, his weapons tucked away once more, and blankets piled over them as the temperature had dropped still further. The next stop would be Penrith. They were nearly there... nearly.

Ellen pressed against him, seeking comfort, her arms about his midriff, but her body felt stiff and her fingers trembled a little, implying her shock had not really ebbed.

Neither had his.

She went to sleep, her head resting against his chest. He laid his arm over her shoulders, and took comfort in her beauty.

As she slept, he could not. The call of battle still raged in his blood. There had never been any real danger, he was by a mile more experienced in a fight than the highwayman, but a murderous desire had swept over him; the same which captured him on a battlefield.

Kill or be killed.

Ellen was right; he was skilled enough to have maimed the man and no more. But the thought of her in danger... *God*, he could not bear it. He had not stopped for one moment to consider doing anything less than kill. Visions of battlefields, of corpses, and men's eyes clouding with death before they fell, had played through his head, but his heart had only felt Ellen and nothing of the bitter world he fought in.

He'd fought for her, to keep her safe, to get to her, to return to the beauty he'd found and forget death.

What was his intent for the future then?

To keep her safe he would have to march across enemy lines

and slay every man.

A throaty sound of self-deprecation erupted from his chest. *Bloody hell.* It was what he wished to do, but he would end up dead from such stupid ideas, and that would hardly protect her, and what was the point of her companionship and comfort if he was dead?

He looked out the window, his gaze scanning the passing tree-line. He'd left the lantern smothered, and the curtain open, so he might look out for any risk of attack, merely to ease his battle ready nerves. But now what he saw was snow. *Ahh. Damn.* Why tonight? Why could it not have waited one more day?

As the carriage rolled on at its hard pace, bouncing over the frozen ruts in the road, he watched the large white flakes fall. They settled. It was the sort of snow which could form deep drifts. But maybe it was a blessing. If it fell thick it would hold her father back too. If... he'd followed.

The snow formed a swirling cloud of white and Paul's heartbeat pulsed, his blood racing as hard as the carriage horses' pace. This was not now only a race against her father, but a race against the weather. How soon before the roads become impassable?

He watched the white flurries for what must have been two hours, as they swept against the pane of glass in the carriage door. Then the snow subsided and instead he watched the blue glow which shone back off the white blanket covering everything. The carriage slid a number of times but fortunately the frozen ruts in the road, beneath the white layer, gave the horses and carriage wheels grip.

He remembered all the travelling he'd done in the years of the Peninsular War, marching hundreds of miles. He'd not been tucked inside a warm carriage. He'd been outside trudging through the cold and urging his men to ignore their numb feet, when his were also numb and his fingers burning with cold too.

How would Ellen survive days like that? True she would be with the baggage train and have the luxury of a respite in the carts. But

47

there were times when the carts got stuck and the women had to get out and walk through knee deep mud, snow or thickets, and then in the summer there were days of blistering heat…

He'd been a fool, to bring her with him. Cruel. Selfish. But yet again he shoved the thought aside as he did with the haunting memories of war. She was happy to be with him. He would not take her back. She was his now, his comfort, and he would be hers. She would be the thing that brought his mind back from war to peace.

Maybe it had been a good thing that she'd faced the encounter with the highwayman, maybe it meant, when she faced the reality of war and wished she'd not left England, he could say, "But you did know…"

Had he become such a selfish bloody bastard then?

Yes, where Ellen was concerned. A thousand times, yes. He loved her.

It was not until the sunshine finally began glinting on the snow, reflecting gold light as it rose above the horizon, that Paul finally rested his shoulder against the corner of the carriage, lifted one foot up onto the opposite seat and fell asleep.

Chapter Four

Ellen woke to find the carriage flooded with natural light. It was appeared to be late morning. When she sat upright she saw a carpet of snow outside. Everything was white. The world looked pure again, denying the memories of a man lying still on the ground beside a dark pool of blood as Paul stood over him with a sword and a pistol still gripped in his hands.

She shivered at the memory but her stomach growled, despite her revulsion. She'd eaten nothing since it had happened, and she'd been sick last night.

She looked at Paul. He slept, leaning against the corner of the carriage, one elbow resting on a sill beside him, so his curled fist could support his chin. His other hand now lay slack on his thigh since she'd risen. One booted foot rested on the opposite seat, with his leg bent, the other still rested on the carriage floor. His thigh had been a pillow for her head.

Every muscle and sinew in his body was honed. He was a soldier. Even in sleep he looked able to fight. Now she knew what that meant, she'd seen the aftermath of his killing.

But her heart chose him. She could not deny him now.

In his sleep he looked younger, as he'd done last night. He was merely twenty-one, just a little older than her, and yet he'd endured so much…

He needed a sanctuary and he'd chosen her. She would willingly play that role, even if at the present moment, the idea of his capability to kill scared her.

The carriage jolted and instantly his eyes opened. He sat up, his hand going to his hip, as though to grasp a sword or pistol. But then he saw her and smiled. His hand lifted instead and raked through his hair, hiding the instinct to be ready to fight.

As the image of the dead highwayman hovered, she wondered how many pictures of battlefields played through his head.

She could perhaps understand a little more of the soldier, now she knew what that meant.

She smiled.

"How are you?" he asked. "You slept well. You have been asleep nearly all night."

"Were you awake then?"

"Yes. I did not like to sleep while it was dark, in case, well…" He did not end the sentence but she understood. He'd been nervous of more highwaymen. But he could not be worried for himself he was able to defend himself– he'd worried over her.

He looked down, lifted his fob watch from his inside pocket and flicked open the catch. "It's nearly noon."

She wasn't surprised; the hunger in her stomach and the sunlight implied it. But he looked surprised he'd managed to sleep.

She wondered how much last night had disturbed him. He'd seemed cold and unemotional then, but now…

"We'd better stop soon." He leaned over the carriage to open the hatch which let him speak to the man on the box. "Where are we?"

"Two miles from Penrith by the last marker, Captain."

"Stop at the next coaching inn, will you?"

"Aye, Captain."

Paul sat back again and then stretched, lifting his arms and arching his back. It showed off the lean, muscular definition of his torso and his thighs, which his uniform hugged so perfectly.

A warm sensation fluttered low in her stomach. They were

nearly at Gretna. Soon she would know what it would be like to share a bed with him. She smiled, excitement and anxiety skittering through her nerves; warring love and fear. It tangled up like a muddled ball of embroidery threads within her.

"I cannot wait to stretch my legs a little," he murmured as he dropped back against the swabs. Then he looked at her. "I admit I am sick of this carriage."

Her smile parted her lips. "I am also."

"Shall we take a break once we're wed, before we travel to Portsmouth? We may find lodgings for a night. It will be our wedding night."

His blue eyes shone

She nodded, the flutter stirring low in her stomach again – desire and disquiet. "It will be Christmas Eve too. There may be poor service at the inns. Do you feel guilty dragging our drivers away from their families?" He looked at her oddly. "Paul…"

"My apologies. I had completely forgotten about Christmas. My mind has been focused on gathering my men and then coming to fetch you ever since we had the order to sail. I've not known it as a time of celebration for years. My family would not expect me to be there, they'll not miss me. But yours… You will miss your sisters?"

She nodded, her vision clouding suddenly with tears. The twelve days following Christmas were for feasting and celebration and on the twelfth night, at Pembroke Place, they always held a servants' ball, when someone would be crowned the Lord of Misrule and order all the entertainments. Ellen and her sisters were allowed to watch for a little while.

He gripped her into a sharp, hard embrace. "I should not have mentioned them. I–"

She pulled away. "You need not apologise. It is nice to know you think of what will affect me. I do miss them. I will miss Penny most. I wish I had been able to explain to her. But I do not regret leaving with you. I will be happy with you."

His palm rested on her hair. "You can write to your sister, when we're married."

"Yes. What of your family?"

He laughed, a low deep pitch. "My family are long forgotten."

"But you came with them in the summer…"

"Yes, because I'd returned to England and sought my old self, the privileged sixth son of the Earl of Craster, but I am not that now. I am first a soldier. My family is the army, and my men. Christmas with my family would feel like living in the past."

"You are no longer close to them?"

"As close as it is possible to be when I lead a very different life to them. They will not miss me, and I will not miss them." His fingers gripped her chin, and then he looked into her eyes. "But you will be my family now, and I will be yours. We will be each other's comfort and companion. That is what I wish for us."

His words sent shivers running across her skin. "Yes, that is what I want too – to make you happy,"

"And I wish more than anything to make you happy, so we have hope, Ellen." His head lowered and he kissed her.

The ache in her stomach swept out to her limbs – yet along with the pleasure of his warmth and gentleness came concern; his gentle hands could kill a man…

When they pulled into an inn a little while later, having driven into the town of Penrith, Paul moved immediately, letting her go so she could sit up. He climbed out of the carriage in a moment, lowered the step, and then lifted his hand to help her.

She took it and smiled as he smiled at her. "Let us go in search of refreshment."

The cobbles of the courtyard were slippery from the snow, so they walked tentatively. He kept a hold of her hand. It was protective, –the way he had been with her ever since they'd been together.

She'd never seen her father be even slightly attentive to her mother. She'd only seen her father give orders and her mother obey and defer to his wishes. This side of Paul, the man she had first met in the summer, was precious gold in her eyes. If only there was not also the part of him that frightened her a little – the image of the highwayman lying dead in his blood still hovered in her head.

Paul ordered cured ham, cheese and freshly baked bread to break their fast, and then asked how many miles they were away from the Scottish border and how long it would take them to get there. The innkeeper implied they could make it by nightfall, if the snow neither melted nor started falling again.

By nightfall. In hours they might be wed.

They ate hurriedly, not wishing to delay. But then, watching her closely, looking into her eyes, Paul suggested they walk away from the inn, and a little way up the road, so he could stretch out before having to endure the cramped carriage again.

His long legged stride made it difficult for her to keep up, especially as the layer of snow caught on the hem of her skirt making her velvet habit heavy as it soaked up the moisture. But she liked the gentle give of the crisp snow beneath her half boots and slid her feet through it. She slipped. Her fingers gripped the firm muscle of his forearm.

His solidity and security gripped at her heart.

Oh, but his strength enabled him to kill men.

Her gaze turned to the picturesque village green on the far side of the road. Its fresh white coat looked beautiful, pure and peaceful.

"Shall we cross?" Paul asked. "I think it is too late now to make any difference if anyone were to remember us."

Ellen nodded, her fingers gripping his arm more firmly, denying her thoughts of the warrior within him.

"Come then." He turned and led her over. On the far side his arm dropped from her grip as he bent, then he quickly grasped a hand full of snow, turned, and tossed it at her; a huge smile cutting his face and laughter glimmering in his eyes. Ellen squealed turning away as it hit the side of her bonnet.

"Oh you brigand!" She laughed. He did too, bending to gather another handful of snow.

Ellen bent and grasped some too, crushing it in her fingers to make it denser. Then she threw it at him.

He threw his. It hit her breast. The snow stuck to her cloak.

The cold, the exercise and the laughter tumbled through her senses in an exhilarating rush.

He still laughed as he brushed snow from his shoulder and she ran a few steps away then turned and threw another handful at him. It nearly missed him only brushing his ear as he ducked. She bent and filled two hands, as a missile of cold snow hit her back.

She laughed again, smiling so widely it made her cheeks begin to ache, and lifted both her hands, full of snow. Still laughing she ran at him. He did not try to avoid her ambush as she neared and thrust the snow at his face, he only shut his eyes and his lips.

She laughed even more as the snow fell away, but then a look of retribution slipped across his face, although his blue eyes glinted with laughter and a smile hovered at the corners of his mouth.

His smile parting his lips, he gripped her shoulders and tumbled her backwards so she fell onto the snow. He fell with her, on top of her, though he did not crush her.

All the air left her lungs as her gaze caught his. Laughter no longer lingered in his eyes, but something else shone in them, something deep, warm and heartfelt. Her laughter died too, a moment before his lips pressed to hers. It was unlike any kiss they'd shared in the carriage. They lay on a green before the inn, with several cottages about them. He just pressed his lips over hers for a moment. But the pressure of his lean athletic body, and the knowledge that last night he had killed a man, and that in a few hours they would be married fought a battle of emotion inside her. Her heartbeat thundered.

He pulled away, kneeling first and then getting up, before offering her his hand. Once he'd pulled her up he began dusting snow from her cloak.

It had been good to laugh. She'd needed laughter, and perhaps

54

he'd known. Perhaps he'd needed laughter too. This beautiful, young, elemental, warrior was not invincible. He felt pain and hurt over the loss of life. He must be weighed down by memories. He needed her. She would protect him too, love him and comfort him, and she would make him happy.

"We'd better be on our way," he prompted, his voice implying the threat which still hung over them, of being caught by her father.

She nodded, taking his offered hand.

"Things will be good between us, Ellen. I promise. I know last night was abhorrent to you. Death is a terrible thing, no matter that a man is your enemy, and even if he is trying to kill you. I hope you will not have to face it often, and I will do everything I can to protect you. I love you."

"I know."

She could face living on the edge of a battlefield, as long as he had to endure fighting on one, and when he came back she would help him fight the ghosts.

"You will endure, Ellen, and we will be happy. I swear it to you."

~

It had turned to dusk as the carriage dashed the last few miles towards Gretna, and Paul urged it on mentally, as he could not give physical encouragement. But it felt far too slow, and he would have gladly given anything to be up on the box shouting at the horses and flicking a whip. There had been no more snow, *thank God*, and no thaw to make the roads turn to a quagmire of muddy slush but even so the weather hindered their pace. The tracks they travelled over were hard yet slippery, so they could not race at full tilt.

Hurry. Hurry. He still had no idea if her father followed. But they'd lost time last night and it would be the worst thing to be caught just before Gretna.

Come on. Faster.

He wanted to jump out and pull the damned horses. *Come on.*

Ellen sat beside him, and his hand held hers, probably too tightly. He relaxed his grip, but he knew she was anxious too. They both sat forward looking from opposite windows, listening for the noise of a carriage or riders in pursuit. But surely no one could gain any ground on them; their carriage had been forced to go slower but it was not slow.

Come on.

Ellen glanced across at him. He smiled at her, trying to reassure her, though he doubted he succeeded, he did not feel assured himself.

Hurry up.

They could not be far from the border, but night had begun to creep across the sky, turning the vista eerie and he was not sure they'd find a witness if they crossed after dark. Would anyone rise from their bed at night to perform the favour, and confirm the ceremony? For enough money, maybe; but he would be spending the precious funds he needed to cloth Ellen. Heaven knew he had spent enough years penniless during the Peninsular War. He'd only received his accrued arrears of wages a few weeks back. He'd also had a small inheritance from a deceased aunt. Still he was not rich.

Come on.

The sky became darker and bleak; they'd passed Carlisle hours ago. In the deep blue light of sundown, he recognised his first sight of the sea on the horizon, and then the inlet of a river mouth; the estuary which marked the Scottish border. He looked at Ellen, the tension inside him spinning in a sudden eddy, disorientation tumbling over him for a moment. Ellen leaned across him and looked out the window on his side.

The driver slid the hatch open. "We've crossed the border, Captain."

Thank God. "Hurry then. Stop at the first place you think we will find a witness."

Anyone could bear witness to a wedding under Scottish law.

As long as the bride was older than five and ten. If he and Ellen stood before a Scotsman and said they wished to marry, then the deed was done, and English law had to recognise it. They had no need for parental consent or a priest. That was why they'd come.

The carriage hurried on, travelling past the estuary, where a few small boats rested on the sand, left stranded by the low tide.

Paul let go of Ellen's hand and drew the window down, to look ahead. They passed over the bridge beneath which the river ran out to sea. He saw nothing as the chill night air rushed into the carriage.

Behind him, he heard Ellen slide down the opposite window. A harsh cold draft swirled through the carriage penetrating his clothing.

Come on. He leaned out the window and looked back along the track, but no carriage, or horses, pursued them.

"I see something!" Ellen called. "A little forge beside the road."

He looked ahead and saw nothing on his side. Looking up at the box he yelled, "Driver. We will stop at the forge!"

Slipping back into the carriage he turned to Ellen.

She smiled broadly, her fingers gripping the sill of the open window as the breeze swept a few loose strands of hair off her face. She'd taken her bonnet off. It rested on the carriage seat opposite.

She glanced at him, her pale blue eyes engaging with the last eerie blue light of early evening. She was magnificent; he'd never seen a woman as beautiful as she. Every man in his regiment would envy him, and when he went into battle he would have this beauty to come back to, to refresh his battered soul.

He gripped her hand again as they travelled the last few yards in silence, in the freezing cold carriage.

A few moments only and they would be safe. Married.

The carriage slowed and pulled up, sliding a little, and Paul braced his hand on the side, holding himself steady. It was a squat, whitewashed building, little bigger than a stable, with a thatched roof. "Stay here," he said as he let go of her hand, and moved to open the door.

He climbed out onto the road but shut the door, leaving Ellen inside until the arrangements were made. As he walked about the carriage, the blacksmith came out, wiping his hands on a rag. His face and hands were dirt stained, dusted with dark smut, and he wore an old leather apron.

"Ye looking to get y'urself hitched?" The question was bluntly put, implying this man had done the deed a thousand times.

"Yes. Will you bear witness?"

"For a price… What will ye give me?"

What Paul offered first the man rejected. Paul's uniform marked him as an officer, and the man assumed he'd pay more. But unwilling to throw money away Paul haggled until they reached a price he was prepared to agree.

"Bring your woman," the blacksmith said as they shook hands, "and let's get it done."

After handing over the payment, Paul turned to the carriage. His heart jolted and a tight sensation gripped in his chest. She watched from the open window. He smiled. Her smile rose like sunshine in answer, cutting through the dusk. She was not only beautiful on the outside, but on the inside too; life brimmed inside her, like a brook bubbling and spilling over the top of a pool. A refreshing pool he wished to bathe in. It was like slipping away from the army camp on the edge of war to swim naked in a cold river – exhilarating sensations tumbled through him.

The horses stamped at the ground and shook out their manes, rattling their harness and tack, restless from their hard ride. They whinnied into the cold air as Paul moved to help Ellen from the carriage.

The spare rider, already on the ground, had lowered the step, and now he opened the door for her.

"Wait." Paul stopped the man with a hand on his shoulder to move him aside, then he lifted that hand to Ellen. "Will you marry me?"

Her smile shone in her eyes. If she'd been unsure when they'd left, she was not anymore. "Oh, yes."

"Come then. Let me make you my wife."

She laughed, gripping his fingers and then looking down to watch her step.

The snow crunched underfoot as he walked her to the forge, holding her hand as he might to parade about a ballroom. Of course they had never done that; she was not officially out. He'd snatched her from the nest, as it were.

"Stand here," the blacksmith called from within. The man had not even washed his hands, or his face. He'd become absorbed in the shadows, cast by the orange glow emanating from the fire of the forge. "There." He directed them to stand before an anvil, on the opposite side to himself.

Paul changed his grip on Ellen's hand, weaving his fingers between hers, uniting them before the words were even said.

"Have you a ring then?"

Yes, he had; where were his wits? Letting go of her hand, he took off his gloves, as she removed hers. He took the ring out of the inside pocket of his coat. It was a simple band of gold, nothing special.

A plump woman came into the smithy through a door at the back, and as he and Ellen turned, she smiled. "Another couple come to exchange vows then." Two young children followed her. A girl who was probably eight or nine, and a boy of about five.

"Aye," the blacksmith answered in a gruff voice. The children hovered near their mother watching as she came closer.

"Margaret can bear ye witness too." The blacksmith said, calling Paul's attention back. "Say y'ur piece and I'll pronounce ye man and wife." The cold dispassionate words turned Paul's stomach. He needed this to feel a little more than something rash and hurried. He wished it to be a moment Ellen would look back on with fondness. He wished to make a memory they could treasure their entire lives.

He faced her, searching for the right words. Words that would profess all he felt, but he had never been a poet. "I love you, Ellen." Her eyes searched his, the pale blue shining even in the low light of the smithy, and her lips pressed together, slightly curved. His chest filled with a warm sensation. "I promise to protect you. I swear I shall cherish you every day of my life. You may trust me, you may rely on me. I am yours. I wish to give myself to you – my life to you. Will you be my wife? Will you marry me?"

Her lips parted in a smile.

A few strands of hair had fallen about her face, the ebony curls cupped her jaw, caressing her neck. She stole his breath away.

"Yes," she whispered. But she did not hold her fingers out for him to put the ring on. "I love you, Paul. I wish to be your comfort and your sanctuary. I pledge my life to you. I will be your wife. Will you be my husband? Will you marry me?"

A smile touched his lips. "Yes. I will. Give me your hand."

She lifted her fingers, holding them out straight. He gripped her palm with one hand and slid the ring on her finger with the other. It stuck a little on her knuckle, but then slid over. A pain, like a sharp blade, pierced his heart as her hand dropped.

He had not expected love and marriage to feel like this.

Forgetting the other occupants of the smithy he gripped her shoulders and pressed a hard kiss on her lips. But then a loud ringing clang, a hammer hitting the iron anvil, broke them apart as Ellen jumped.

"I pronounce ye man and wife, forged together now ye are." They both looked at the blacksmith, and his lips lifted in a smile of acknowledgement. The deed was done. Her father could not prevent it now. They were married.

"Congratulations," the blacksmith's wife said.

"Thank you," Ellen answered, looking at the woman before glancing back at Paul, and giving him a self-conscious smile, her cheeks turning pink. He loved her like this, a bit tousled and unkempt, and looking young and slightly lacking confidence. To see her perfect beauty a little awry made her appear more human, more touchable.

"I shall fetch ye a piece of parchment to show we witnessed y'ur vows," the woman said, before turning and hurrying back inside the living space of the forge; it must be no more than one or two rooms.

Ellen's hand gripped Paul's and he looked down at her. Her eyes said she truly thought he could master the world if he wished, her trust appeared absolute. She was so innocent. He prayed her faith would be honoured. *Please, let all be well.*

"Here ye are, Donald, here's the marriage paper. I've signed it."

The blacksmith took the parchment from the woman's hand, and then held it out to Paul. "Ye sign it first. Then I'll put me mark."

The woman had brought a quill and ink as well as the parchment. Paul took the paper and moved to a wooden table then took the quill and ink from the blacksmith's wife to sign his name. The woman's name had been carefully written in a very precise script; it was probably the sum of her education. Paul handed the quill to Ellen who signed it too, then she passed it onto the blacksmith's smutty hand, it marked the paper as he scrawled a virtually unrecognisable name. But it did not matter; it was evidence enough to prove they were married within English law.

Paul lifted the paper and blew on the ink, as outside they heard horses. He handed the document to Ellen.

The blacksmith looked at him, a dark eyebrow lifting. "An angry Papa? Or another couple come?"

Paul's heartbeat stilled for a moment, then pounded. *Damn.* He'd hoped to save Ellen from any scene with her father. He turned and followed the blacksmith outside only a little behind the man. Ellen walked behind them. An unmarked carriage was indeed racing along the road. Not her father. If it had been her father, the Pembroke coat of arms would be emblazoned on the door. Yet it looked like a private vehicle, it glowed with fresh polish, shining in the last rays of light.

It would be dark in moments.

The postilion rider, who sat astride the right-hand lead horse, began pulling on the reins as the carriage drew closer. Paul took a breath and held it, an uncomfortable feeling running up his spine. Ellen gripped his elbow. She'd put her gloves back on.

Silent, Paul watched the carriage slow as it slid on the snow covered ground.

"They are my father's men." Ellen's grip tightened on his arm.

Paul straightened, feeling the lack of his sword and pistol. Both were in the carriage. Not that Pembroke would fight, Paul was married to Ellen and any thought of annulment would be foolish, it could not be undone; she had been on the road alone with him for days. She was ruined regardless.

Whoever was within waited for one of the men to climb down from the box.

Accustomed to charging into battle, Paul's arm slipped from Ellen's grip as he walked forward. He reached the carriage at the moment the man opened the door. Another stepped out. Not Ellen's father. Though this man had blue eyes very like Ellen's.

"Harding?"

Paul glanced into the carriage and saw no one else within. The Duke had sent someone for her, not come himself.

"Mr Wareham," Ellen said.

"Lady Eleanor." The man's gaze passed across Paul's shoulder, to Ellen, his expression stiff. "I have come to prevent this nonsense—"

"You're too late," Paul answered.

The man glanced at him, then looked at Ellen. "Am I, Lady Eleanor?"

She nodded, holding out the document on which the ink still dried. "The evidence is here."

"My journey is wasted then."

Paul did not answer, neither did Ellen, and for a moment the man just stood there looking at them as if he expected something else.

62

Then he said, "Very well…" and reached into his inside pocket. "I have this for you. I was to give it to you when I found you, if you were already wed." He held out a folded letter, the red wax seal on the top had been stamped with the Duke of Pembroke's mark. Ellen took it.

"I will leave you then."

"Wait," Ellen said. "Will you take letters for me, Mr Wareham, if I write them quickly?"

The man had already moved away, but he turned back, glaring at her but agreeing with a nod. "If you wish."

"I will only be a moment." Ellen looked at the blacksmith. "May I purchase some paper?"

The man nodded, looking at Paul to complete the deal. Wareham turned away again as Paul walked inside with Ellen and the blacksmith.

It did not take her long to write three separate letters and fold them. The first she wrote to her father as Paul watched, asking for his forgiveness. The second she addressed to her mother asking for understanding. The third was to her sister, Penny, expressing regret over leaving her behind.

The weight of her youth and innocence hovered over his own youth and experience. He remembered writing letters home when he'd joined the regiment. They'd been full of light and hope as hers were. He'd given up writing after he'd been posted abroad. Who at home wished to hear of his desperate need to keep his men fed, and alive, and how many men had been killed in battle, or how far they'd marched? Ellen would lose her naivety when she learned his life and the hope would die from her words.

Selfish fool. But he refused to think of consequence or future now. This was their wedding day, their wedding night, and tomorrow was Christmas, the first day of the twelve days of feasting; a time to count blessings.

"Here, Mr Wareham." Ellen rushed back out into the road, bearing her letters. Paul could see her willing her family to support her marriage as she handed them over, but he'd seen her father's face when the man had turned his offer down, as though it was piss he'd offered. Her father would never approve.

The Duke's man took them, neither smiling nor looking at her, only taking the folded pieces of paper before he turned away, saying no more.

Ellen looked at Paul. She bit her lip. He moved forward, leaving the blacksmith behind. It was night now, darkness had fallen, though the white snow reflected the moonlight. It gave the world an eerie blue glow. "Ellen." He took both her hands. "Do you regret—"

"No." The denial came immediately, even before he'd finished the question.

He smiled, ignoring the Duke's carriage pulling away behind her. "Shall we go to Carlisle and find an inn?"

"Yes."

He turned towards their carriage, still gripping one of her hands. "Who was he?"

"My father's steward."

"Do you think he even tried to get here in time to stop you? He did not seem bothered."

She glanced up. "He is committed to my father. He's worked for him for several years—"

"Time is not the thing that makes a man loyal; trust and respect make a man loyal." Officers died in battle constantly and the men had to look to a new commander.

It did not matter. The man was naught to do with Paul, and he had been too late.

Chapter Five

Ellen's heart pounded. A part of it was heavy with sadness because they'd married without her family there. But it had been beautiful and Paul's vows had sent joy overflowing in her heart, pushing her guilt and fear aside.

Becoming Paul's wife outweighed the scales. She loved him. She did not regret it.

Paul had left the carriage curtains open and the lamp unlit again; so she opened her father's letter and held it to the moonlight which reflected back off the snow, resting her shoulder against the edge of the carriage and holding the paper near the window. There were just two lines of his precise, formal script.

Eleanor
You have made your decision and by doing so, made me look a fool. Do not expect a welcome back. You are no longer permitted here.
The Duke of Pembroke

His words hurt. He had not even signed it *your father*.

They'd been brought up by her mother to call him Papa; he'd not once used the childish name himself. Father, he would concede, but he never said it with emotion.

"What does it say?"

Ellen looked at Paul. "That he wishes nothing more to do with me. I think it would have been the same even if Mr Wareham had arrived before we wed."

"Then why send him?"

"Perhaps just to look as though he tried to stop me; for appearance sake…" She shrugged. She'd never understood her father. She'd have to be much wiser to fathom his depths.

Paul smiled. "Put him from your mind. You have no need to worry over him now."

She was not worrying over him but she was concerned about her sisters and her mother.

Paul gripped her hand and lifted it to his lips. The warmth of his breath seeped through her glove. Then he turned her hand and kissed her wrist above it. Sensation skimmed up her arm. "Do not fret about your sisters either. They have time to mature, and I am certain, your eldest, Penny, is tough enough to fight her own battles. She did not seem demurring when I met her."

Ellen smiled, although moisture filled her eyes. Then she laughed, just a sudden sharp sound. "No, she is not demure, she will stand against him if he tries to force her hand, and she will use my disobedience as her example."

"And the others will learn from her…"

"Yes."

Paul had such an aura of confidence; it filled the air around him.

"Very well then. No more sulking."

Her smile lifted. "No."

"And no more tears," he added, wiping one away from the corner of her eye with his thumb.

Her next laugh was a little chocked, and then foolishly she burst into tears. But she was happy too; they were part happy tears. He pulled her close and held her, as the carriage rolled on.

Another hour or more passed before they reached Carlisle and the snowy frost bound mud roads, turned to cobble. The noise about the carriage changed as it rolled through streets, and the

66

strike of the horses hooves, tack and carriage wheels bounced back from brick houses.

When they turned into an inn, Paul pulled away from her and gave her a smile. It burned with compassion. "I know you've left a lot behind, Ellen, but now is the time to begin our new life."

"I know." She was his wife and she was about to become his wife in full. A pleasant ache gripped low in her stomach. She took a breath and her breasts pressed against her bodice.

The carriage halted and all outside was noise. Within, her nerves rioted in anticipation.

"Come." He leaned across her to open the carriage door, then climbed out before her and lifted his hand, as he'd done so many times during their journey to the border. She stepped out, her head spinning.

"Do you wish to eat in a parlour or in our room?"

"In our room."

"Well then we had better claim one."

"Yes."

He walked her across the courtyard. It had been cleared of snow. Grooms moved to help free the horses.

Her heart raced. She was not hungry. Her stomach had tied in knots.

He ordered the gammon pie for them both, and asked for a room for Captain and Mrs Harding. That was her name now. Her lips lifted a little as the novelty flowed through her.

In a moment they were shown to a room at the front of the inn, overlooking the dark street. It had a huge four-poster bed, carved in the Tudor style with garish looking men and women, and oddly shaped animals and birds. Beyond the bed, two chairs stood before a small hearth. The candelabrum on the mantle spread flickering gold light, and a fire burned in the grate, doing its best to fend off the freezing cold winter air.

"Your dinner will be up shortly, Captain." The maid bobbed a curtsy.

As soon as the door shut, Paul turned and gripped Ellen by the waist, then swept her off her feet and spun her in a circle. "My bride. My wife." He grinned broadly. Her happiness burst into a smile.

"I am in love," he said, when he put her back on her feet, and then he kissed her, hard, pressing his lips against hers at first, but then opening his mouth. It became a kiss like those they'd shared in the carriage. Her hands gripped his shoulders as it continued and he pushed her back against the solid plaster wall.

All the air left her lungs and a spiralling sensation twisted through her middle, tumbling down as her fingers slipped into his short hair. He plundered her mouth and she fought to keep up, yet she could sense his restraint as his fingers gripped and held her hips, pressing her back against the wall. She wished to be against him, to press her body up against his.

A knock struck the door.

He broke away with a sideways smile and a dimple cut into his cheek as his hair fell over his brow. He swept his hair back as he turned to the door and called, "Come in."

A blush heated Ellen's cheeks as men clothed in the inn's livery entered, carrying Paul's trunk, and other articles from the carriage. A few moments later another man arrived with a table to set up in their room and then their dinner came.

It was Christmas Eve. Ellen stripped off her gloves and dropped them on Paul's trunk, where her bonnet had been left. Her sisters would be at home in their beds.

"Eat," Paul ordered, with a smile, pulling out a chair for her.

Ellen glanced at the bed as she moved to the table. *Soon…*

Paul slid the chair in as she sat and then moved to sit in the chair opposite, before slicing up the pie.

He put a piece on her plate.

"Thank you."

"No need to thank me…" He smiled, but there was an odd look in his eyes of questions and need. "Has anyone ever spoken to you about what will happen?"

The heat of another blush crept over her skin. "No."

"Then I will be mindful, Ellen, but you have no need to fear it."

"I know. You have been..." Her words dried not knowing how to express the things she felt.

"A physical relationship between a man and a woman can be a beautiful thing. I think it will be beautiful between us."

Her face grew warmer still.

"But I've said, enough, haven't I? Eat and then you will find out for yourself."

Now she could eat nothing, each mouthful was tasteless as she forced herself to chew and swallow.

He ate heartily, discussing America. After tomorrow they would travel to Portsmouth, to meet his regiment and then catch a ship to Cork, in Ireland. Then from Ireland they would sail hundreds of miles over the Atlantic.

When he pushed his empty plate away, Ellen ceased shifting the last of her food about her plate and pushed hers away too.

"You did not eat much. Are you anxious?"

Her stomach was empty, and yet she was not hungry, because she was so nervous and she could not smile.

He did. "I'll have them clear the table. I'll be back in a moment."

Anxiety hit her even harder when he'd gone.

She rose and turned to the window, then walked across the room. She could not see anything; clouds had hidden the moon. Instead she saw her image reflected in the light of the candelabrum.

She did not look like herself anymore; the Duke's daughter who must always be perfect. The woman who faced her had hair falling from its pins and wore a creased habit, stained from days of travel. This woman would follow the drum and live on the edge of battlefields. She was the woman who would give solace to a soldier. Mrs Paul Harding, not Eleanor Pembroke.

The door opened behind her and she turned as Paul entered, followed by two of the inn's attendants. He directed them to clear the table. One carried their plates and leftovers away, the other folded the table and took that too.

The door closed behind them and Paul looked at her. Ellen's stomach somersaulted. She gripped her fingers together to stop them trembling.

He smiled, the same one he'd given her before he'd gone – the one that said, don't worry, trust me; you'll be safe.

She knew it, but it did not prevent a rush of anxiety through her nerves.

He walked towards her, intent shining in his eyes.

He leaned past her and pulled the curtains closed, then looked at her. The awe she saw in his eyes reflected the love she felt for him. He leaned down and kissed her, his palm embracing the back of her neck.

It was just a brief kiss, before he said over her lips, "I am utterly in love with you."

She smiled. "I also – I mean, I am in love with you."

His smile tilted sideways, then he looked down and his fingers began tugging the buttons securing the front of her habit loose.

Her heart pulsed so hard it pounded in her ears.

"Relax," he whispered, as he looked up to her face, but continued freeing buttons.

She could not. Her heart beat far too quickly.

Beneath her habit she wore only her chemise. She had not been able put on her light corset.

The last button slipped free, then his fingers cupped her breast over the cotton. He looked into her eyes as his fingers gripped and released and his thumb brushed across her nipple.

A sharp little pain caught like a pin-prick.

What he did felt beautiful.

His hands lifted and slid the short coat which formed her bodice from her shoulders then down her arms. It fell to the floor. The cold air touched her bare arms. "Turn and I'll undo your skirt."

She shivered as she did so.

"Cold?"

"Not really."

"We will get into bed soon, and then you will be warm."

She nodded as her stomach did another somersault.

Once her skirt had fallen to the floor, he kissed her bare shoulder and then turned her to him. He smiled as his hands slid to grip her buttocks over her cotton chemise and pulled her close. Then he kissed her again. A kiss like the one they'd shared when they'd first come into the room, his tongue pressing into her mouth.

When he pulled back all the air had gone from her lungs.

"Ellen…" he whispered, it was a question but she didn't know what he asked. "Take my coat off for me," he encouraged then.

She bit her lip, realising she was too naïve. Of course he would expect her to take part. Her fingers lifted to the glinting brass buttons of his military coat, as her gaze fell, but her hands shook too much to free them. A sound of amusement left his throat as he took over the task. She could not meet his gaze as he took it off. An aura of strength and masculinity radiated from him and it travelled through her flesh to her bones. Then he stripped his shirt off too…

Heavens. He *was* beautiful. She touched him. His stomach and chest were ripples of muscle, and his flesh warm.

He smiled at her when she looked up, with humour in his eyes. She smiled too.

"Will you help me with my boots?"

She nodded as he turned to sit in one of the chairs. He began tugging at the heel of one boot. She helped him.

After his second boot fell to the floor he stood again, and still smiling gripped her chemise by her hips. Her stomach flipped another turn when he lifted it. But she raised her arms so he could strip it off over her head. It left her naked.

"You are beautiful; you have the look of a goddess." His fingers touched her breast, slipping over the lower curve and then her nipple, before his thumb pressed down to tease it to a peak. She rose to her toes and kissed him. She needed that contact to ground

71

her again, and hold her nerves steady.

He conceded, kissing her back, his tongue pressing into her mouth as his hand gripped and kneaded her breast more firmly, while the other cupped her nape.

I love you. The words roared through her mind. She was not afraid of him.

When he broke the kiss, gentleness, and love, shone in his eyes. This battered, hardened, young, warrior, who had the marks of war in scars on his skin, who she'd seen kill a man – had a heart of gold. "Take off your stockings on the bed, then get beneath the covers, so you do not get cold. I'll stoke the fire."

As she sat, he moved to the hearth. She untied the ribbons forming her garters and then slipped her stockings off. He tipped coal from a scuttle onto the embers. She let her stockings fall onto the floorboards and moved beneath the sheet.

He reached for a poker and stirred up the embers so flames flickered into life.

Her father would have called for a maid to do it, and been angry that a servant had not already thought of it. He would never tend a fire himself. But then Paul had been his own master and servant for years.

The sheets were cold, and the dense feather filled quilt which covered them pressed the cold sheet against her naked skin. She shivered as her nipples peaked.

Paul stood and turned back to face her. He smiled as he crossed the room.

She'd lifted the covers up to her chin.

When he reached the bed he unbuttoned his falls holding her gaze, then slid both his pantaloons and his underwear down. The air caught in her lungs and her heart thundered again. She'd thought his chest beautiful – but the movement of the muscle in his buttocks and his thighs as he bent… then he pushed all his clothing off his feet and stood…

She could not breathe.

He lifted the covers and she moved back to make room for him beside her. He'd not snuffed the candles, but left them burning.

Immediately his lips pressed against hers and his warm hand ran over her cold skin, from her hip to her breast, then he kneaded it once more.

The blissful sensation twisted in her stomach as she rolled to face him and reached her arms about his neck.

His kiss travelled from her lips across her chin, down her neck to her shoulder. Her back arched as if she knew what he was about to do, but she did not, not until the moment his lips touched her breast once quickly and then closed over her nipple. The pressure as he sucked was warm and gentle as his hand slid lower, brushing across her hip, making her shiver. Then it touched her inner thigh.

"Paul?"

He did not answer, merely continued sucking her breast as his fingers brushed over the private place between her legs. The place she knew a man and woman would join, but she knew no more than that.

His fingertips sent tingles across her skin and an ache skipping upwards through her body.

She was warmer now. Her fingers ran through his hair.

Then he looked up. "Do you, trust me, Ellen?"

She nodded, staring into his blue eyes and looking at the curve and length of his brown eyelashes. "Yes."

Oh, his fingers slid into her, and hers gripped hard on his shoulders.

"I'll not hurt you."

She nodded; she knew that. But she bit her lip as his fingers drew in and out, gently and intimately, invading then retreating.

His lips returned to hers, his tongue pressing into her mouth, distracting her mind. *Paul*. She did love him. She did.

His mouth left hers and returned to her breast, as his fingers continued their caress. He was cherishing her; absorbed in her, she could feel it. Warmth spread throughout her body, reaching

73

in ripples as far out as her fingers and toes. Her legs bent and her knees parted wider for him, as his invasion grew in intensity, in speed and depth.

She was damp where he touched her, and the dampness increased as the warmth did too.

His head lifted. "Ellen…" His fingers slipped free of her then gripped her own and set them against the part of him which would join them. He curled her fingers around him and moved her hand up and down.

Shyness prevailed over every other sense, and anxiety stirred. His fingers slipped back inside her and then she touched him as he touched her. It was awkward, unreal and strange…

"Lie on your back, Ellen."

She rolled backwards letting go of him and opening her legs wider as he came over her, so he could settle between her thighs.

"It may hurt for a moment."

She nodded as that part of him touched her, and then as she looked into his eyes, he thrust in, and yes it did hurt, a bursting sensation pierced her, and then there was an uncomfortable pressure.

She felt a little sick. But it was done now; they were man and wife.

He withdrew then pressed in again.

She gripped his arms, realising it would not just be a single invasion. His jaw had been taut before but now a smile played with the edge of his lips as he withdrew again, and pressed in. Her fingers lifted to his hair.

"I love you, Ellen. You are the most beautiful woman I've ever seen."

She smiled, her shyness receding, and her senses absorbing the odd new feelings. "I love you, also."

"I will look after you, I swear it."

She nodded, watching his face as he worked, casting spells in her body.

She could not take her gaze from his and he did not look away from her. She loved him so much. "It's wonderful."

He smiled more, and moved more quickly, pressing in and pulling out, again, and again, and her fingernails dug into his shoulders, as her knees bent higher so her toes could curl into the sheet, against the wool filled mattress beneath it.

Her body was flooded with lovely sensations; they gripped in her lungs, caught her breath, and trembled through her stomach. She had no breath left when he thrust hard, once, twice and then pushing deep, his body went as stiff as stone and his eyes shut as he sucked in a harsh breath before releasing it in a sigh which brushed over her skin. The part of him inside her pulsed.

He didn't move for a long while, and while he lay still, the pleasurable feelings he'd engendered tingled through her nerves then ebbed away.

He opened his eyes and smiled, then withdrew suddenly and rolled to his back beside her. "Come." He lifted his arm. "We'll sleep now."

She pillowed her head on his chest. She felt odd. Like a new person – a person who'd been shown a precious secret other people had been keeping.

He fell asleep and she listened to his breathing, watching the flickering orange candlelight dance about the room.

She was his wife.

~

Ellen woke in a silent room as daylight peaked about the curtains. She'd curled up against Paul who'd turned on to his side. It was Christmas. Her sisters would be waking. They'd have come to her room if she'd been at home. She presumed Sylvia and Rebecca would go to Penny instead. They'd attend mass and eat an informal luncheon with her mother, then dine formally in the afternoon with her father too, and there would be guests invited from local

75

families.

"Good morning."

Paul turned to face her.

"Hello. Good tidings," she whispered her seasonal greeting, embarrassment sweeping over her.

His fingers stroked her hair back from her face as a smile curved his lips.

"Merry Christmas." He kissed her for a while, then the weight of his hips rolled her backwards, and he was between her legs once more and pressing into her. She lost her breath.

He did delicious things, moving within her, the soft hair on his chest brushing against her breasts as he did so.

Her fingers gripped his nape as she held his gaze. He was so steady and strong. Her fingers slid down his back, exploring.

When his end came this time he growled, his eyes shutting again as he ground against her for a moment, then stilled.

He sighed when he rolled off her.

"We will stay here today," he said, after a moment. "I'll order breakfast. I'm starving, and then I'll ask for a bath and we can bathe together."

That sounded naughty and decadent. She was certain no married couples she knew bathed together. She laughed with happiness.

She missed her sisters and her mother, but she was with Paul and she was his wife.

They spent the rest of the day doing as he'd said; relaxing. They ate breakfast in their room, she back in her habit for propriety's sake as he sat in his pantaloons and shirt. Then the inn's attendants brought up a copper bath, and pails and pails of steaming water along with some lavender water to scent it. It was a tight squeeze for them both to fit in it. But Paul sat behind her with his legs bent and parted, and she draped her shins over the edge of the tub. They lay in the water for an age as he ran the soap across her skin and brushed the water over her breasts.

They made love again when they got out, and stayed in bed until he was hungry once more and wanted supper. Then they returned to bed and languished there without sleeping for hours.

She *was* happy.

Chapter Six

"It is a shame you have to endure another long journey so soon, Ellen." A look of tiredness caught in her eyes. He'd kept her awake half the night. He smiled. She did too. She did not look unhappy about it.

The inn's grooms were readying their carriage behind her.

"It doesn't matter. I knew it would be so."

He nodded and tapped her under the chin.

The snow had melted yesterday, the tracks would now be slush and mud, and it would be a much slower journey to Portsmouth. Travelling was a game of endurance she was going to have to become used to.

It took five days. Five days of dull inactivity within a carriage. Five days in which he was unable to fully appreciate the beauty of his wife. Although, on two occasions as they'd travelled through the night, he had persuaded her to sit astride him and lift her skirts. She'd blushed both times he'd asked, so he'd tamped the lamp to save her embarrassment. He praised God for her precious innocence, yet a part of him knew such moments would often be hurried and stolen when they joined the regiment – she'd have to adjust.

The carriage pulled into the courtyard of an inn near the docks in Portsmouth. The time for her innocence and carefree living was at an end.

Once it came to a halt, he opened the door, climbed down and handed her out. "I'll settle you into a room, then leave you while I find the Lieutenant Colonel. I need to tell him I'm here and find my men. I'll come back afterwards." Lifting his fob watch from his pocket he flicked it open to check the time. It was two after midday. "I should return for dinner. But if I have not, order a meal and eat in our room."

She nodded, but he could see she was nervous. She caught her lower lip between her teeth, as if holding back the words, *don't go*. He did not wish to leave. Yet this was his life, many times she would be left alone.

She smiled. It trembled a little. "I know you must go, it is your duty." Her answer implied she'd read his mind, and he thanked God she was brave enough to override the words her heart wished to say.

At least she understood. "Come then."

He settled her into a room, which looked out onto the busy street, although to the far right you could glimpse the sea, then said, "Goodbye," after kissing her lips.

He wished to stay, but her words were true – he had a duty. That came first and pleasure afterwards.

It took a half-hour to walk through the docks and up the hill to the barracks. The other officers were there, with the Lieutenant Colonel. Paul was told who'd arrived and who was still to come, the date they would sail, and the name of the ship he and his men were to use. Then he went to visit his men who shared a room in the barracks.

They greeted him, after saluting, with smiles and laughter, and he was smacked on the shoulder a dozen times when he told them he'd married a few days before. The 52nd was different. They had a rule that officers drilled with their men, and it developed a cama-raderie and friendship which did not exist in other troops. As Ellen had said, he could have ridden in the cavalry, but the closeness of these men had got him through the last years. They'd endured horror together, lost comrades, and survived to fight again.

He could not walk out and leave them when he'd told them of the plans for their sailing, so he sat down and shared a drink with them, then played a hand of cards, but all the time his blood itched to be back at the inn with Ellen.

When he finally found an excuse to leave, it was dark. He looked at his watch. Seven. She would be bored and lonely. He quickened his pace.

In fact she was asleep. She lay on top of the large bed in their room, fully clothed. The innkeeper had told Paul she'd not eaten before he'd come up and so he'd ordered a meal.

She'd taken the pins out of her ebony hair and it had spread across the quilt, her pale skin was a stark contrast to it. He'd not seen her hair loose since Christmas. She was such a precious sight. He let her beauty ease his soul; the memories of war, the sound of cannon fire and rifles that had invaded his head when he'd sat among his men, slipped away.

"Ellen."

Her eyelids fluttered and lifted, long dark lashes framing her very pale blue eyes. She took his breath when he turned and saw her for the first time each day. She was a balm to sooth his battle sore soul. "I've ordered dinner."

She sat up and blinked.

He sat on the edge of the bed. "Is sleeping all that you've done?"

She nodded. "I was tired."

He lifted her hand and kissed her fingers. "We are to sail in four days. Tomorrow I will take you to meet the other officers and my men." She looked nervous. "They will like you, Ellen."

She nodded. A knock struck the door, announcing the arrival of their dinner.

~

When Paul ushered her into his Lieutenant Colonel's quarters, cold fear tightened in Ellen's stomach. It had been one thing to travel with Paul, it was completely another to become a part of his life. She stepped into a world far beyond her father's sheltered realm. A world she did not know, with Paul the warrior who still frightened her a little.

Paul's body stiffened as he entered. It felt as if his thoughts detached from her. Here, he was the soldier who had killed the highwayman, not the young man who'd turned music pages for her in her father's drawing room – the man who had made her smile and laugh.

All the men she was introduced to were just as intimidating, dressed in their smart red and gold regimental coats, looking tall and confident. But all of them smiled and bowed over her hand, wishing her well, and giving both her and Paul words of congratulations. Only his commanding officer, the Lieutenant Colonel, made her continue to feel uncomfortable, because he never stopped watching her from the moment she and Paul had entered until the moment they left. But the conversation progressed and all the men were polite and jovial. Particularly a man Paul called his closest friend, Captain George Montgomery. He followed them out of the office and onto the parade ground.

"I am pleased for you, Paul. You've picked a pretty little piece…" His smile was for Paul, but passed onto Ellen. "We'll have a ray of sunshine to look forward to in our baggage train, ma'am." He gave Ellen another swift bow.

"She will be *my* ray of sunshine though," Paul answered, the jest sounded half joke and half warning. His friend winked in Ellen's direction. A blush burned her skin.

"Quite the diamond." Captain Montgomery commented looking back at Paul. "And all yours, yes, I know. No wonder you do not wish to leave your wife behind."

"Come." Paul gripped her arm gently. "Let me introduce you to my men. Good day George." Glancing back at his friend, he nodded, his fingers already encouraging Ellen to move.

"Good day, Paul." His friend's smile passed between them again. "Ma'am."

She smiled. He was a rogue; she could see the twinkle in his eye, and as they walked away Paul confirmed it. "George is a charmer, but you are to pay no mind to it, he is harmless in reality. Simply a slave to a pretty face–"

"A sublime face!"

The shout came from behind them, and they both looked back. Captain Montgomery grinned, lifting a hand in a gesture that said good-bye. Paul scowled when she looked up at him, but when they turned away, his gaze grew depth, warmth and humour. "It is true though – it is a sublime face."

A smile she could not have held back parted her lips. She could live in Paul's world when there was a soft look in his eyes to carry her through. He let go of her arm, and instead she gripped his, as he pointed to a two-storey red brick building on the far side of the parade ground. "My men are quartered there. Tomorrow I shall have to be here at eight to run them through their paces. They'll have been lax during leave, I imagine. It's time we returned to routine."

Routine? She could not even begin to imagine the routine of her new life.

When they entered the room full of soldiers, it was very different from meeting the officers. There were shouts and whoops and a mass of masculine energy surrounded her. She pressed close to Paul, gripping the sleeve of his scarlet coat tighter as his other arm lifted, calling for quiet.

"Show my wife some courtesy!"

The men then paraded past her, and Paul gave their names as they bowed.

She did not lift her hand to any of them, but feeling wide-eyed and unnerved nodded at their comments and congratulations. Her mind span with names at the end of it, and she could not recall a single one.

"Will you stay and take a drink with us?" Paul's sergeant asked, looking at Paul.

Paul looked at her, a question in his eyes. *Are you comfortable?*

She was to live amongst these men, in closer quarters than she'd lived with her family. She refused to be feeble. She nodded.

The Sergeant flicked his hand at one of the soldiers who moved to begin pouring from a jug, and others then moved too, refilling pewter beakers. She was given one full of frothing small beer, as was Paul, and then the sergeant encouraged them to take a seat on a long bench beside a long wooden table. They did.

The sergeant stood to make a toast, holding up his dented tankard.

"To the Captain and his wife."

"To the Captain and his wife!" The room chorused at a deafening pitch.

Ellen looked along the table, at least fifty faces stared back, smiling. She was probably as red as it was possible to be, but still she lifted her beaker. "Thank you."

"Aye, thank you, for your good wishes," Paul added, and then they both drank.

Ellen looked at him as he set down his empty tankard. She set down hers, still half full.

He appeared different amongst his men – more vital. Energy, mastery, and pride, oozed from his stance. He was definitely the warrior here, and he looked older.

He turned to her, as if he sensed her staring, gripped her hand and lifted it onto his thigh, his hold gentle but secure.

Love welled up inside her. Yes, he was a soldier, but his strength was protective, and with her, his touch was always gentle.

They walked along the waterfront once they'd left the barracks, then returned to the inn and ate dinner in a private parlour.

"Tomorrow I'll have to leave early, Ellen, to drill the men."

Ellen nodded, she could do little but accept his life.

"You can come if you wish?"

Her eyes opened wider.

"Not to stand on the ground, you understand, but you may watch from the barrack room I'll have been allocated. You will be among the men all the time as we travel, it's best you adjust to it."

She smiled. "Yes." She wished to be able to fit in, at the moment it was all alien compared to the sheltered life she'd left, and here Paul was so different to the man she'd thought she knew.

A smile tilted his lips, forming the dimple that stirred her heart with tenderness. Warmth and depth filled his eyes. "Shall we retire?"

That same warmth turned her stomach over as he took her hand and kissed her knuckles. She rose and followed him upstairs.

~

In the morning when Ellen woke, Paul stood before the wash bowl in the corner, he held a razor in his hand, as he looked at his image in a small mirror, shaving.

He wore no shirt, only his grey pantaloons with his braces hanging loose, and his feet were bare.

She watched the muscles moving in his back, and his shoulders, and looked at the strong defined curves of his upper arms as the etched lines shifted beneath his skin.

Her husband was superb, physically as perfect as the statues lining the halls in her father's Palladian mansion.

Ellen turned and stretched and he must have caught her movement in the mirror, he looked at her through his reflection and smiled. "Good morning, my love."

My love. Those words made her stomach tumble over and the sight of his smile clutched tight in her chest.

"Once I'm clothed, I'll order breakfast. We'll eat in the parlour. I'll send a maid up to help you dress."

Ellen nodded, and then sitting up in bed watched him finish shaving and dress. Pride flared in her chest as well as love. He secured the buttons of his scarlet coat, smiling at her.

"I'll go down then and send up a maid." He came to the bed and brushed a kiss on her cheek.

As soon as he'd gone, Ellen rose to wash and prepare herself, her heart pacing swiftly in her chest. She would truly start her life as a soldier's wife today.

After breakfast they walked up the hill to the barracks. As they walked through the gate, the guards saluted Paul, and he them in reply. Within, he led her to a small room, which was empty bar a narrow, cot-like bed.

Light broke into the dingy room through a small window in the outer wall. When Paul left, she leaned her elbow on the sill and looked down onto the parade ground.

In a few minutes she saw him down there, walking into the centre of the parade ground. His men came from the far corner gathering in lines. But he did not merely stand and order them to walk as so, but marched with them in several formats and called for them to lift and aim their guns, before checking that they all stood as they should. Then he made them kneel and rise a dozen times, calling them to aim, and then kneel again, and form a square.

It was an impressive spectacle, but again she had a sense, she didn't really know the man she watched.

At the end of the activity he walked about, speaking with each man and checking their equipment before letting them leave. Of course here it merely looked like a rehearsal for a theatrical show, but it was preparation for battle, not entertainment.

When he came to fetch her, he still hid behind the guise of a military man and although she wished to hug him she did not. She did not think he'd welcome it. But he did offer his arm when they went outside, and said he would walk her back to the inn and take luncheon with her before returning alone to speak with the officers.

So would this be her new life, watching his through occasional windows, while he fulfilled his duty and excluded her with stiff, silent, coldness?

To do his duty he closed his true self off, hiding emotion and feelings – she did not like the soldier side of him.

He did not leave her with nothing to do though, he ordered her to make a list of everything she'd need to take to America, and bid her write an advertisement for a woman to help her. He said they would recruit someone to act as her maid when the regiment reached Cork.

Chapter Seven

Ellen stood on the deck clutching the rail, watching England disappear. It had been two days since she'd first watched the regiment parade. Four days since she'd met the other side of her husband fully.

It was midday, and Paul had spent the last hour instructing his men and ensuring they were all aboard and their kit stowed away before the ship sailed on the high tide.

She'd met the other wives who were travelling with the regiment, all married to men of a lower rank than Paul. There were only four and they were on deck now too, keeping out of the way as the men worked below decks to organise the space the regiment had to share.

Only an hour ago Ellen had learned she and Paul were to sleep in the open galley with his men. There would be no privacy. But they would reach Cork in two or three days. Yet when they sailed to America there would be weeks with no privacy.

Her fingers gripped the rail over-tightly. She thought of Penny at home, possibly sitting before a warm fire working on her embroidery at this hour of day, or perhaps she practiced the pianoforte.

A longing for home caught in Ellen's breast.

Something touched her waist and then a tall strong presence settled behind her. Her husband. She looked up and back. "You look sorrowful, Ellen."

Air left her lungs, a breath she hadn't even known she'd held in. *I am a little sorrowful*, but only because she could not yet picture the future. She was happy with him, but there were so many unknowns, and her family had been left behind. She did not admit her insecurity though; that would be disrespectful.... "I'm well. It is simply odd to leave England when a month ago I'd travelled barely ten miles from home."

His fingers tucked a lock of hair, which kept catching the breeze and blowing across her face, behind her ear. "This must be difficult for you."

Ellen held his blue gaze. "I'm not afraid."

"I think you are, if you take the trouble to say you are not." His fingers slipped over her cheek to tap beneath her chin. "Remember I've seen enough recruits preparing for battle to know the signs, Ellen."

She swallowed, then licked her lips to stop them feeling dry and saw his gaze lower to watch the gesture, before she spoke again. "I am afraid. A little. But only of what I do not know – what life will be like." He'd become more and more the soldier she did not know well, and less and less the man she had met in her father's beautiful state drawing room back at home.

"Ask the other women. They shall tell you. Make friends. I know at times it will not be easy but I shall do my best to make you happy."

"I know, I will be happy, I have you. I am not afraid of that."

"Then I am content. I must go and speak to the Lieutenant Colonel. You will forgive–"

"You do not need to ask forgiveness for fulfilling your duty, Paul."

His fingertips cradled her cheek as he smiled, before walking away.

Her heart thumped steadily. The other women had not really spoken to her, she presumed because they thought she was too wellborn compared to them, but Paul's men did not seem to judge him by his birth, and Paul had not even told anyone who she was. Yet, her voice, her posture, her clothing, made her stand apart from the other women. She was not and never would be a common soldier's wife. She was an officer's wife, and from a titled family. She would never quite fit in. But she longed to, she missed the company of her sisters, their hurried, whispered conversations and laughter.

She looked back at the thin line of green and grey along the horizon, England.

If her father knew she wished to fit in among commoners, he would send a scalding letter.

~

They dined with the men and doing so gave Ellen opportunity to speak with the women who were clustered at the end of a long trestle table. Paul sat further along among his men.

Now was her chance to try and become a part of them – accepted.

"How do you travel with the men in general?" she asked of the woman beside her, before taking a sip of the watery broth in her bowl.

The woman glanced at her with uncertainty; all the woman had been sitting stiffly since she'd joined them, when on deck earlier, Ellen had heard them talking easily with each other many times.

Ellen longed to simply say, *you need not be afraid of me,* but that would sound crass and patronizing when she was so much younger than most of them. "I have no idea how I shall live…" Ellen added, her uncertainty and fear slipping into her voice.

"Simply, ma'am," the woman said at last, then she took a breath. "We mostly ride upon the baggage carts if the men are on the march, but sometimes we must walk if the terrain is too difficult for the horses or the carts. When we travel by boat, then we must make do with whatever accommodation we can obtain." The woman's hand shook a little as she took another mouthful of her broth, as if she was afraid of speaking.

Ellen looked across the scored dark oak table at another woman; they had all been listening. Ellen asked, "And where do you sleep, and stay when the men are camped?"

"Wherever we may, ma'am. We share our men's tents, and they are put up and taken down often if the men are on the march. Or if they are defending a place or preparing for battle then we camp in one place—"

"But the Captain will be billeted." one of the other women said, looking at her friend not Ellen.

The woman who had spoken initially looked at the other, then nodded at Ellen. "Yes, the officers, if we are to remain in any one place for long, will find a room, or a farmhouse to take them in, or somewhere they may be put up. They are only in their tents if the regiment is marching and nowhere is near… If the men are in barracks though, they must find us accommodation nearby"

Ellen looked along the table at Paul. He talked animatedly with the men, then laughed before he took a sip from a tankard.

Swallowing another mouthful of the foul broth, Ellen then asked. "What have you seen?"

All the women glanced at one another. They *were* uneasy. They did not like speaking with her and from their hesitance and nervousness, she guessed they were uncomfortable because she was an officer's wife, and a wellborn woman. But one of the women answered in a whisper, "Many horrible things, ma'am. Many things a woman would not wish to see… But that is war, and I would rather be with my Michael here, than in England, not knowing if he is alive or dead, or will ever return to me."

"And I could not bear to let Tommy go to America and never see him for months or years, ma'am." Another woman chimed in, smiling nervously at Ellen.

She looked the closest to Ellen in age, perhaps only a few years older. Nancy. Her name flew into Ellen's head, plucked from all those she'd been told in the last few days. She had been introduced as Mistress Bowman, but asked Ellen to call her by her given name.

Ellen *was* making them feel awkward sitting among them, Nancy's voice had quivered.

"And what do you all do?" The question came out on a breath of longing, as the life Ellen had left behind tumbled through her thoughts – memories of playing her pianoforte, sitting and working silently on embroidery among her sisters; learning to dance with the master who had come to the house once a week; sitting and reading aloud to her sisters before they went to sleep...

All the women looked at her oddly. "Why, we wash the men's clothing, and cook for them. There is little time for anything else, ma'am."

The question proved Ellen's naivety. They had never played a pianoforte, or perhaps even seen one, and they had certainly never sat in the warmth of the sun engrossed in a book – they could not read. Blushing, Ellen changed her question to ask about what the men did.

When it came time to sleep, the tables and benches were collapsed and secured along the sides of the galley.

The low ceilinged room which forced Paul to bend over constantly then became a dormitory for a hundred or more men, all rolling out pallets. Ellen watched as Paul laid out theirs. It was only wide enough for one.

"Do you wish to undress?" he whispered as he slipped the buttons on the coat of his uniform free.

Biting her lip, Ellen shook her head. She'd shared a room with her sisters when she was younger, but this... she would suffer two nights in her dress rather than disrobe down to her chemise. The women's conversation haunted her. What if it was always to be like this?

And what would happen when they sailed to America?

"The women said that when the regiment camp, you are billeted.

Do you share that accommodation too?"

He looked up and smiled. "Sometimes, but that is only during war, when we are fighting. In America we will most often be in barracks, and then I will hire lodgings to share with you and not live among the men. America will different to the Peninsular War. The situation is not the same."

"And the woman you said you will hire for me…"

"Will have her own room. She will be your maid of all work, Ellen. You shall not live exactly as the wives of the soldiers live."

She longed for the woman who Paul intended to hire to help her when they reached Cork. She was out of her depth without servants and she did not think herself proud, but she had come from a sheltered life. This was so different from her father's Palladian mansion with its many rooms, and statement of wealth – this low ceilinged space, was too enclosed. With so many others here, it felt overcrowded and as if the walls closed in.

She would beg Paul to secure them a cabin for the longer journey.

Most of the lanterns hanging from the low beams had been extinguished, but a few still burned, one near the ladder leading to the upper deck and a couple beside some of the men's pallets.

All about her the men were in varying states of dress and undress as they retired, though none were naked.

She turned her eyes to Paul, and watched him lie down and lift the wool blanket for her. Nervousness warring with embarrassment, she knelt and then lay down beside him trying to look only at the wooden planking of the ship. Her pillow was his muscular arm as it rested beneath her head. His other arm surrounded her, his hand on her stomach, as she lay with her back against his chest. His shallow breathing stirred her hair.

She did not sleep, merely lay there, her thoughts absorbed by the odd rock and sway of the ship, and the sound of so many men breathing heavily in the shadow filled space.

When she woke, Paul was rising, moving from behind her, and

about them others stirred. She felt as if she'd had just a moment's sleep. "I'm sorry you must get up," he whispered to her as she watched him slipping on his scarlet coat. "You will learn to shut your eyes and sleep no matter where you are in the end, because if you do not, you'll never rest."

Ellen nodded and sat up, rubbing her eyes. Then she stretched. He'd said this life would be hard. She had not imagined it like this…

"Go with one of the women freshen up, while we set up the benches." He looked away. "Mistress Porter, would you help my wife?"

This was all so strange.

~

The ship swayed constantly – it was no different than Ellen's emotions, trepidation rocked inside her. Soon they would be sailing for America and travelling for weeks. She was doing her best to fit in among the women, but everything was so alien it was not easy.

Paul had spent a couple of hours with her on deck, as she stood at the rail, just watching the acres of ocean reaching to the horizon, but beyond those hours she'd stood alone mostly. When she approached the other women, their conversation dropped to silence before they curtsied. They were clearly uncomfortable around her and she did not like to upset them.

When it was time to retire, she slipped beneath the blanket quickly, leaving him to undress.

When he lay behind her he wore only his underwear and a shirt – she could feel the muscular definition of his body. His hand gently pressed against her stomach. The breathing of the men about them calmed as people drifted into sleep and the movement in the room stilled as the last few lamps were extinguished. Without the lamplight, the galley sunk into a depth of pitch black.

She had not heard Paul's breathing change.

He pressed a kiss on her neck.

Her stomach turned a somersault.

Then his fingers urged her body back tighter against his.

His arousal pressed against her back and bottom through the layers of her gown and her petticoats.

"Lie back," he whispered into her ear.

She did as he urged, rolling onto her back, and he moved over her.

"*Here…*" The word was spoken on her breath.

"Here or never, Ellen, there will be hundreds of nights like this when the men are about us; simply be quiet." His words were spoken in a very low whisper.

Ellen longed to look and check if anyone watched them, but it was too dark to see and no sound indicated they did.

"Raise your skirt and petticoat."

Her heart pounded as she did so, looking up, but she could not even see his face.

His fingers slipped between her legs, rubbing for a moment, and then sliding inside her, the movement slow and gentle, drawing her thoughts away from the room and anyone but him. Then he slipped his underwear lower on his hips. The same hand gripped her thigh and moved her legs further apart.

She bit her lip when he entered her, and she carried on biting it as he moved within her, in a slow steady motion. Her heart thumped and her breathing grew short, as if the air disappeared from the galley.

They were covered by the blanket and it was dark, none of the men would see anything if they did watch. But they might know what was happening.

He pressed a kiss on her temple as he continued moving, as though he sensed her insecurity, but he did not speak, probably to avoid increasing the risk of waking his men.

The spell he could create began to weave its charm, whispering through her blood and spinning into her limbs.

Her fingers gripped his hips, grasping the muscle moving

beneath his skin.

"*Paul*." She could not prevent his name escaping.

"Hush, Ellen."

She closed her eyes and bit her lip again, absorbing every heavenly sensation, and he moved more quickly.

She opened her eyes her fingers touching a hollow in his cheek. It implied he'd gritted his teeth.

Her thighs gripped about his hips involuntarily as the sensation inside her swelled, and then there was one deep last push and his seed spilled into her. She opened her mouth, her breath releasing – while his body shuddered. Then his weight came down onto her and she held him as he lay still for a moment.

When he moved, he brushed a kiss on her cheek before laying on his side, as she turned to hers. Her back brushed against his chest.

"I love you," he whispered to her hair.

Tears slipped from Ellen's eyes.

"Are you well?" He could not have seen her tears, though perhaps he sensed them.

"Yes, I am well." She was. She was happier than she'd ever been, no matter the oddness of his world – she could still feel the intensity of his love for her.

"Sleep now."

She understood there were two sides to Paul; here he must be the soldier, but he had wanted her to know the other half of him was still there. The man who loved and needed her.

She did sleep and she slept well, wrapped in his arms.

Chapter Eight

Ellen sat with a quill poised in her fingers and an empty page lay on the oak table before her. After four weeks in Cork, the weather had not been good enough to sail. She'd written to her mother and to Penny. She'd told her mother she was well, but impatient to complete their journey. To Penny she'd written a dozen amusing little stories of her adventures, describing Paul's men and their atrocious ability to maintain polite language in her hearing – and about the women, who were kind and supportive yet kept their distance. She had a woman to help her now, as maid, cook, washerwoman and everything else, though currently, while they lived in the inn, her only duties were as a companion and ladies' maid.

Ellen looked at the blank page. She'd no idea what to say to her father. She'd received no response to her last letters.

The quill twirled in her fingers. No words came.

She looked out the window at the busy street. She knew Paul was restless. He wanted to be on his way. The waiting was difficult.

Words came at last and she looked back at the paper and dipped the quill in the ink then wiped the nib clear of drops, before writing simply.

Dear Father,
I hope you will forgive me for marrying Paul. But I am happy.

We are happy. I have told Mama how we are waiting to sail to
America, but the winds will not calm enough to allow it. I think
we shall be here another couple of weeks, if you wish to write to me
before we leave?
   Your daughter
   Eleanor

She looked at the words for a moment, before blotting them
and then folding the letter. She sealed it by heating the red wax
over a flame lit from a flint, and letting a couple of drops fall
onto the folded page.

Once she'd addressed it, she placed it with the others and moved
to fetch her cloak. Then she went in search of her maid, to ask
the woman to accompany her to put them in the post. She could
have asked the woman to simply take them, but Ellen wished for
air, and Paul would not be back until dinner.

~

Ellen stood on the edge of the harbour wall watching the waves
crash against it. The sea was still too angry for the ships to sail.
Foam and spray spewed over the top of the wall as the waves hit
it, and tiny droplets of salty water blew into her face.

This was her favourite thing to do, to come down to the harbour
and watch the sea. She liked to come during the hours Paul drilled
his men because at this early hour, the harbour was less busy as
long as the tide was out.

Another four weeks had passed and more since she'd written to
her family, but there had been no reply. Each day she looked out
across the sea thinking of her mother and her sisters, wondering
how they were, and what they thought of her desertion. Were they
angry with her? Was that why they had not written? Ships reached
Cork from England every week but no letters came.

Ellen stood for a little while longer, just watching the tug of war the tide played with the waves, throwing them against the harbour wall, before pulling them back.

She felt like the sea. She was happy with Paul, and this life had become normal, yet when they left for America it would be abnormal again. The part of her which missed her mother and her sisters still tried to pull her back.

Ellen turned her back on the water and faced her maid. The woman stood a few steps back. "Jennifer, I'm sorry to leave you standing in the cold. We will go home." *Home?* An inn was not a home – yet they'd been here so many weeks.

But when would she have a home again, if they were to always travel?

Home.

Paul was home – and so the inn was home – that was the answer. She did not need a place, just him.

To stave off boredom, she'd begun sewing shirts and cravats for Paul. The task filled the hours she sat alone. At home she would have embroidered, but embroidery had little purpose here; it would appear ostentatious. Sewing was the occupation she decided to return to as she walked back through the cobbled streets, with Jennifer keeping pace beside her.

The streets were busier than they would normally be and everyone seemed to be huddled together in small groups and talking in hurried whispers. A group they passed splintered and began another conversation with others. Ellen could not hear.

"What are they talking about, Jennifer?"

"I don't know, ma'am."

It had rained last night, and the cobbles were damp and glistening with a metallic glow as the grey stormy sky reflected back. A sense of doom, of eerie disappointment, settled over Ellen as she walked the last hundred yards. Something was happening, something ominous.

When she reached the inn instead of going to their room, she sat in the parlour Paul had hired for their use and gathered up her sewing, but her fingers shook, making it difficult to thread a needle. It was silly to feel anxious merely because people talked in the street, and yet after luncheon, as the afternoon turned to evening and Paul had not returned, her anxiety grew.

She kept looking towards the door of the parlour each time she heard footsteps on the flagstones beyond the door, her heart setting up a sharp rhythm...

He was late.

"Should I order your dinner, ma'am," Jennifer sat in a chair across the room, also sewing.

"No Jennifer, I will wait for my husband."

But half an hour later and Paul had still not come.

Ellen wondered if she should ask someone in the inn to send a message to the barracks. But surely he would have sent word if anything was wrong.

She put her sewing down on the arm of the chair, to go and ask. Then finally she heard familiar strong heavy footsteps in the hall. *Paul.*

She stood just as the door opened.

The scent and chill of cold air seeped from his greatcoat. It had been trapped in the cloth. "Paul?" She moved towards him as his blue eyes settled on her. His whole body implied concern. Something was wrong...

"Ellen, have you heard?" He spoke sharply – the military officer.

"Heard?"

"You have not?"

She shook her head.

"Napoleon is free."

"Free..." But the war with France was over. Napoleon was imprisoned. *We are to sail to America.*

"He escaped Elba at the end of February. He's already gathering an army. We are no longer going to America. We have orders to sail to Ostend."

"To Ostend?" A lead weight fell in her stomach. She'd heard how

99

many men had been killed before. The papers spoke of crippled soldiers begging in the streets and announced the loss of husbands, sons and brothers in obituaries.

He took her hands. "You must pack tonight and make ready. I'm not sure when we will sail. As soon as we may."

Such a sudden change.

"I'm sorry, I cannot stay to dine. I'll eat with the officers. We need to plan. But I wished to let you know what is happening, so you might prepare."

Fear rushed through her – a sense she would lose him. But how silly. He'd survived years of the Peninsular War. She knew he was capable. Even so she hugged him, her arms reaching about his neck. "I love you."

"And I you, Ellen. I shall return as quickly as I can, but eat without me. Do not wait." His arms came about her for a moment, but he held her stiffly, then set her away, smiling quickly, before he left.

Ellen turned and saw Jennifer look away. A warm blush touched Ellen's cheeks. Her intimacy had been inappropriate before a servant, and it had hurt that he'd set her away. But he'd done it because he was a soldier today and he needed to focus on his work, not her. If they were to sail towards a war there would be many more moments like this. She would simply cling harder, to *her* Paul, when she lay in bed at night with him – the man she'd met first.

The pain of brewing tears hurt Ellen's throat and pressed at the back of her eyes, but she swallowed them away and breathed. "Would you order dinner for me, Jennifer?"

After dining alone, and eating very little, Ellen retired to their chamber asking Jennifer to help her undress. Once the maid had gone, she slipped between the cold sheets and waited for Paul, and the moment the soldier became just the man to her.

Chapter Nine

Ellen lay asleep in the bed. Paul carefully closed the door to their chamber, trying not to wake her.

She'd left a candle burning for him.

Quietly he slipped off his greatcoat and laid it over the arm of a chair. His heart thumped hard. It had been doing so all day. The news still shocked him. Napoleon had escaped when they had thought that battle won. It should be over. He'd spent enough years starving and exhausted battling his own men, to keep them fighting when at times they'd have rather turned and run, as well as battling the French and their allies. Images and memories of the horrors of war had been spinning through his head all day, the sounds of imaginary cannons deafening him at times.

He did not want to go back, and yet he would not allow that damned tyrant have his way. The whole regiment was angry and ready to fight again to put the man back in his jail. But it was galling that they had to. Napoleon had already been defeated.

Paul's fingers slipped the brass buttons of his military coat free.

He just wished to be in bed with his wife, and feel her softness. She was his safe harbour, his sanctuary. His sanity. All he lived for now. He'd known she would be from the first moment he'd seen her at her father's house.

When he set his coat aside, exhaustion hit him. He ran his

fingers up over his face and through his hair. It had been a long day, but there would be many more long days in the next months. Napoleon was gathering an army to return to Paris. The message had said *hundreds of men*.

Paul pulled his shirt over his head and let that fall on top of his military coat. Then he unbuttoned his falls, watching Ellen in the bed they'd shared for weeks.

Her dark hair rested across her shoulder in a braid and her breaths lifted it a little, as her bosom rose, lifting the sheets too. She looked so young.

He slipped off his pantaloons, underwear and stockings all in one.

She was young. Perhaps too young to face the conditions on the continent. They'd been bled dry by the previous years of war. But he'd been her age when he'd first left England – he'd survived and he'd trained recruits still younger than him. They'd had to walk into a battle, kill men, and risk being killed.

She would cope. She was strong. He said the words to reassure himself. But still there was a fear low in his stomach that he'd never known before; a fear for her, not for himself. It accused him of being juvenile and incapable.

When he moved across the room, he was careful not to let the floorboards creak, and then he blew out the candle, casting the room into darkness, before climbing into bed beside her. The sheets were cold at the edge of the bed, but near Ellen they were warm, so he moved closer. She lay on her side. He shaped his body to hers and gently rested his arm about her. She did not wake.

When he woke in the morning, Ellen turned beneath his outstretched arm, and as he opened his eyes, he faced the very pale blue of hers.

Her gaze was warm and welcoming. "Good morning," she whispered.

"Good morning."

"What hour did you return?"

"Past ten."

Her fingers brushed across the stubble on his jaw. "As I have said before, you need not feel guilty for doing your duty."

He smiled, his hand embracing the curve of her waist, beneath the sheets. "Things will become hard over the next few months."

"I know."

"And you will cope?"

"I will cope, because I have you."

Again, there was that clasp of fear, low in his stomach, the one he'd never known before. It did not trust his judgement, or his ability to keep her safe.

But he was not the only man in the army and she would be in a camp away from the battle. There would be hundreds of men between her and danger.

She would be safe.

For now though he needed to feel her security. The light in the room implied it was a little past dawn; there was time. "Let me love you," he whispered, moving over her. Perhaps it was selfish to press straight into her when she opened her thighs, and yet it was what he needed.

The weight of her arms rested on his shoulders, crossing behind his neck, her fingers brushing his back. The rock of his hips as he moved slowly rocked her body too, making her breasts stir.

He adored her. There was a blissful intensity when they did this. Because it was love making, it was nothing like any encounters he'd known with whores. This was his wife he honoured, and she was warm and wet for his invasion. Little sighs left her lips, as colour scored her cheekbones. Her eyes had been open, looking up into his, but now they closed, dark lashes settling on her pale skin, and she bit her lip to keep her silence.

This is what she'd learned from the time they'd made love on the ship – to always be silent. He did not admonish her, nor encourage her to be more vocal. There would be many times they must be silent. It was better she had this skill.

103

Yet he saw her fighting it. The heat between her legs increased and he worked harder, pulling out and pressing in, captured by the primal call of her body. Three. Four more strokes. And then… *Oh*. He firmed the muscle in his arms to stop himself from falling, as her gentle fingers ran over his hair.

She was so beautiful.

~

Paul slipped out of the bed as carefully as he could, trying not to wake Ellen. As he moved she rolled to her back and stretched her arms, her sleepy eyes opening and looking up at him, the pale blue slightly misty. Her skin was reddened in places from the heat of his embrace and the brush of his stubble.

When she lay in bed looking like this, with her hair only loosely braided and escaping about her face, he loved her more – the imperfect, approachable, Ellen.

He turned back, leaned down, and pressed a kiss on her forehead, longing to return to the bed but knowing he could not; he had things to do. "Be ready in case we are to sail today, I shall send word as soon as I know."

She nodded.

As he washed and dressed, she sat more upright in bed, watching him, her pale skinned arms lying over the covers. He kept occasionally smiling at her in the mirror. They would be well. They would be happy. And he would keep her safe. He would accept no other conclusion. But even as he assured himself, his mind threw images of dead and dying men at him.

When he looked at her, and walked back to the bedside, she looked up at him with a *wonder* that suggested he was something stupendous. The look spoke to his heart as it had done in the summer, stealing away all the memories of war. He bent and kissed her forehead. "Goodbye, Ellen. I doubt I shall return for luncheon, not unless we are to sail. But I shall send word."

She nodded again then said, "Good day."

As he turned away, there was the sensation low in his stomach. Fear. He didn't like it. Perhaps it was the vulnerability he sensed in her. She was quiet and she had a way of hiding even when she was in a crowd of people, withdrawing into her thoughts. Yet despite her shyness, his men loved her, and the other officers were all enamoured too – though they'd expressed shock over her decision to follow the drum.

Perhaps that was why he felt concern – because it had not been her choice. She'd chosen only to be his wife, the outcome of that had been decided for her.

Casting the thought aside, he left the room.

It was too late to worry over such things. Their course was set.

~

When a soldier arrived, almost bursting into the small parlour, dressed in the scarlet coat and blue-grey pantaloons of Paul's regiment, Ellen stood, setting aside her sewing without thought. Jennifer stood too.

He smelt of cold and damp, as Paul had done the day before.

"Madam." He bowed deeply.

"Tell me your news. I presume my husband sent you; Captain Harding?"

"Ma'am." He bowed again. "The Captain did. He asked me to inform you that the regiment is to sail on the high tide at six this evening."

It was today then "Very well. Did he say how our things are to be taken to the dock?"

"Some of the men will come with the Captain after four, and bring a cart to take your items, madam."

Ellen nodded. That was it then. The end of the peace they'd known here.

"And there are these, ma'am." He held out two letters.

"Letters from my husband?"

"No, ma'am, they came with the regimental mail."

She took them from his outstretched hand and turned one over. The coat of arms imprinted in the seal was one she'd known all her life… her father's. She recognised the writing on the other; Penny's.

Ellen's heart leapt then pounded as she looked back up at the young soldier. "Thank you." Her voice came out much quieter than she'd expected and a little shakily with the emotion gripping in her chest. She urged more strength into it. "I'm grateful. Please tell Captain Harding, I shall be ready."

The soldier bowed again, sharply, with a stiff posture, and then he walked from the room.

Ellen turned to Jennifer. "Would you fetch us tea?"

As soon as the maid had gone Ellen walked across the room to the hearth and broke the seal on her father's letter. It was short and sharp.

I did not, and do not, welcome your letters. They have all been destroyed and you are not to contact your mother or your sisters. Do you understand? I do not wish to hear from a disobedient child, and I shall not have your ill behaviour reflect on the others.

You have made your choice, now live it, and be done.

The Duke of Pembroke

"The Duke of Pembroke…" The words escaped from her mouth. "You are my father, Papa."

She held the letter against her bosom for a moment, thinking of her mother, Penny, Rebecca and Sylvia. Tears clouded her vision, then slipped onto her cheeks. Her heart ached. This was the moment a tide, like the sea, tried to pull her back, but soon there would be even more miles between herself and them.

She looked at the second letter. It was also marked with the Duke of Pembroke's seal. But the address *was* in Penny's hand.

Ellen's heart pumped hard as she broke the seal, a beat of

excitement and anxiety drumming through her limbs, even into her fingertips, making the paper tremble.

Tears traced sensation down her cheeks…

Eleanor, my dearest sister,

I am sure you must feel guilty for leaving us, but do not. I am glad you have run off with Paul. Papa is furious; he has not let any of us mention your name, not even Mama. But I know she has cried, and I have tried to comfort her, but she must obey father and so she will not let me say your name to her, though I see it in her eyes all the time.

When I saw him scribbling a letter with a look of steel on his face, then I knew he must be writing to you, and so I wrote my own and hid it in the packet with his. He does not know I have written, and I am sure you will not be able to write back. This is just to tell you that I understand and miss you terribly, but I would not have it different for the world. I hope you are happy.

I saw an article in Papa's paper; there was a paragraph. 'Lady P, the daughter of the Duke of P, is known to have run off with the 6th son of the Earl of C, without the consent of either influential home. One does wonder over the abilities of these noble lords if they cannot even control their sons and daughters. The eloped couple are now believed to be abroad.'

Papa threw the paper at a footman. I have never seen him so obviously angry. You know what he is like for cold disdain, but this was definitely heated.

Oh, Ellen, I miss having you to talk to, so much, but you must not come back. You must stay away and enjoy your life. I wish you happiness. I can hardly imagine what it must be like to be an officer's wife. You shall have a life of adventure, while I pine away for you. But do not let that put you off, you must enjoy every moment.

All my love,
Your sister
Penelope

Ellen collapsed into a chair, tears tracking pathways down her cheeks, as her heart bled for her home, her sisters and her mother.

~

"Are you ready, Ellen?"

Ellen turned to look at Paul as he entered the chamber. She'd heard his arrival with his men through the window and his boot heels striking the wooden floorboards in the hall.

"I am, yes." Externally – but not internally.

"Come in!" He looked back and called to the open door. Immediately she heard men moving and her heart began pounding.

She was dressed to leave. She wore a pelisse, which he'd bought for her to wear when travelling, it had a military theme with frogging like a hussars' uniform, gold braid and brass buttons, and beneath it, her travelling dress was made from calico. It was thicker than muslin, so the chilly sea breezes would not penetrate the cloth. When he turned back to look at her, moving out of the way of his men he smiled. A torch lit in her heart, light and warmth, and she smiled too.

The smile was Paul's, the man she'd met at her parents' home. It was the same smile that had captured her heart the first time she'd seen him.

The soldiers lifted the trunks and carried them out. Once they'd passed, Paul lifted his arm. "Come then."

Her fingers gently embraced the firm muscle beneath his layers of clothing as she walked out of the inn room beside him, then downstairs and out into the cobbled street, leaving Jennifer to oversee the loading of their items.

They walked on towards the dock. It was only a couple of streets away.

"My father wrote to me. That was one of the letters your man brought."

Paul looked down at her. "And…"

108

"He told me I may not write, not to him, nor Mama, nor any of my sisters."

His arm dropped away from beneath her fingers and he turned sharply and held her briefly. It was so uncommon for him to show her affection in public when he was in the guise of a soldier; it made her wish to cry. But her father would have frowned upon crying in public, and Paul would not wish a weeping wife when they boarded the ship. She wiped away her tears as he let her go, not looking at him.

"But the other letter was from Penny, she wished me to know that she is happy for me, and wishes me well…" Fresh tears flooded Ellen's eyes and tumbled over.

Paul gripped her hands. "I know you miss your sisters. If he had accepted my offer–"

Ellen met his gaze. "It is not your fault he refused you, and to acknowledge us. You are more than worthy."

His blue eyes shone with passionate, heart-felt, anger.

"The fault is my father's rigid judgement." Ellen concluded.

Paul touched beneath her chin. "Even so, I regret that this is the outcome of marrying me."

"I do not regret. I am happy to be your wife."

"And I am a very lucky man."

"Well that makes us equal, because I know I am lucky."

She could tell from his eyes he wished to kiss her, but that would be a step too far for a conversation in the street when he was in the persona of a soldier.

"Come." He smiled, before turning away to continue.

She gripped his forearm, wiping the tears from her cheeks once more.

When they reached the dock, the other officers were present and casting various orders. Instantly she noticed his Lieutenant Colonel on the deck of the ship. She sensed his gaze on her but did not look up as Paul acknowledged him. She was under no obligation to do so, and there was just something about the man

109

which made her skin feel uncomfortable, as though it did not fit her body suddenly. He always watched her and it felt invasive.

Paul's arm fell from beneath her fingers then he walked a little ahead. Isolation swamped her as she stood, waiting, under the scrutiny of his Lieutenant Colonel.

Paul called a couple of the soldiers over to tell them his belongings would arrive soon and where to put them.

When he returned to her he bent to whisper. "I have managed to secure us a cabin as you were so uncomfortable with our conditions previously, Ellen."

Her gaze met his, and beyond him, that of his senior officer, who did not look away even then. She focused on, Paul. "Thank you."

"Shall I take you to it? Or would you rather wait on deck until we sail."

"Take me there."

"Very well then." Instead of offering his arm, he took her hand, and she was well aware of her fingers shaking despite her brave words.

He led her up the gangplank and stopped before the Lieutenant Colonel for her to curtsy. She did so, briefly, without looking up to meet his gaze, she looked instead at his cravat.

"Good day, Madam Harding, I hope our weather is fair and the journey shall not be difficult for you."

He said nothing wrong – nothing offensive – there was nothing factual to cause her discomfort, except that he stared. But that tremor of disgust which kept running up her spine whenever he was near, tingled through her nerves.

"I will show Ellen to our cabin and then return and instruct the men."

"Indeed." With that she was dismissed.

Paul's hand tightened around hers gently leading her across the deck. The cabin was tiny, probably only a yard wide, with one narrow cot and another above it, but at least it would be private.

"We will be at sea for three to four days, Ellen. I shall send

Jennifer to you once she arrives." Paul closed the door, leaving her alone. She sat on the lower bunk.

Everything felt so strange. She supposed this would be the way it was now – she would become used to one place and then it would be time to move to another.

She lay down on the bunk. If he wished for relations tonight it would be impossible as her bleed had begun. Her lower back ached a little as she rolled to her side.

Chapter Ten

Paul looked about the port for what seemed like the fiftieth time. It overwhelmed, even him. The place was teeming with soldiers and among the men in uniform, were dozens of people here for pleasure. It seemed as though half the fashionable world had descended on Ostend, as well as the military. He'd intended to leave Ellen on the ship, but she had not wished to stay while he went ashore.

She'd not been well during their journey; she'd had her bleed and her stomach had been painful and queasy. It was a problem which would arrive each month as they travelled, a thing a man would never need to think of – another thing to make him wonder if he'd done right by her.

But this was no time to fret over her stamina. He needed to find somewhere for them to stay until he knew where the regiment was to go next – and there were so many others here hunting for accommodation.

"This is madness," Ellen said, clinging to his hand.

"It is." The noise about them was deafening, with so many voices all shouting over one another seeking someone to carry luggage, and directions; while working men shouted orders over that, to load and unload ships. "This way." At least Paul knew his way around Ostend.

On a street away from the docks he managed to hire a hansom cab, but the streets were overflowing with carriages and people, just like the docks, and it took an age for the man to navigate through it. The world had truly gone mad.

It was only a few streets. They would have probably been better walking. But to his relief the boarding house he'd used previously still had a room. It was nothing grand, yet it was adequate and they would not be in Ostend for long.

"Stay here. I'll go back and bring our things." Ellen only nodded. She looked exhausted. "Rest. I know you have not slept well during the journey." He had slept in the bunk above her as she'd been bleeding but he'd heard her moving restlessly each night.

She nodded and then bent to unlace her half boots. He moved forward, knelt, and took over the task. Once her boots were off she unbuttoned her pelisse and he slipped it from her shoulders. Then she lay down on the bed, not even looking at him, she was so tired. He watched her, unwilling to leave her, but he needed to go back and tell the men where to bring their possessions, and of course he had to fetch Jennifer and bring her here too.

"Do you have the headache still?" He leaned and brushed a lock of hair from her brow, gently stroking her temple. She nodded. "I shall have a maid bring up some remedy." She nodded again, her eyes closing.

There was a pain in his stomach once more; the one that kept challenging his ability to protect her.

Ignoring it, he left her.

Two hours later, Paul returned to the room to wake her, before allowing his men in with their private articles.

When he let them in to set the items down, Ellen sat in the only chair in the room, still looking pale and tired.

They were to move on in four days. Then Ellen would discover what it truly was to be the wife of an army officer; there would be no laying abed.

Once his men had gone, he shut the door. He'd left Jennifer

with the female proprietor, to be shown to her own room in the servants' quarters. He could stay with Ellen now, until tomorrow.

"Is this all too much for you?"

Her eyes focused on him. "No, I am simply unwell. I shall be well again tomorrow now we are off the ship, and my bleed will cease in a day or two."

Fortunately before it was time to depart. At least they'd have a month before she would have to endure this again.

Hopefully within that month they'd reach Brussels. The plan was for the Allied Forces to wait there while their leaders argued over the politics of Europe at the Congress of Vienna. Napoleon had already been named an outlaw though, it was only a matter of time before war began again.

"Let me help you undress, and then you may rest properly."

She stood and let him begin releasing the buttons at her back. Once they were all undone, he helped her step out of her dress and put it aside, then unlaced her light corset. When it slid off, he kissed the skin above the line of her chemise at her shoulder. She shivered beneath his touch.

He knew she was in no condition to be bedded, but his body longed for it. "Lie down, Ellen."

Thoughts of war, memories, dreams, had been haunting him since they'd left Cork.

She slipped beneath the sheet and the coarse blankets covering the bed, shut her eyes and fell asleep in moments.

It was only three in the afternoon. He could go out, but he did not like to; he preferred to stay here and watch over her. There would be so many times to come when he would not have that choice.

He sat in the chair she'd vacated, and ran his fingers over his face. *Damn it.* Why had that bastard Napoleon had to continue this bloody war? Paul was tired of the endless hunger and effort, and the need to close himself off to avoid the pain of seeing constant death.

He looked out from the window at the street below. Numerous people flooded it, people who thought this fun. Ostend held a party atmosphere. These people had come to cheer on the soldiers while the soldiers, all tired of war, longed to sit back and let others fight.

Paul could not help being reminded of the amphitheatres he'd seen on the continent, those he'd heard, that hundreds of years ago, would entertain the crowds with men battling until death. It was macabre. These people had come to play audience to men killing and being killed. It turned his stomach. It did not hearten him.

Chapter Eleven

By the time they reached Ghent for the first time in his life, Paul regretted joining the army. They'd travelled from Ostend by barge to reduce the time it would take to reach Brussels but Ellen had not been allowed to travel with the regiment; she'd journeyed on another craft, and the isolation from her had been unbearable. He'd worried over her, although by all accounts it was as good as a pleasure cruise with excellent food and entertainment, as if this was no more than a festival parade.

There were so many tourists.

They did not understand war.

He did not wish them to.

He wished them a hundred miles away.

At least now though, having reached Ghent, he could be with Ellen again.

Paul sighed and let his hands settle at his waist as he watched Ellen sorting out items to be laundered and passing them to Jennifer. They had four days in Ghent. He was to meet with the other officers in an hour and speak with other regiments and find out how the 52nd fitted within the whole, and obtain their orders before progressing.

He knew Ellen was relieved to have a break from travelling, but he did not really know what to say to her. He did not apologise for what could not be different. He did not think she expected him to. She had been stoic and resilient throughout their journey. He had no complaints. It was just that damned tense queasy feeling in his stomach that feared for her and wished to protect her – and it was from things he had no capability to protect her.

"I shall come with you, Jennifer, when you seek supplies."

Ellen had already changed. She'd learned how important it was to plan ahead. She'd travelled to Ghent with the other women and they had clearly been educating her about the next weeks they would spend marching.

"Is there anything I may fetch you?" he said at last.

She turned and looked at him, smiling, though it was not the carefree stunning smile he'd received at the time they'd wed. It was careworn. He smiled back, feeling the same weight she probably felt in her chest. Tonight he would retire early with her and love her. That would make them both feel better.

"There is nothing I can think of…"

"Well then, if I can be of no assistance here, I shall return and meet with the officers."

She nodded.

"Goodbye, Ellen." He longed to move forward and kiss her, but Jennifer was still in the room. "I will return soon."

She nodded again.

~

Ellen clasped the edge of the cart. She was sitting beside the driver and the Lieutenant Colonel's servant. Two of the other wives and Jennifer sat in the back on top of some of the regiment's supplies.

Ellen gripped more tightly as the cart rocked, jolted, and creaked along the muddy track. They'd had to stop and climb down from it on three occasions today to lessen the weight so the horses could pull the cart out of the mud. She'd secured the skirt of her dress by tying a knot at her waist so it would not spoil, but her petticoats were stained with mud and there would be nowhere to wash them. A year ago she would not have worried, but now… everything was precious. She could not simply buy more.

She'd not imagined an army life would be as hard as this, yet it had not even really begun; the regiment were not fighting.

She gritted her teeth as the cart jolted heavily to the left. She had not complained to Paul. That would be unfair. He was marching towards a battle, wading through the mud, and striving to keep others moving. *She* had the luxury of a cart. But she was black and blue with bruises from being thrown about on it, and he knew that, and at night he would kiss all of her bruises in the privacy of their narrow canvas tent.

Then there were the times when they sat about the campfire among his men, with Jennifer and the other wives. Those times felt special. They would huddle together against the cold and Paul would be beside her, his muscular thigh against her softer one, and at times, because it was dark he'd even put an arm about her waist, when others might not see.

The conversations around the campfire were unlike any she'd known before. Her father would have called the language coarse, but it ran so easily among the men, and Paul would laugh with them; a laugh which seemed to come from low in his stomach. His laughter had become a precious sound.

"Lieutenant Colonel."

Ellen jumped a little as one of the women in the back of the cart spoke.

"Mistress Porter."

The man beside her looked back. "Sir." Ellen's knuckles whitened as they gripped the edge of the cart harder.

The Lieutenant Colonel was the only man on horseback; he often road alongside the cart. Ellen's teeth clenched. It was an involuntary thing. But each time he chose to ride beside them her skin prickled, as if a million beetles crawled over her. She wished him to stay away.

She could feel his eyes on her.

He stared all the time and he spent hours riding beside the cart as the men marched. She felt as though he only rode beside it to watch her.

Why did he watch her? That thought had slipped through her head a thousand times since they'd begun this journey.

Paul had deliberately chosen not to tell anyone in the regiment which family she came from. He thought she would be safer if no one knew her status, so if anyone was captured during a battle, they would not be tempted to tell the enemy. In battle, if anyone was captured, they would not be tempted to give away her status.

She wondered if the Lieutenant Colonel suspected. Her father's black hair and pale eyes were distinctive and she and all her sisters had inherited his colouring. That still did not really explain it, though. Even if he knew, why did he stare constantly?

She'd thought of saying something to Paul. He had no idea how many hours the Lieutenant Colonel spent beside the cart watching her. Yet this was his superior officer.

If the Lieutenant Colonel spoke, it would be easier. It would at least break the unbearable atmosphere. But he did not speak, merely rode in silence, staring.

She'd thought of speaking, but she had no idea what to say to him. So she said nothing, only speaking with the women. He did not participate in their conversation, and that was always stilted anyway because of the gapping class divide between her and them.

As they rode on, she wondered if the others in the cart found his presence uncomfortable. If they did though, they would not share their thoughts with her – an officer's wife.

"Nancy, is your wrist better?" Ellen looked back at the woman, trying to set aside her awareness of the Lieutenant Colonel. Nancy sat behind Ellen on top of a chest in the cart.

"It is a little, ma'am."

"Well Jennifer will help you with the meal and washing if you need her to, if it is still too painful for you to work."

119

"Yes, ma'am," Jennifer responded from her position on the opposite side of the cart.

"Thank you, ma'am," Nancy answered. Nancy was only a couple of years older than Ellen, and she had fallen onto her wrist as they'd walked earlier, twisting it, meaning she'd have difficulty fulfilling her role in supporting her husband and the regiment. The soldiers' wives did not just help their own men, but others too.

Of course as an officer's wife, and genteelly bred, it was not for Ellen to do the same, but she loaned them Jennifer, and supported where she could.

She had not really formed friendships with the other women, they were too mindful of her class, but they did speak to her, and she spoke to them.

When they set up camp later, she helped Jennifer sort out the bedding once the men had put up the tent she shared with Paul.

Ellen wondered again whether or not to say something to Paul about the Lieutenant Colonel.

When she came out of the tent, with Jennifer beside her, the sky was a rich deep blue waiting to turn to black as dusk hovered. Ellen looked for Paul. He was nowhere in sight.

"The Captain will be among the officers, Jennifer. Shall we stretch our legs a little and walk across?" The woman nodded.

She got on well enough with Jennifer, but not as well as she had with Pippa, her nurse since childhood. She had felt a part of her family to Ellen, but Jennifer was simply a maid; she did not welcome Ellen's conversation although she spoke with the other wives. She walked with Ellen now because it was her responsibility. Having been brought up, waited on and cared for by servants, Ellen wondered if the maid's awkwardness was her fault. She had never had company or friends beyond her sisters, perhaps it was because *she* did not know how to speak and act among others.

Mistress Porter looked up as Ellen passed. Ellen lifted a hand. Mistress Porter smiled, stopping in her task of sorting through cooking provisions, straightened and bobbed a shallow curtsy.

Smiling too, Ellen acknowledged the gesture with a little nod.

Facing ahead, Ellen walked on. She could think of nothing to say to break the silence between herself and Jennifer. She was imprisoned by it – by her past – she was unable to really fit within this life. Would she ever?

Sometimes her heart longed for all the luxuries she'd left behind – quiet rooms, tea, and easy conversation. She missed warm baths to bathe in, spare hours to embroider pretty images, her pianoforte to play music – music she could escape into; afternoons spent with her sisters talking of the fashion, and the books they'd read.

Her pace increased as she hurried to see Paul, longing for his company – and the time of day that made up for all other times.

The officers stood gathered about a large table within the marquee that was set up for the use of the Lieutenant Colonel. This was his living space.

Ellen was permitted entry. She'd left Jennifer to return to the area where Paul's men camped.

Only the Lieutenant Colonel and one other officer were married. Their wives had been left at home. Perhaps that was why the Lieutenant Colonel stared; because he disapproved of her presence? She was more of a burden to the regiment than an aid, the other women worked for the men. She did not. Lieutenant Colonel Hillier looked up and gave her a stiff smile, "Mrs Harding." He was the only one who had been able to see her at that point. The others leaned over the table before him, on which a large map was spread. They all straightened, looking back at her.

Paul turned. "Ellen…"

She smiled, looking only at her husband. "Sorry to interrupt."

The Lieutenant Colonel answered, "It is not an issue. We are almost done."

She looked at the Lieutenant Colonel. She could judge nothing from his eyes. There was no warmth or depth in his expression.

Paul looked back too. "Is there anything else you need from me, Lieutenant Colonel?"

"I think not, Captain Harding. You may go."

"Thank you, sir."

Paul saluted and then nodded to the other officers in parting. Ellen noticed a man standing across the room, wearing a different uniform from the 52nd. It was spattered with mud. He was clearly a messenger who'd been sent back to give the regiment direction.

Paul's fingers gripped her arm. "Ready."

She smiled. "Yes." As they stepped outside she added, "I'm sorry, should I not have come? Was I intruding? Were you talking secrets?"

"If we had been talking secrets you would not have been allowed in." Paul leaned to whisper to her ear, his fingers still gently gripping her arm.

She looked up at him, engulfed by the warmth of his proximity. Whenever he was close, heat ran within her blood and chased up her heartbeat. "Are you tired?"

"Starving. I wonder what the men have found to eat."

"When I left them, they were bargaining for a pig from a farmer, with the promise of recompense."

"Well as we know, Wellington is generous in that…"

The regiment had resorted to begging and hunting, because no pay had come down the line. But the Duke of Wellington was insistent local people were refunded for any loss the army caused as they progressed. Money was always found so the soldiers did not insight unnecessary bitterness and create more enemies of the British.

"Well, I am remaining hopeful there is pork for dinner."

He smiled at her. "Then I shall hope for your sake."

No one was looking at them, so she stopped, turned and hugged him briefly, slipping her arms about the sinuous muscle of his waist. He'd become leaner and firmer since he'd been marching daily.

She let him go, turning and walking on again.

"Your petticoats are filthy."

"We had to stop the cart, and get out so the horses could pull it from the mud."

He caught her arm, stopped her and turned her back. Then he cradled her chin with one palm, lifting her gaze so she looked directly into the turquoise blue of his eyes. "Such a decline from the pretty parlour I found you in. Do you miss those comforts and your pianoforte?"

How did he know she had just been doing so? But she would not admit it to him; that would be disloyal, and she wished more than anything to make him happy and be a dutiful wife so he need not worry over her. She merely rode in a cart all day and had to bear the lack of the friendship of others; he had to march and prepare his men for war.

I have his friendship.

She shook her head, lifting her chin from his touch. "Not when I would have to trade them for your presence. "

He smiled. "I would trade nothing to have it different. I wish you here." Then he said more gently. "I need you here…"

She wished to lift up on to her toes and kiss his lips but it would be wrong to do so here, and so instead she longed for privacy – for the time they would retire to their tent – their cocoon – the place where they could be private and express their love. The place where he always made her feel beautiful and happy. "And I need you…"

~

As Paul made love to his wife, thoughts of war plagued him. The messenger who'd come yesterday had said, since Napoleon had reclaimed Paris on the 20th March, he'd recruited and begun training men for a new army.

The other European states still fought their verbal battle in Vienna over who would own what land when this was done, leaving their armies to fight for it.

The Lieutenant Colonel received new information daily from the spies the Allied army sent out. But the Duke of Wellington's decision was not to race towards Napoleon, but to hold back and wait. That way, they could prepare and be ready, and they could pick their ground.

Damn it, focus.

He had begun this with Ellen to forget these things, to escape thoughts of war, if only for a short while, but it was becoming harder to – even though he had Ellen's beauty to bathe in. Bird song seeped through the canvas about them, increasing from odd chirps to a constant vibrant swelling sound. It was the first true sign of spring. It was a time of rebirth. But for a soldier, time always held a measure of death.

Quiet. He did not wish to think of war, only Ellen. Only the body he moved within, a body which was soft and giving, and hot and damp for him.

Her fingers brushed through his hair, as if she knew his thoughts were splintered and she sought to bring him back.

He focused on her eyes, losing his thoughts in the pale blue and his thrusts sharpened, as the sound of yawns invaded their haven and fires being stirred up for kettles to be heated, and slopping water against metal.

Ellen became breathless, but she bit her lip to stop any sound as his strokes grew more urgent, hard and firm, and, and… Release came in a rush, flooding into him and onto him all at once. Relief. Escape. Freedom. He shut his eyes and let it fill him for a moment, resting his forehead on hers. She kissed his cheek. He rolled on to his back, and she turned to her side holding him. They had not undressed. It was too cold and so their clothing mostly covered them as well as the blankets.

She kissed his jaw with such tenderness it made his heart ache. He was tired now. He hoped exerting this energy would not affect his stamina today. He did not normally make love to her in the morning, but today the thought of what was to come and the haunting memories of battles had brought on an intense desire to seek the safe harbour of Ellen's body, and he had let himself

124

indulge.

He held her close for a moment more, willing time to cease for just a little while, but the sounds outside their tent grew stronger, men speaking and washing, and the edge of kettles striking tin cups.

"We had better rise," he whispered to Ellen.

She held him tighter, clearly wishing time to be held back too.

He ran his fingers through her hair, and sighed, then kissed the crown of her head. "We have no choice, darling." As he spoke he was already moving, sitting up to right his clothes. Ellen rolled to her back. He looked down at her. "I shall send Jennifer to you."

She nodded.

Chapter Twelve

Captain George Montgomery bowed over Ellen's hand. "Will you dance with me, Mrs Harding?"

Ellen glanced at Paul, who smiled to give his consent. "Go along, have fun."

Looking back at Paul's best friend, she agreed, "Of course."

His grip firming on her fingers, he stepped back a few paces, pulling her away from Paul. His hand lifted hers and his other arm came about her to provide the secure frame for a waltz. Her heart thundered. She had danced the waltz more than a dozen times. Paul had taught her in their rooms. It was the thing here, the rage. Everyone danced it, and at the Lieutenant Colonel's parties he insisted it was the only dance.

Her heartbeat thundered as they began to move. She was not comfortable being on show in a room full of people, nor with the intimacy the waltz created with a partner as it made her feel awkward. Yet the steps were swift and there was something enchanting about being spun through the dance, so she did have fun once she forgot who she was with and where she was.

She glanced at the other couples dancing and those looking on.

Brussels was as busy as Ostend, Bruges and Ghent, or perhaps even more so. There were people everywhere. When she'd imagined her role as a camp follower, she'd thought, that she would be one of a small number, but there were thousands of people here to support the army.

But the army itself was not based in Brussels; it had been dispersed over miles. There were over a hundred thousand in the Duke of Wellington's army, Paul had told her, and even more than that in Blücher's Prussian army. All of these men sought food and lived on depleting local resources, while their audience lived lavishly in the decadent city and danced the waltz.

Paul had said the way people lived here out-did even the rash extremes of the London life he'd experienced during the season last summer. She'd never known anything like it. But of course she'd only lived in her father's house, sheltered from all this.

There were balls and parties daily, picnics, and the theatre continued as if there were not two hundred and fifty thousand men camped in an arc about the city preparing for war.

During the day, these fashionable people walked about in the parks, laughing and thoroughly enjoying themselves. Women flirted with the soldiers in the city, and men thought themselves something important because they were here, absorbing the atmosphere. But they would not be the ones who fought.

They had been here weeks, though, and there was no news of when Napoleon might come or when the army would invade France. The 52nd was camped five miles outside the city, in the direction of Nemur, and each day, while the hordes of novelty seekers sought entertainment, Paul rode out to his men, and Ellen waited in Brussels for his return.

He'd told her they'd been exploring the local terrain, learning every hill and hollow so they would have the advantage if Napoleon brought the battle to them.

She felt surplus. There was nothing she could do to help him except love him, and be a companion for him when he returned, to take his mind from the preparation for war.

In the evenings, they generally avoided entertainment like this. But they did walk through the parks, along paths edged with early flowers, and a few times Paul had taken her to the theatre. They'd seen the Duke of Wellington once, in a box there. Paul had pointed him out. She'd been in awe of the nation's hero.

She'd said a prayer that night – that the Duke of Wellington would be wise. Because Paul's life lay in his hands and the skill of his decisions.

"It is a rare treat to have you in my arms, Mrs Harding…"

Ellen merely smiled at Captain Montgomery's flirtation.

Paul had urged her to participate more in the social life. At the first party, the Lieutenant Colonel had walked her about himself introducing her to everyone, as though she was something special to him, and then some people had invited her to afternoon teas and picnics. She'd never gone. She did not think all this merriment right, and she knew Paul did not. It would be disloyal to him, and his men.

"It would just be you entertaining yourself while I work, I would not mind, Ellen." Paul had said, but still the thought of spending time among people she did not really know, and certainly did not care for, did not appeal. She was not unhappy to sit and wait for him. She had Jennifer for company, and she read and sewed, and walked outside, perhaps along the river. It was not an unbearable life. She had a roof over her head, a comfortable bed to sleep in, food in her stomach, even though they were now living upon credit as the army had not paid Paul's wages… and every evening Paul came home to her.

But then there were nights like this, when the Lieutenant Colonel hosted a lavish dinner party in the house he'd rented, a very pretty and rather large townhouse, and the officers and his guests would be expected to dance almost until dawn.

"I never realised until I came to Brussels that ostriches came in every colour of the rainbow. Have you ever seen a blue or pink one in a zoological garden?"

Ellen focused on Captain Montgomery and bit her lip to stop herself from laughing, though she knew he must see the humour in her eyes. She understood why Paul liked him, because he was always light-hearted, and always making jokes. "You are naughty…" But even as she spoke, her gaze passed over his shoulder glancing at a dozen ostrich feathers waving like the regimental flag on its staff, from the highly coifed hair of so many over-dressed women. They did look a little silly.

She smiled at him, and then for the rest of the dance they talked, mostly about others in the room – the pleasure-seeking people she thought fools.

But then perhaps her view was coloured by Paul's who said that continually.

When the dance was at an end, Captain Montgomery bowed swiftly, lifting her hand and kissing the back of it. "Paul is a very lucky man." He said the same at the end of every dance they'd shared before giving her a swift smile. Paul knew he said it, because he said the same to Paul. She smiled, the heat of a blush warming her cheeks.

"Come, seeing as you have a husband, and he is my friend, I am duty bound to return you to him. I had better do so."

"Paul," she acknowledged as they walked nearer and he stepped forward to take the hand which was on Captain Montgomery's arm. She moved away from Captain Montgomery. Paul's smile passed from her to his friend.

"I have just said to her again, you are a lucky devil. I cannot believe you have the pleasure of looking into those fine eyes for hours at a time. I am envious of you."

"Well you may remain envious, for the lady is mine." The two of them laughed.

"Are you warm now, Ellen?" Paul asked her, "Shall we fetch you a glass of punch?" The two men turned as she nodded, both walking with her as Paul let her hand go. Instead she gripped his forearm. Then her gaze struck the Lieutenant Colonel's. He was seated at a card table in a room beside the one in which they danced.

She smiled, and he smiled in return.

She had become more accustomed to his measured stares, but perhaps that was because she did not have to endure them overmuch. Since they'd reached Brussels she rarely saw him. It was only when the officers were invited to his parties, or to dine here that she encountered him. She looked at Paul, listening to him speak with his friend. He'd not noticed her exchange with the Lieutenant Colonel.

Paul had told her the Lieutenant Colonel had submerged himself in the hedonistic life here. He socialised and was constantly playing cards, gambling, as he was now, until the early hours, and he'd encouraged his officers to participate. Paul had excused himself, giving Ellen as his reason.

If this was a window into the life of his senior officer, she preferred her own. She and Paul were happy. If only there was not a war looming like a dark, swirling storm cloud.

Chapter Thirteen

On the 10th of June, word reached Brussels that the Congress of Vienna had signed a final agreement over the state of Europe. It gave Napoleon no rights to France. But prior to this Napoleon had signed a new constitution for the Empire he'd claimed, and paraded through Paris to celebrate, cheered by thousands of supporters who'd come out on to the streets to see him.

In response, the parks and streets of Brussels were full of people eager to discuss the news with excitement and expectation, all gossiping in high-pitched hurried voices, wondering what would happen next.

Ellen hated their speculation.

She walked with Paul in a park at six, enjoying the evening light and the last of the sun's warmth.

It had rained a lot recently so the clear night was a novelty. Paul said the fields and tracks they were scouting were muddy, and terrain would not be at its best if war began now. But it was likely it would. The French were renowned for moving quickly.

Ellen held his arm, but as they passed another huddle of obnoxious observers, she slid her fingers down to grip his hand.

She'd heard at least half a dozen voices in the group all agreeing that the battle would be soon.

Her heart had been pounding for hours as she tried not think of it.

Paul gripped her fingers firmly then glanced down at her as they walked on.

"You know, Ellen, if I could assure you of my safety I would say it…" She wished to stop and cover her ears. She'd known this conversation would come but she did not want to hear it. Yet she could not tear her gaze away from his vivid turquoise blue eyes – lost in the emotion burning out of them. It would be cowardice not to listen.

"There can be no guarantees in war, Ellen."

She knew.

"I have written to my father, and asked him to help you, financially. If anything happens to me you must write to him. You understand?"

She nodded, unable to speak past the lump of tears gathering in her throat. She bit her lip to hold them back, biting down hard to distract them as her fingers gripped his more tightly.

"I've asked George to see you safe if things do not go well. He will organise a route to get you home, and if anything were to happen to George then any of the officers would help you, you may appeal to any of them."

Again she nodded. A hole opened in her stomach, an emptiness. She could not and would not imagine him gone. She could not live without him. He was her whole life. She sometimes thought of her old home, but it was beyond reality, it was with dreamlike affection.

"And you must write to your father, and tell him, and encourage him to forgive you and show compassion…"

She did not think her father capable of compassion, but again she nodded.

"I've written a will, George has it, and it was properly witnessed. I do not have much. We have too many debts. But the few things I have you can sell to help pay your way home."

He spoke as though it would happen, as though this was a plan, not a contingency. She gripped his hand in both of hers and held his gaze, fighting against the lump in her throat. "But you will not die. I shall not let you. I cannot… I am too much in love with you. I cannot lose you. You will survive."

His hand slipped free of hers and his eyes suddenly glowed aquamarine, then he held her, gripping her tightly against his chest, ignoring anyone in the park who might see. For a moment that was all he did, then he whispered to her ear. "And I love you, more than mere words can ever express, but I cannot control fate, Ellen. Believe me, I shall fight as hard as I can, both to beat back the enemy so they can never reach you, and to stay alive. But we must be sensible and plan if…" He did not say the words.

She was betraying him by letting emotion get the best of her. She needed to be brave for him. Not send him into battle with tears that might distract his thoughts, but with love. She pulled away and her hands cupped his soft shaven cheeks. "You must not fear for me. You must focus on yourself. I will manage here."

~

Ellen's eyes were bright with unshed tears, they sparkled in the evening sun which flooded down on the busy park. This woman had so much beauty inside her, and so much love for him. It glimmered there.

After she'd spoken, she bit her lower lip, and he could see how hard by the white line beneath the press of her teeth.

She was being brave for him. He could ask no more.

His hands braced her pretty pale skinned face. She was such a delicate looking woman, and yet she was not delicate at all. Inside, she was strong, and he knew she would survive. "If the whole army fails, Ellen, you must leave as soon as you hear the news. Do you understand? I'll leave you what money I have and you are to buy a passage on any coach or cart you can find. Do you hear me?"

"Yes." Her soft lips trembled as they parted to answer him, and a single tear slipped from her eye.

"I will have to leave you in Brussels soon, in the next few days I think, and you may stay here. But if you hear that ill fate has befallen us, then you must go. Yes?"

She nodded, her hands falling to grip his biceps through his coat, as if she might collapse. He held her to his chest again, fiercely, as the pain he'd become used to gripped in his stomach. He hated that he could not protect her, that he could not offer her any certainty of his return. He hated having to leave her every day. But in a few days it might be to never return, and he was not afraid for himself, but for her. What would happen then?

He held her for a long time, ignoring the stares of others in the park. Perhaps they should have had this conversation in private, but when he'd heard the voices, he'd known what was passing through Ellen's mind and he'd not been able to hold his words back any longer. They'd been passing through his head for hours too, for weeks, during all the time of their preparation.

When he released her, he pressed a brief kiss to her temple, then said briskly, "Let us think and talk of other things…" It was better having said what needed to be said that they did not dwell on it. What was the point? He would live or he would not.

~

Ellen had prayed last night, over and over, while Paul slept, whispering the words out loud in case God could not hear them if they were spoken in her mind. She pleaded and begged God to keep him alive and bring him back.

When she went out for a walk with Jennifer just after midday, an exodus had begun; carriages and carts were being loaded with furniture and baggage. People were fleeing the city before the fighting began – all the people who had laughed and danced as though they had no fear.

Not everyone was leaving though; there were still many hardy revellers in the parks.

But watching others leaving increased the fear Ellen struggled to hold back. It slept inside her, still gently breathing, and then occasionally something would stir it and it would wake, running into her blood, gripping about her heart, and capturing the air in her lungs. But she continued walking beside Jennifer as if nothing was wrong, refusing to acknowledge any chance Paul might not return. He would. She would not accept another outcome.

When they returned to their rooms, Ellen picked up her sewing with an aim to focus her mind away from fear.

She'd been sick this morning, fortunately it was after Paul had gone. She knew he worried about her too and she did not want him to worry more.

Chapter Fourteen

Ellen looked up as Paul entered their room. Jennifer stood. His hand lifted. He held two gilded slips of paper. "We are invited to the Richmond ball."

They'd laughed about the lavish event and the battles to obtain invitations a week ago. Those who'd remained in the city had not stopped their parties; if anything they'd entertained themselves even more determinedly and the Duchess of Richmond's was the ball everyone wished to attend.

The Duke of Richmond rented a property in the Rue des Cendres and the ball was to be there.

Ellen set down her sewing and stood. "How? I thought you did not wish to go." At least the Duke and Duchess were holding it for the right reason. Paul had told Ellen, the Duke commanded the troops who were to remain in the city and defend Brussels, should Napoleon reach this far. His wife was entertaining solely to hearten the soldiers and keep their minds off war for a few hours. It was to be held in four days, on the 15th of June.

"I did not. I do not. But the Lieutenant Colonel wishes my presence… our presence. He insists all his officers attend."

"So Captain Montgomery will be there too?"

"And the others. We are to make it appear as though nothing is afoot beyond us enjoying ourselves."

"But that is silly."

"Apparently, even the Duke of Wellington wishes it so."

"Then we must go."

"Yes." He dropped the invitations on a side table. "But for now… You may go Jennifer." The maid dropped a swift curtsy in both their directions, then left the room, closing the door behind her. "For now, Ellen…" Paul continued, walking across the room to her. He captured her chin in the grip of his finger and thumb. "I wish to feel the flesh of my wife against my flesh."

"Do you not wish for dinner first?" Ellen looked into eyes full of longing.

He shook his head. But then he smiled. "I suppose you would rather I was civilized though and let you dine first."

She gripped the sides of his scarlet coat. "I can wait, if I must." She would let him do anything he wished for as many days as she had him still. The tears which had been threatening to fall all day, finally flooded her eyes.

She blinked them away and turned her back. "Let me ring for supper to be brought here, then you can at least eat soon."

When Jennifer returned, Paul was already seated on the bed undressing, Ellen opened the door slightly and whispered. "Will you bring us something hot from a local inn for dinner, a pie perhaps? Leave it outside the door and knock. Oh and purchase wine too."

When she shut the door she leaned back against it, watching him sitting in his pantaloons, bare chested, as he worked to pull off his boots.

He looked up at her. "All I have thought of all day is you, and being back in bed."

She smiled. It was good to know he thought of her, and now she could help him escape. She watched the muscle move beneath the skin of his torso. The hard contours were more defined since he'd lost weight from working so hard, but it only made him more beautiful. Yet he looked so young today. He was young. Young and too full of life to face death.

"Take your dress off, Ellen." She shook her head, smiling, but began unbuttoning it as he watched, leaning his hands back on to the bed.

She undressed slowly, then turned her back to him so he might unlace her light corset. The moment it fell away there was a knock on the door.

"Your dinner, ma'am, Captain."

"Thank you, Jennifer. Set it down and go!" Ellen turned away from Paul. She wore only her chemise as she crossed the room quietly. She listened to Jennifer walking away before opening the door to collect their food. The smell of hot cooked mutton filled the room as she carried it in.

"Well now you have my stomach rumbling," Paul said, rising.

They ate at a table in the room, facing one another. She'd shared many moments with him in the past six months, but none had felt as intimate as this as he sat shirtless before her eating hungrily and speaking of his day. At the end of the meal his hand swept through his hair and his gaze settled on her.

She stood. "Let me rub your shoulders."

He smiled.

She walked behind him and gripped the tightly bunched muscle. "Relax."

He leaned his head back against her bosom, and as she kneaded his flesh, the muscle beneath her fingers softened, his breathing slowed and he shut his eyes.

"I love you," she said to the air above his head.

"And I you," he answered, his eyes opening and looking up at her. She smiled. She'd never been in doubt of his affection. It had been constant, solid and reassuring. "May we go to bed now? I know it is early, but I ache for you, Ellen."

"And how can I deny such an offer."

His smile widened, and then he stood suddenly, turning to kiss her, gripping her hair and holding her mouth to his.

138

He made love slowly, just touching and kissing her for a long time, before moving over her. She opened her legs so he could come between them, and held his gaze, offering comfort with her eyes as well as her body. His gaze clung to hers as he moved, pushing in, and pulling out, over and over, in the pattern which drove her senses towards delirium. Her fingers lifted and stroked through his hair.

It was precious, what he did to her - precious and beautiful. She would hold on to this moment for the rest of her life.

His movements stayed slow and deliberate as her fingers clung to his shoulders and she looked into his blue eyes.

He was hiding from reality. But she wished to hide with him and keep it at bay for as long as they could.

She pressed back against his movement as he continued. An animalistic sound left his lungs, before her name... "Ellen."

She moved more forcefully with him. Wishing to help him escape and escape too.

"You are a wonderful wife."

She laughed, her fingers clasping in his hair. "You are the perfect husband."

His gaze became matt for a moment. "And I will try to continue to be, Ellen."

Damn it, she'd let reality into the room. She did not wish to think of the battle, or Napoleon, or anything beyond their bed...

"You *will* continue to be," she filled her voice with strength pulling his mouth to hers and slipped her tongue across his lips.

His movement became more urgent in reply, his hips working swiftly as her hands dropped to grip his waist and the muscle stirred beneath his skin.

Oh, he made her feel so... so...

He broke within her in a flood of warm sensation, and his weight came down on top of her, pinning her into the mattress. She did not mind. She liked the feel of him lying over her, and his presence between her thighs. But then after a moment he rose and rolled on to his back.

She rolled over to hold him, pillowing her head on his shoulder, her arm resting on his chest, as his came about her. She fell asleep thus.

~

It was warm the night of the ball, so they walked rather than tried to obtain the credit to hire a carriage. Paul had purchased a new dress for her though, on good will and I-owe-you payment. It was the fashion, white muslin, and the fabric was virtually translucent, light and fluid. It clung to her petticoats and her bust. She loved it. She felt beautiful in it, walking beside him, holding his arm.

Nearly every hour he'd spent at home, since they'd had that conversation in the park, had been spent in bed. He'd loved her constantly, and they'd laughed and kissed, and acted as though fate could not throw them a fatal hand.

And here they were, attending a ball, as if this was something normal in their lives. Although for both of them it should have been, if he had not become a soldier and she had not chosen to marry and follow the drum with him.

She and Penny had once crept downstairs and watched a ball at her father's house, peering about the door which opened onto the musicians' gallery. The images span through Ellen's head.

Her parents' world, her childhood, seemed as if it had been a fairytale now.

Her fingers gripped Paul's arm more tightly as they climbed the steps to the door of the Duke of Richmond's home, others were arriving too, some in carriages and some on foot.

"This way, sir, madam." A man in livery bowed to them, and then held his arm towards the back of the entrance hall. "The ball is being held outside."

"Outside?" Paul whispered, smiling as they followed his direction and walked on.

140

Ellen smiled up at him, wondering where on earth the ball was to be held. It was warm but the weather had been temperamental for weeks. What if it rained?

Another footman held out a hand directing them towards a narrow door. "This way."

As they stepped outside into a small cobbled stable-yard another man in red livery directed them on, but now they could hear the sound of the party. Voices and muted music rose on the air. People talked and laughed. It came from a long building, which looked like a coach house. Another man held a door open for them, and others who followed them.

The inside looked nothing like a coach house. It had been papered with an ivy print; there was a wooden floor for dancing upon, and the room was illuminated by hundreds of candles.

The music she'd heard was a jig and when she passed through the crowd with Paul, she saw the Highlanders regiment in their kilts, dancing about their swords.

She looked up at Paul. He glanced down at her. "A worthy entertainment, but do not expect to see me manoeuvring a riffle to amuse you."

She laughed.

"Come, let us find a drink and others we know."

It was an exclusive company they walked through. Paul acknowledged several people and introduced her to a few. Then he whispered, "The Duke of Wellington," leaning towards her.

"Oh." She turned and looked. The Duke of Wellington stood across the room speaking with a number of women.

"And there is the Duke of Brunswick." Paul nodded in another direction. Her gaze turned to the second commander. She knew Paul revered these men.

"Sir Thomas Picton is here too, look."

She did. They all meant very little to her, but they were the men who would be responsible for making the right choices to keep Paul alive.

She looked up at him. "Do you hope for promotion if we win?"

He smiled. "I would not be adverse to it."

"Then I will one day be a Colonel's wife." After their conversation in the park, neither of them had spoken of the possibility he might die. They were denying it. Ellen was glad.

"You may only hope." His smile filled with warmth.

"Do you think my father might receive us then?"

"I would need to be a General and have earned myself a dukedom like Wellington, for your father to accept me."

She turned and faced him as the music changed tempo and the Highlanders cleared the floor searching for partners among the women.

"Dance with me, Captain Harding, before anyone else might spot us and ask me."

"Of course Mrs Harding." With that she was swept away into a waltz. It was most beautiful when she danced it with her husband, holding his gaze and feeling the gentle pressure of his hands gripping her as they span. This night was precious. She would hold on to the memory of it.

When the dance came to its conclusion, Captain Montgomery appeared beside them and held out his hand. "I claim the next, ma'am."

She smiled and agreed, though as she moved away she looked back over her shoulder at Paul. He smiled. It wrenched her heart to walk away from him. *Have fun* he mouthed silently. She did not feel as though she could without him. But then she remembered Captain Montgomery would be fighting soon too. He smiled at her over-brightly. She focused her attention on him. He deserved that much when he was to go to war.

When the dance ended, the Lieutenant Colonel came to ask for her hand, she even felt more disposed to be kind to him. After all, everyone was at risk on a battlefield, and he was not so bad, he was polite when he did speak to her. It was just his stare she did not like. As they danced she looked across his shoulder, while his gaze seemed to hover on the curve of her jaw and her neck.

She was glad, though, when the dance was over, and then she clung to Paul's arm and lifted to her toes to whisper in his ear. "If anyone else asks me to dance, say, no, say you wish to keep me for yourself."

He looked down at her with a question in his eyes. "But there are a couple of hundred men in here, Ellen, all seeking pretty partners and a moment to escape."

He made her feel guilty, and for the first time as she glanced around the makeshift ballroom, she realised there was a forced, overly exuberant feeling within it. All these men were a little afraid but being brave and forcing fear aside.

She looked up at Paul and realised he was too. That was why they'd spent most of the week in bed. "I'm sorry, I shall dance again if anyone wishes me to. But first will you take me to get some lemonade?"

There was a lot of high-pitched laughter in the room, from both men and women, and many of the young officers drank heavily.

She was sorry for them. All of them.

When they reached the refreshment table, Paul accepted a small sculpted glass in the shape of an open tulip and handed it to her. The lemonade's tartness tingled on her tongue. It was cool and refreshing as the room was hot with so many people gathered.

They turned as the orchestra struck up another jig to jubilant calls from the crowd, and the Highlanders came forth again to entertain.

Paul drank the lemonade too. It was only sweetened flavoured water. He was avoiding the wine. She looked about the room – most of the senior officers present were avoiding it too. *They* awaited the moment they were called to fight.

Paul's fingers gripped her elbow. "Let's watch." He drew her forward. The men stepped and danced over crossed swords which they'd laid out on the floor. The crowd kept gasping and then laughing as the Highlanders' feet moved between the blades, while clapping along. But again, there was that otherworldly abandonment in the atmosphere.

She leaned into Paul's side more closely, and his arm unusually came about her, his fingers clasping at her waist as they continued to watch. She pressed her temple to his shoulder, still watching the men but feeling love sweep through her blood. She was so much happier than she had thought it ever possible to be.

When the jig had finished, she would have asked Paul to dance with her again but one of the Highlanders came over to her and asked for her hand. She could not refuse, not now she'd realised what tonight meant.

After she'd danced with the Highlander, Paul's Lieutenant Colonel came to ask for her hand in the next waltz, and so again she had to leave Paul. Her heart longed for him all the time she danced, but she tried to smile, and speak brightly. These men were willing to give their lives for her and others.

She was breathless when the Lieutenant Colonel returned her to Paul, his fingers gripping her elbow. The grip seemed to hold a little too long as they stood facing Paul. "Your wife, returned, Captain."

Paul saluted, then bowed a little, and the Lieutenant Colonel's grip fell away.

As he walked away, Ellen longed to hug her husband. She wished it was time they could go home but the ball was nowhere near ready to break up; it would look odd if they left so early.

"May I dance with you once more, or are you too tired?"

She smiled at his hesitant but urging look. "Not too tired. I would love to dance with you."

"Come then." His embrace was firm as he took her waist and her hand then span her into another waltz. Paul had said London society would be shocked to its core by the army's addiction to the waltz. But everything was different here and when Ellen danced it with Paul, it was heaven.

When they finished, heat flushed into her cheeks. The air in the room had become overly warm, and not only from dancing.

She smiled at Paul, laughing as he breathed more heavily also and his blue gaze clung to hers. "We shall leave soon."

Directly behind him there was a flurry of whispers. Ellen looked over his shoulder. The group of people about the Duke of Wellington were all turning to others and passing some message on while the Duke spoke with the Duke of Richmond, looking concerned.

Then both men turned to leave the room.

"Paul…" she said, gripping his arm a moment before he turned to look.

He did not hesitate when he saw what was happening but broke free and began crossing the room in quick strides. She followed, hurrying to keep up. Captain Montgomery was already there.

"What is it, George?"

"Word has come."

As she heard the answer to Paul's question, Ellen saw a man in a muddy uniform standing among a huddle of women who had been gossiping. Now they were offering him food and a drink, while behind him the orchestra still played and people danced, even as the news passed about the edges of the room.

"Napoleon has already struck our left side. He's caught the Duke of Wellington off guard. We are to march. There will be a battle within hours."

Ellen's heart dropped into the soles of her dancing slippers. *No!*

~

Ellen had known the battle would come. But knowing, and accepting it was a reality, were very different things. At the ball Paul had left her sitting in a chair for nearly an hour, as he'd found the other officers of the 52nd and then disappeared with the Lieutenant Colonel in search of the Duke of Wellington. When he'd returned, he'd carried an air of determination. His jaw had

145

been taut and the grip on her arm firm, as he'd told her they must go home.

She'd known then they were not only leaving the ball, he was about to leave her.

Yet what could she do? Nothing. It would be wrong to plead with him to stay; it was his duty to go, and it was honourable and right. But the thought made her heart hurt so much.

What if he never comes back?

Ellen pushed the thought away – she did not want to even think it.

As they walked back through shadows the moonlight cast across the streets, she didn't speak, afraid that if she did she would sob.

He was silent too. She could tell from the tenseness in his muscles and the intent look in his eyes as he stared ahead, his mind was on the future. On war.

When they reached their rooms, he changed immediately, stripping off his best uniform coat. Then he put on another. When he strapped his sword on, something tumbled over in her stomach. Horror. Fear. Her voice came out at last. She could not let him leave without speaking. "May I do anything to help you?"

He looked up at her as if only now he remembered she was there. He'd been leaning forward, throwing a few things into a canvas bag. "No, Ellen." He straightened, then his eyes glowed a beautiful heated blue, and he opened his arms. "Come here."

She went to him, her arms slipping about his lean waist. She could not hold the tears back.

"You will manage, Ellen, whatever happens, because you must. Do you understand?"

She nodded against his chest. She knew she would; he'd told her what to do if he did not come back. But… She did not wish to lose him. Physically she knew what to do… But, her heart… how could she breathe if anything happened to him?

His fingers stroked through her hair, knocking out pins as she wept against his uniform which smelt of soap and starch from

146

washing.

He'd had it washed to wear into battle. To perhaps die…

She could not think of it.

But even as she pushed the thought away, her mind saw the image of the highwayman lying dead on the road, so many months ago.

Paul held her away a little, looking into her eyes. His own burned with concern – with the word he never spoke. *Sorry.* Only thrice in their marriage had they argued and on each occasion it had been Paul who began it, and mostly because he was tired and she had not been ready to dine, or had been speaking of something he considered mundane when he'd merely wanted to eat and rest. His mood afterward was always apologetic, but he never said sorry. Now though his touch said the words *I am sorry I brought you here.*

She wiped the tears from her cheeks. She must cease crying. It was making this worse for him. She met his gaze. "I do not regret marrying you, not at all. You've made me happier than I ever thought it possible to be." He leaned and pressed a kiss on her lips, a chaste kiss. When he pulled away, she said. "And you will fight for our country, and I shall be proud of you, and you will come back and make me even happier."

He nodded, but then his head bent and this kiss was not chaste at all but searing with intensity. "I love you," he said in an earthy voice when he broke it.

"I love you too."

His eyes looked regretful again, yet he smiled, before saying, "I'd better pack." She nodded, but he was already letting her go and turning away.

"I've told you what you must do." He stated as he continued throwing spare items of his uniform into the bag. He did not say – *if I die.*

She knew. "Yes."

"And you remember…" he glanced over his shoulder meeting her gaze for a moment.

"Yes."

He looked towards his packing again. "And swear to me, if there is any news that we've lost, you will do everything possible to get out of Brussels and back to Ostend, with anyone who will take you. When you reach there, sell whatever you have to get a passage back to England and go to my father. If I survive I will come and find you there."

She gripped his arm to stop his hurried packing. "You *will* survive."

He did stop, straightening again and looking at her. "If fate and God are on my side, but I have long ago learned there is no ordering either of them. As I have said before, Ellen, what will be, will be – we must make the best of it."

His hand lifted then and brushed over the skin of her cheek. "You are so beautiful. I have been a very lucky man these last few months. I do not regret marrying you either, though I feel that I should."

"You should not." Ellen answered, vehemently.

He smiled, but then turned back to his packing.

~

It took Paul an hour and half to walk back from the ball and pack his kit, much longer than it should have taken. His mind was only half on his duty, the other half was focused on his pretty wife who hovered close, like a delicate butterfly drawn by the colour of his scarlet coat.

When he'd packed his canvas bag, he pulled the drawstring closed and tied it off. He had to ride out to his men. They were to march at three; the army was being moved to defend the critical crossroads of Quatre Bras, and his regiment was to be used to form part of a cavalry screen to the west and south west of Brussels. Wellington's orders wished them in position before six as Napoleon's army was known for moving early.

Paul straightened and turned. Ellen had not moved from beside him. Her arms hung limp and helpless at her sides.

He wondered if he should have called Jennifer for her. Now the last moments were here, he did not know what to say. Sorry? But sorry was a useless, pointless word – he had done what he had done. There was never any going back, only forward. Yet this could be the last time he looked at her face, and those perfect pale eyes. "I love you." The words whispered over his lips, as he opened his arms to her once more and fear gripped cold and hard in his stomach. His fingers ran over her hair, which was a mess from his earlier embrace.

"As I love you," her words were warmth and vibration seeping through the fabric of his coat.

He held her tightly for a moment more, her soft weight pressing against him, as her breaths filled her lungs, her breasts pressing against his chest, and her back lifting beneath his fingers.

He did not in general pray before a battle, he was never convinced that God would take sides in war, but he prayed now, not for himself, but for her. That she would be safe. That he would come back to her. *Let me return to her.* The words whispered through his thoughts as he looked up to the ceiling, as if God really lived upwards within their room and he might see Him.

Sighing when there was no immediate echoing voice announcing that He had heard, and it would be so, Paul let his hand run over Ellen's hair once more, possibly touching it for the last time. He lifted her chin and kissed her, deeply, slipping his tongue into the haven of her mouth and wishing he could slip into the haven of her body too. But there was no time.

He broke the kiss. "I must go."

She nodded, although he saw the sheen of tears glittering in her eyes. He knew she tried to fight them.

"Goodbye," she whispered as he turned to collect his bag and then threw it over his shoulder.

He turned back. The tight feeling in his stomach became

excruciatingly painful. He had never imagined, when he'd decided to allow himself the luxury of a wife, that it would feel like this when it came time to fight – so horrible to leave her behind. But leave her behind he must. And then again, he had never made a decision to take a wife, he had just wanted Ellen. And now… now she was the whole world to him, and he might never come back.

"Goodbye." What a final word. He would not have it be his last to her. "My beautiful, precious wife, I shall hold you in my heart as I fight. I shall not be alone on the field."

Tears sparkled even more intensely in her eyes, and she merely nodded. Then when he turned and left the room, she followed him down the stairs to the street. At the door, when he turned to say a final goodbye, she threw her arms about his neck and sobbed against his collar.

"Come now, Ellen. This is not how I wish to leave you." His voice seemed to roll out over gravel as emotion welled in his throat too. "Let me remember your smile as I leave."

She pulled away nodding, swallowing back and wiping away tears. Then she bit her lip as she fought to control her emotion.

"I must go."

"I know. I shall be thinking of you, and praying for you, and waiting to hear word."

He smiled.

At last she smiled too, a pretty smile, though there was still moisture in her eyes.

"I will do my best to come back to you."

She nodded, and then he bent and pressed a last kiss on her lips. But as he did so, the feeling of love within his chest swelled. His hand lifted to cup her scalp as his tongue swept over her lips to part them.

He showed her with his last kiss how little he wished to leave her too, even if he could not bring himself to admit such dishonour in words.

Her arms slipped from his neck as he pulled away.

"God go with you." She whispered.

But he wished God to stay with her. Could God's grace be in two places at once – *in a hundred thousand places?* Every man on the battlefield probably prayed for divine protection.

His hand ran over her hair. "I love you. I will always be with you in my heart, Ellen, no matter what." He turned away then, because he had to, if he did not, he would never leave.

Chapter Fifteen

Ellen returned to their room exhausted and empty, having watched him from the door until he turned the corner at the end of the street. She lay down on the bed, her arms cradling her stomach, and prayed, whispering the words aloud.

"Protect him. Save him. Bring him home. Bring him back to me…" Tears slipped from her eyes rolling onto her cheeks, a gentle sensation of pain.

She'd not realised she'd slept until the call of a bugle woke her, the loud piercing ringing sound echoing ominously about the streets outside. She rose, still wearing her ball gown and moved to look down from the window. There was another bugle call, shouting for the military men.

Leaning her shoulder against the edge of the window she watched the street, listening out for the calls which roused any soldier who may not have heard the news. But surely it must have travelled about Brussels last night like a flood, sweeping into every street and alley.

At only a little after three, when it was barely dawn, and still mostly dark, men came marching along the street, rifles clutched in their hands and balanced on their shoulders. The beat of the drum she'd become so used to on their journey here paced their steps, while notes of tin whistles echoed on the air.

Paul would be with his men, marching. Her stomach tumbled over. More men passed through the street, and women hung out of windows wearing their nightdresses, waving and blowing kisses at the men below. A soldier looked up and his gaze caught Ellen's as she looked through the glass. *Let me remember your smile as I leave.* This soldier looked younger than her and fear shone in his eyes.

She lifted her hand and smiled at him, mouthing silently, "Good luck."

He smiled too, then looked away.

The men kept coming and she opened her window, crying out God's blessings to them as others were. Some people had even hurriedly dressed and gone down into the street. She did not go down.

When the last man walked past, almost an hour after the first, her heart bled like an open wound and her stomach turned with sickness. But resolutely, she shut the window. Her misery would not help Paul; he'd told her she had the strength to carry on, she would keep breathing, and living… She moved to call for Jennifer. She would change and go for a walk in the park. She needed air, and she needed to feel Paul, and somehow, if she was outside, knowing he was outside would make her feel closer to him.

It was not until one past midday that they heard the first cannons firing; deep heavy booming sounds which rumbled over the city.

As they'd walked through the streets earlier, with dawn fully broken, more people had been leaving.

It was desertion to leave behind the men they had all cheered only hours before. But by midday the exodus had broadened and just like the moment when the news had come of Napoleon's parade through Paris, there was now at least one cart being loaded in every street.

It was cowardice to leave the soldiers behind. They risked their lives.

Ellen looked at Jennifer. They were sewing. The sound of

153

another cannon firing resonated through the window. Jennifer looked anxious. There was another. They became constant; the sound rumbling over the city like a persistent thunderstorm. But there was no guessing the distance the noise came from – how close they were to the battle. Ellen's heart was held in a firm embrace that made it hesitate a little each moment before it beat, and she had to force air into her lungs as she worked on another shirt for Paul and refused to think of him fighting amidst that cannon fire.

Another boom rattled her nerves as Jennifer made a little frightened sound.

Ellen began talking, they'd hardly ever sat and spoken. Jennifer had made it clear by her stilted answers, she felt uncomfortable speaking. But today was different; they both needed to absorb their minds with something. Ellen spoke about the ball…

It was about two when the gunfire ceased, and then an ominous quiet fell over the city as people waited for news. *What was happening?* The words swept through Ellen's mind a thousand times as the clock in the room ticked away minutes which felt like hours.

At three, she stood. "Let us walk out again, Jennifer."

It was not for air this time. It was for the possibility of hearing news. Any news.

But when they got outside the streets were virtually empty, eerily so. They went down to the nearest park and walked all about it in silence again, as Ellen could think of nothing to say and Jennifer would not speak.

When they walked back towards the lodgings though, there was a different atmosphere. More people were about, and some moved from group to group, while others knocked on doors.

Ellen walked towards one man dressed in livery, who had knocked on a door and spoken to a woman then moved to knock on the next.

She stopped, standing in his path. "Is there news?"

"The Allied army has been overcome. We are to leave the city.

Everyone must leave." He walked around her moving onto the next door.

She had no idea who he was or where he had come from. Or most importantly whether she should believe what he'd said. So many thoughts fought for attention in her head as her heart kicked. Something punched in her stomach. Paul had said she must leave if such a message came; he'd made her promise – and yet... *How can I go?*

People who'd come out into the street were now turning and hurrying home, and the conversations became louder.

"Let us go home," was all Ellen said to Jennifer, but when she reached there she could not sit and sew. She went to the window and looked down on the street as Jennifer hovered by the door. People hurried past, and some doors were open as urgent, rushed, conversations took place. Then others hurried off.

Within an hour the mood in the city had turned to panic. There had been no sign of any soldiers, but a new exodus began and this one was more urgent than the previous evacuations.

The street before Ellen's window was packed with carriages and carts all badly piled with crates, furniture, trunks and bags, as people hurried to flee the city before the French arrived. Around the vehicles were others on foot, begging for horses, or space. They waved watches, notes and jewellery for any of those things.

It was bedlam, a nightmare – *disloyal.*

Paul would have had her doing the same, but she could not bring herself to go.

Four times Jennifer suggested they pack. Four times Ellen denied the suggestion, her stomach tied in a tight knot, full of fear – not for herself, but for Paul...

She could not get the vision of the highwayman's bloody body from her mind, only it had Paul's face. But he could not be dead. She would know. She would feel it.

She turned to Jennifer her heartbeat pacing out the seconds. "Let us go back out and see if it is like this all over Brussels."

"Ma'am, we should not go out, we should leave with everyone else. If the city is over run we shall be…" *Raped and murdered.* Jennifer did not have to say the words, they had both heard many rumours of the Peninsular War on their journey here, and Ellen knew that was why Paul had told her to run. But how could she desert him? It would be a betrayal to leave him behind, as though she believed he was dead. She refused to believe that.

"Just humour me, Jennifer, let us go out on to the streets."

For the third time that day Jennifer held up Ellen's pelisse for her to put on, but the maid was not happy.

When they stepped onto the street they were immediately jostled by the crowd, as a man who had been trying to free a horse from its harness received a blow from a sharp flip of the driver's whip.

"Ma'am, we should go back and pack," Jennifer said more urgently.

"Let us just see what is happening," Ellen ordered, refusing to give in. With that, she pushed her way through the crowd, not looking to even see if Jennifer followed; working her way along the street as if around the corner, the next street would be quiet. Of course it was not, it was the same. Ellen saw a woman holding up her wedding ring, a woman Ellen had seen a dozen times, walking along the streets on the arm of a soldier. "Give me a seat on your carriage, sir. I only ask to sit beside the coachman?"

The man yelled at her, "Get back or I'll drive the horses over you!" though no vehicle moved at more than a crawl. There were too many people on the street.

People were doing anything, at any cost, to escape the city.

Paul had urged Ellen to do the same, but the woman had been denied anyway.

"Ma'am!" Jennifer gripped Ellen's arm. "If you will not leave the city, then I must leave your service. I shall find my own way back to a port."

Horror hit Ellen. But how could she force Jennifer to stay if she wished to go? "Of course."

Paul would shout at her if he thought she'd chosen to stay here alone without a woman to accompany her. He would think it foolish. But the pain in her heart, the warm light that burned for him, calling him home, could not leave him behind.

"If that is what you wish, Jennifer. We shall go back."

"Come with me, ma'am." Jennifer's grip firmed on Ellen's arm, urging Ellen physically too.

"No, I will stay and wait for the Captain."

"And if he does not return?" Those words kicked with the same force as the horses who fought a path through the panicking crowd.

"He will." Ellen turned and began pushing through the crowd towards the place she and Paul had called home for weeks. Jennifer followed.

Within their room, Ellen searched for what little money she had and then went down to Jennifer, to give it to her.

Jennifer had not been paid for four weeks; the money would be compensation. It would be unthinkable to let her go without the means to obtain a passage home.

"Madam, you need not give me all of this."

"Just take it, Jennifer."

"But you will need some for yourself."

"I shall be fine once my husband returns."

Jennifer stopped packing and gripped Ellen's arm. "Ma'am, come with me? You should not stay. If the Captain is alive he will find you. It is better you go."

Tears clouded Ellen's vision. "I cannot." It would be as if she admitted he was gone.

"Ma'am-"

"Jennifer! I will not. There is no point in urging me. I cannot leave." The words came out in a cross voice, but only because she was in so much pain. *How will I cope? How?*

"Very well." The maid let go of Ellen's arm and turned to push a few more things into the leather bag she'd packed hurriedly. Ellen watched as she'd watched Paul.

Time felt unreal. Life felt unreal. This could not be happening.

When Jennifer's bag was full, she secured the leather buckles, pulling them tight. She already wore her bonnet and cloak. She turned towards Ellen. "You are sure you will not come?"

Shaking her head in denial, inside uncertainty roared in Ellen's ears. She was empty. Alone.

"Very well then." With that Jennifer went too, she walked out of the room, across the hall to the front door, and then out of that. Gone.

As the door closed behind her, the breath slipped from Ellen's lungs. She was truly alone now. Her limbs shaking, she stumbled backwards and sat on the stairs, almost collapsing.

Fear hung as a weight on her shoulders and something eating at her innards as she stared at the door.

She was not completely alone. The woman who owned the establishment lived in the basement below, and although everyone who'd rented other rooms seemed to have fled, she did not think the woman who owned the house would have left. It was mostly the British who were fleeing.

She covered her face with her hands. But she did not cry. She was beyond crying. The fear inside her hovered with a sense of waiting, wishing to know whether there was a need to cry or not?

Is he alive or not?

~

"Rise up!" The Lieutenant Colonel's voice echoed through the trees. "Rise up!"

The cannons had begun pounding at about one, but Paul's men had not been amongst the fighting; they'd been kept in the woods just north of Lac Materne, lining the Namur road, defending it in case the French broke through. For hours they'd been lying down beyond the sunken road, in amongst the trees, to avoid becoming targets for the cannon fire, listening to the battle unfold in the distance, defying the urge to move without an order.

"I said rise up men!" Now the order had come it resonated all about Paul as he moved instinctively.

Within a moment the French riflemen poured over the brow of the hill, and in the next instant after hours of waiting – no, after months of waiting – they were at war, each man fighting for his life. Kill or be killed.

"Rifles! Present!" Paul called to his men to make ready. Then having given them a moment to prepare, he yelled. "Fire!" The front row of men charging towards them fell, their screams of pain echoing as they clasped at wounds. Others looked their last at Paul with horror.

God, he'd forgotten the stench of gunpowder and blood – death.

"Make ready!" he called again, raising his arm as the second row of his men, stepped through the first who'd begun reloading. The sound of the regiment moving always stirred the patriotism in his blood. *For Britain and for victory.* "Present! Fire!" Another round was released. More men collapsed to their knees. Smoke rose on the air from all the rifles. The caustic smell of gunpowder burned at the back of his throat, making his stomach lurch.

A volley released from the platoon beside theirs, as Paul's third row stepped forward. "Prepare! Fire!" Rifle shots reverberated all around him as the third round blasted into the French.

There was time for two more rounds. Two more.

"Ready!" He yelled again, as the first row stepped through the third. "Fire!" The volley rang out.

One more. He held his nerve, willing his men to do so too. They trusted him implicitly; he knew they would. "Prepare!" The sound of rifles being lifted to shoulders and aimed repeated along the line either side of him. "Fire!" The final shots were deafening, ringing in his ears. Paul looked into a man's eyes and watched the man's gaze shutter with pain, the light within his soul dying out. He fell.

There was no time for compassion. None for thought. Breathe and fight. That was all he must do. He was a soldier. A British soldier. Nothing else. He lived as part of a whole on a battlefield.

"Draw arms!" Paul yelled for his men to lower their rifles and present their bayonets. The enemy were too close now for bullets.

The French shouted. "Vive l'Empereur!"

"Attack!"

"On to victory!" his men yelled, "Give them the bayonet!" The words echoed over the cries of the wounded men they ran across, and blood streamed in rivers through the mud that squelched beneath Paul's boots.

An unearthly cry came from behind Paul's men, shrill hollers and whoops. Then Picton's Highlanders, the men who had been dancing jigs last night to entertain the women, came charging through the lines of Paul's riflemen at a run, swords drawn to repel the French.

The fighting was fierce, but Paul held back, prepared to defend if the Highlanders failed, rather than waste himself by getting caught up with Picton's men.

Paul watched as the Highlanders wore the French down with their vicious energy in an unrelenting onslaught; they hacked and parried, pushing the French back, away from the 52nd riflemen. But then the sound of thundering hoof beats vibrated through the ground.

"Form a square!" he yelled. "A square! Now! As swift as you can!"

As he hollered out the order, Picton called. "Retreat! Move amongst the 52nd!"

It was the turn of Paul's men again. Even as they moved he shouted. "Make ready!"

There was only time for action, as men ran about him; those either side of him dropping to their knees, their rifles already raised to their shoulders as above them the regiment's flag caught on the wind, held aloft by their pole bearer.

Other men crowded in behind Paul, and the Highlanders ran back, seeking refuge amongst the riflemen.

On all four sides of the square his men had formed, there were now men on their knees. As the Highlanders ran through their boundary, the cavalry came over the hill, hooves trampling the dead and dying.

Standing with a rifle, facing a man on a horse, was terrifying, if that man got too close… "Fire!" Paul yelled. The cavalry were only paces away. Horses screamed and fell, writhing on the ground as Paul called his second line forward.

"Present."

Men trapped beneath their mounts cried out from positions half buried within the corpses already strewn across the ground.

"Fire!" Another volley and more men and horses fell. But there was no time for another, as the cavalry thundered into the front of his men. Swords slashed and hacked, while his men presented a boundary of lethally pointed bayonets. The metal glinted catching the sunlight, trying to protect the Highlanders hidden within the square. Some had not made it.

Paul watched them cut down on the field.

"Present!" Paul yelled to the men about him, three back within the square as those at the front were still kneeling, jabbing at men and horses with the tips of the piercing blades on the ends of the rifles. "Fire." More horses and men went down, some crushing his men.

"Make ready!" he called again, determined to keep as many men as possible alive. Determined to win. "Fire!"

His mouth was dry and his voice hoarse from breathing in the gunpowder.

Wave after wave of French assaulted their surviving square. But they were not alone. Beside them, along the brow of the hill, Paul could see other regiments also formed into squares, fighting just as hard.

The bombardment went on for hours, as they repelled line after line of the French, and after a while he heard the cannon booming to the north of them again. But there was no time for fear. No time to wonder if they would survive – if the French would tire before he did. Only time to fight.

"Fire!" he called the word again, his throat painful with thirst.

They would run out of ammunition soon.

"Fire!"

He could see his men were pale and worn.

"Fire!"

How much more?

"Fire!"

Then suddenly another charge came over the hill, a fresh wave of cavalry. But only a single battalion charging against the squares Paul could see.

There must be many more Allied squares along the line.

"Fire!" Another volley rang out, in denial of the yells of those charging, as the horses pounded over the dead and wounded, racing towards the British at a gallop. The horses were already blowing, they must have been raced at a gallop all the way up the hill.

"Fire."

Even with another wave of cavalry charging towards them, even though they must be tired to their bones, Paul's men did not falter. They stayed steady, bayonets held upwards and rifles hurriedly recharged.

"Fire!"

More French went down.

Paul prayed for it to be over. They could not hold much longer, but the French cavalry was already thinning.

Instead of attacking directly, the French sought to pass between the Allied lines.

"Present! Left! Right!" he yelled. The same call came from the squares beside his. Shots rang out, bringing down a dozen men or more from their horses.

"Prepare!"

The next row of rifles rose. "Fire!" Another volley and a dozen more men and horses went down as other horses reared and their cries reverberated on the air.

"Prepare!" As Paul called again, the French onslaught slowed. Those remaining turned their horses and raced away.

His heart leapt, and energy – which had been non-existent a moment before – flooded into his veins, as adrenalin pulsed into his limbs.

"Attack! Attack!" The cry came from a man on a horse racing at a gallop behind the lines. "Wellington bids you attack!"

The square closest to the rider was already breaking up, men rising and dispersing – men who had knelt for hours at the front with bayonets, stood, and were now charging forwards on unsteady legs.

"Attack!" Paul took up the cry, beckoning for his men to move forward and release the Highlanders from within. "Attack!"

In moments, they were running, with energy only a quarter-hour ago he would not have thought they had. "Attack!" he yelled again to keep his men on their feet and moving. "Attack!" The cry came from the right of his regiment now too, as the British army raced forward, running over bodies, as though bodies were no more than mud or grass, forcing the French to withdraw further and further back.

Within an hour they were no longer charging but walking, claiming more ground, as the French continued pulling back. The light turned from day to early dusk then twilight, before slipping further and further towards night. It was then the call came to camp. But there were no tents to be put up. Small fires were lit from gathered wood, and he and his men, and others further along the line crowded about them, exhausted from battle, and haunted by death, and lay down on the cold hard ground.

It was only then he thought of Ellen, left behind. A sense of concern – dread – ate into his empty stomach. *Damn. How is she? She must be afraid for me.* He whispered silent prayers for her again, and for his return to her, before his eyes closed. When they did, he thought of her body, of sleeping with her warmth and softness against him, letting her sooth his soul and free him from the images he'd endured today – the faces of the men he'd killed, and those he'd seen dying.

Darkness claimed him.

It was at five, when light had already flooded the sky, that he was shaken awake. As he opened his eyes, he saw men working their way along the line spreading word. "We are to move." The words were whispered to him by a stranger. "The Duke of Wellington's orders are to pull back to the ground by Waterloo."

Paul knew the ground. It was the point the Generals had considered the best place to fight. There was a ridge and another wood, the Forest of Soignes, where men could hide if needs be. It was more defendable and every officer had been made accustomed to the terrain in the months they'd spent about the city.

Paul sat up and rubbed his face, urging himself to wake, as the men around him stretched and yawned, rising slowly. "Eat and drink," he whispered. They looked at him. There was only limited water and dry biscuits in their provisions, but they must do.

It seemed this second day they marched for hours. But it was not so many. Within a day they had re-camped and positioned themselves on the Duke of Wellington's chosen ground to take the enemy. The losses of the day before had not been as bad as Paul feared, only a couple of thousand, some of the wounded had been moved by cart back beyond the lines, but many were bandaged and ready to fight again.

Chapter Sixteen

If people had been in panic yesterday as cannons had echoed over the city, the 17th of June felt like the eye of a terrible storm. The city was quiet and unmoving. Those who were the sort to run had gone, and those who'd chosen to stay remained in their homes, waiting to hear more guns or news. No word or sound came.

Ellen was sick first thing in the morning, probably because she had not eaten anything the day before. Her stomach felt too much like a whirlpool as anxiety swirled inside her. She tried to sew but her fingers shook too much to thread a needle. She tried to read but her mind would not concentrate on a single word. When it reached two past midday, she went for a walk outside, alone, which as a genteelly bred woman she should not do, but with Jennifer gone she had no choice.

The streets, which yesterday had been full of people, were entirely empty. She walked for an hour and saw no one.

When she returned to their rooms, she moved a chair beside the window, and sat upon it with her knees lifted to her chest and gripped in her arms, as she'd sat in her room as a child, if she'd been scalded. Then, with her chin resting on her knees, she watched the street, silent and praying, her heart beating out the time.

"Where are you, Paul?"

"Where?"

"Are you alive?"

She remained where she was as she watched dusk finally fall, and still there had only been the odd servant passing through the street.

As darkness claimed the city, falling like a shroud, Ellen's eyes closed.

When Ellen woke the next morning, she was sick once again, and her stomach ached with cramps of hunger as she vomited bile.

Paul would be angry with her if he knew how poorly she'd been taking care of herself. She should eat.

Paul would be angry with her for not leaving Brussels when she'd had the chance, if he was captured and not dead. But surely if the French had already won, they would be in the city now.

Ellen moved to pull the rope which would call down to the kitchen, and waited uncertain who, if anyone, might come, now that Jennifer had gone.

After a few minutes there was a knock on the door, and Ellen opened it to see a maid in a grey dress and white mobcap. "Madam." She dipped into a curtsy.

"Is there any food in the kitchens? My maid has left…" Paul at least was not in debt for their rooms. The proprietor had no reason to refuse.

"There is bread and cheese, ma'am."

"Anything," Ellen answered as her stomach tightened with pain.

When the woman returned, Ellen accepted the food, and asked if anyone in the house had heard news of the battle. The maid said they had not, but she held a hundred opinions upon the French and proceeded to share them as Ellen sat down to eat. She did not turn the maid away; after Jennifer's constant silence Ellen was relieved to listen to another woman's voice as she broke her fast and drank sweetened, weak, milky tea.

But at half past eleven their conversation was interrupted by the sound of cannon fire. Ellen stood and turned looking towards the window. Another distant boom could be heard. Ellen looked back at the maid for an instant. She had paled to almost white.

Pulled from the room by the sound, Ellen hurried downstairs and out onto the street.

Yes. It was cannon fire. Closer than the other day. Volley after volley sounded over the city.

Ellen looked back at the maid who'd followed, as others came out onto the streets.

What did it mean? Was Paul alive?

~

The first of the cannons rang out at twenty-five minutes past eleven in the morning on the 18th of June. But this time Paul's regiment were more prepared. They had their orders for the battle, the best position to defend, and a day's rest.

But when one hour past midday came, the cannons were still pounding, and Paul's men were on the ground where they'd spent the hours since the cannon fire began; hiding behind the ridge, lying on damp bracken as rain seeped through the cloth of their uniforms. He was cold, but not because the day was cold. It was fear. Anxiety. Expectancy. A need to simply fight, pumped through his blood.

In the hours he'd lain here, he'd thought a hundred times of Ellen in Brussels, hearing the sound of the cannons and thinking of him.

He'd survived one battle; he only had to survive one more. Today, they all believed – would bring success or failure.

All the men about him lay still and silent, listening, waiting.

There were encounters taking place, he could hear rifles, horses, swords and battle cries, men exerting their strength to stay alive, but the battle was not close enough for Paul and his men to be called in to fight.

Aware of every beat of his heart, and every breath he took, Paul listened to the sounds as he waited, including the warning cries of rooks nesting in the trees above him.

At two o'clock finally there was movement close to them. A few hundred yards away there was a cry for Picton's regiment, to "Rise up!" The sound of several hundred men rising followed, and the movement of swords and rifles.

Paul remained on the ground, with his men, watching Picton's men move forward, pacing towards the brow of the hill. Beyond it shouts of "Vive l'Emperuer" rang out.

"Charge! Hurrah!" Picton yelled out suddenly, calling his men over the top. The men ran.

Paul's heart pumped hard, waiting for his moment, certain it would come soon, as he looked right and left for the Lieutenant Colonel. His commander was holding back behind the ranks for orders.

They could hear the fighting increasing in intensity beyond the ridge, screams, shouts and rifle fire as the cannons still boomed.

Damn. Damn. He burned to be able to look through earth and see what was happening, but he'd been a soldier long enough to know how crucial it was to await orders from the men who had the oversight of the whole battle. He and his men simply needed to hold their nerve.

Wait. Wait.

Hollers of another charge came from beyond the ridge of the hill, and amid them more cries of "Vive l'Emperuer."

Paul looked back at his Lieutenant Colonel who looked to the right for some signal. Then he turned sharply, looking at Paul first, and lifted his hand without a word, before looking on to others and bidding them rise with the same signal.

"Up." Paul said in a low voice which swept along the row in a quiet wave of sound, and then the Lieutenant Colonel made a hand gesture encouraging them forward.

"March," Paul ordered as quiet as before, taking a step himself that the men followed a step after, and so, silently, they paced forward, as the cries of the French became louder.

From the sounds, they were running up the hill, believing they were about to claim it.

Lieutenant Colonel Hillier came past Paul, riding at a canter but leaning low in his saddle, and he called them to halt and lift their rifles with another gesture.

"Present." Paul said more firmly. A couple of hundred rifles were lifted to press against shoulders along the line of the 52nd.

Wait. Wait. They could hear the French army coming closer, a mass of sound beyond the brow of the hill...

His heart pulsed.

"Fire!" The cry rang out from half a dozen commanders along the line, as the French rushed over the top, in reams. The volley of shots scythed down men, as a look of horror flooded their eyes. They'd not known the British soldiers had lain hidden over the hill.

"Fire!" Another volley took down more men.

"Forward!" The Lieutenant Colonel shouted over the sounds of battle, and so they began to pace, winning ground a step at a time.

Now they were in the fray and over the hill Paul could see the thousands of dead and dying spread over the fields below.

The French were pushed back, but then they returned with a cavalry assault, forcing Paul to order his men into a square behind the Allied cannons. The cannons kept booming between assaults. When the French attacked, the gunners hid amongst Paul's men as the Highlanders had the day before, but each time the French pulled back for another charge, the Allied gunners ran out to load and fire a round at the French.

Then suddenly from behind, a regiment of British cavalry swept through, mounted on huge grey horses, forcing the French back again. Their charge persisted as Paul watched, chasing the French to the far side of the field.

There, they struck down the gunners who fired the French cannon.

The British lines cheered as the French were called back to the edge of the field to regroup. But it left the British cavalry trapped.

They were killed.

An eerie silence fell on the fields they fought over as Paul glanced back to check his men.

None of the Allied lines were called forward; instead, orders reached Paul to say that Wellington was taking the opportunity to break the soldiers from their squares. As Paul and his men rested and drank water from canteens, messages were passed along the line, checking casualties and positions.

When the battle began again, Paul was on the hill, and like the whole Allied army, back in a square. Though this time, from within, the Lieutenant Colonel shouted orders to move them forward.

All the squares crept forward, pushing the French back and the fight down the hill as the French cavalry continually assaulted them and was repeatedly repelled. Neither side was conceding.

A new wave of French soldiers suddenly poured onto the field at nearly five o'clock and weary but determined, Paul, like the whole of the Allied forces on the hill was ordered to make his men form a line, four deep, as the French charged again. Volleys echoed on the air.

The fight could not go on much longer; they could not fight forever.

~

It was at about four that Ellen first heard of wounded soldiers arriving in the city. She'd seen people in the street and gone to find out the news. Returning to her rooms she'd slipped on her pelisse and hurried out towards the gate leading onto the Nemur road.

There were cartloads of men with limbs missing and open, bandaged and bleeding wounds.

Dear God. Her gaze scanned the men who'd been left lying on the street or were being carried into houses, her heart pounding as she looked for Paul. She did not see him. But as she glanced over the men, she was drawn forwards. She remembered the young soldier she'd waved to from her window. So many were younger than her.

Before she even knew it, she knelt beside a young man, asking what he needed.

"If you wish to help, I have a dozen things you might do…" Ellen turned as a woman spoke. "There's water, and bandages, and we are looking for people to hold men who require treatment. Will you come?"

Ellen rose, and turned. "Of course, but let me bring water to this man first." Like so she was swept into the mayhem of war. It was beyond anything she might have imagined as hundreds of men were brought back into the city, and as she worked, she constantly looked for Paul in each new cartful, and then, at about seven in the evening, the first men began arriving on foot, hobbling, exhausted and bleeding.

Her heart beat out a steady rhythm, the pace of the drum the men had marched to as they'd left, a beat or two away from panic as she waited and helped. Her breathing was held at bay only by the need to do something for these men who'd survived, but were in agony.

"Madam!" A doctor shouted across the drawing room they'd taken over. There were two dozen men lying on the floor. At the same moment the man who had gripped her hand, released his hold, his fingers slipping away. She looked down. His eyes had turned white.

Her heart missing a beat, sickness threatened, and she pressed a hand over his bloody coat. She did not even know if that blood was his, another's, or the blood of a Frenchman, but there was no sense of his heart beating, and no feeling of movement in his lungs.

"Madam!"

She stood not knowing what to do, and moved to the doctor's side. "I think the man I was with may be dying."

He looked over but when he looked back at her there was no hope in his eyes. "There is nothing I can do. I must deal with those who have more chance of survival. This man needs his arm taken off, and I need someone to hold his shoulder while I cut. Will you do it?"

A soldier who had a bloodied bandage over one eye but in all other ways seemed well, was already kneeling holding the man's legs down, their patient looked up at them with wild terrified eyes. But the bone in his forearm was protruding from an open wound, shattered and in splinters.

Ellen's stomach turned again, but she bit her lip and nodded. She would do anything to help these men – in the hope that someone would do the same for Paul if he was wounded, some-where, needing help.

~

At seven the last sunlight painted the clouds above Paul orange. The battle could go either way. For hours he'd fought amongst others, by attack and counter attack; neither side had gained an advantage.

Napoleon's force made another push to break through the centre of the Allied lines, trying to cut Paul and his regiment off on the left. The fight continued as daylight turned to dusk, and then edged towards night, and once again Paul was on the defensive, in a square, watching as a British troop charged past to push the French back down the hill.

A call rang from the left. Paul's Lieutenant Colonel raised his sword, calling Paul's square to break and move about.

Something was afoot.

Paul lifted his own sword high, calling his men to break from the square and move. Then he saw the risk. The French Imperial Guard made a last charge up the hill, seeking to break the Allied forces once and for all.

Paul ran ahead of his men, calling them on, his sword raised. The pole bearer ran beside, holding up their colours, and the flag flew out on the breeze. "Halt and kneel!" Paul bid his front row when they were in close range. "Present All!" Three layers of men at varying heights all raised their rifles a moment before the French fell into the same position. There was a sudden vicious volley of bullets.

A force ripped through Paul's stomach; a solid mass, tearing through his flesh and pushing him backward off his feet, slamming him down onto the muddy ground as the air about him filled with the bitter smell of powder and blood. There was no pain, only shock. Cold, disbelieving, shock.

My God!

"Captain! Captain!"

One of his men was beside him, and Paul saw him for a moment before the world went black. "Captain!"

There was a foul smell in the air. Death. His death. The smell of a gut wound.

Ellen…

He had no feeling in his arms or legs, though his heart beat even in the darkness, but his blood and energy drained away. *I am going to die.*

"Tell my wife…" He forced the words from his dry lips into the emptiness beyond him, and felt a man's hand touch his face. Then… the last image in his head was Ellen, her face, as around him shots still screamed above his ahead, and swords and bayonets clashed.

Life ebbed, creeping away into nothing.

Nothing.

"Captain! *Captain!*"

~

Ellen moved from man to man, and each time she knelt down beside another she prayed it would not be Paul. They were all so bloody and mud stained she could not tell until she was close. *Oh! This was hell on earth.* So many men. So many wounded, and for

173

every man here, they were saying there was a dozen left on the field.

Inside her, two phantom hands clasped hard, not allowing her to breathe, tying her stomach in a knot, and the hands would not release until she saw Paul.

Please God, you are safe and well. Please, God!

"May I fetch you water?" She knelt beside another man. He'd lost a leg; the lower half had been torn off by cannon fire and the rags he lay on and his clothes were covered in blood. The doctor had stopped the bleeding already. He'd tied a tight tourniquet around the man's thigh.

This man must have the rest of that limb severed too, yet he might die from infection in a day or two.

Nausea twisted through the knots in Ellen's stomach.

She would hold Paul so tightly when he came back, and love him even more.

Inside the invisible hands gripped harder about her stomach and her lungs.

The man's skin was starkly pale beneath the stains of gunpowder, mud and blood, and his eyes white from blood loss. A look of panic hovered in his gaze, but he nodded. She smiled, trying to ease his fear, though she was terrified herself. She rose to fetch a cup of water. When she returned she held it to his lips for a moment and let it trickle into his mouth. He sighed and lay back, closing his eyes.

She stood. A surgeon waved her over. "I need bandages. Have we more bandages?"

The women had been ripping up sheets for hours and she rushed now to fetch some of the strips that were left; there were not many.

Paul's image constantly held in her head. Her heart prayed for his safety. It was a continuous cry to God. *Keep him safe. Keep him safe, and bring him back to me.*

She handed the bandages to the surgeon and watched him wrap them about a wound he'd just removed a bullet from. Then behind her, another man was brought into the room, shouting out in agony. The doctor looked at her. "Carry on, here."

"Tie a tourniquet," Paul had said months ago, when she had mourned a single highwayman. She had not imagined this when he'd said it.

Paul.

Chapter Seventeen

Finally when it was dark, the sound of cannons in the distance ceased but the wounded still flooded into the city.

Everyone helping in the house in which she worked stopped and looked at one another as the world fell silent apart from the groans of the men in the room. Her heart skipped a beat. *Was it over? Had the Allied forces won? Was Paul alive?*

But she had no time for such thoughts – there were men here who needed help.

Three hours later, word reached the city that the Allied forces had won, and a cry rang out in the streets, even from the wounded.

Ellen's heart filled with warmth and hope.

Four hours later troops began marching back into the city, bringing still more wounded.

Numerous times she rushed to the window to see if it was the 52nd as men were cheered and applauded.

But by midday, when she had gone for a day and half without sleep, there had been no sign of Paul's regiment.

She'd asked some of the returning soldiers, but the numbers of men fighting were so many and no one she'd asked had seen or knew the fate of the 52nd Oxfordshire Regiment of Foot.

"Mrs Harding, go and rest." Ellen turned to face Mrs Beard. She was the wife of a colonel from another regiment. It was her house that had become a makeshift hospital in the last four and twenty hours, like a dozen more along the street.

Now Ellen wished she had socialised more during their time in Brussels. Not at the parties but among the officers' wives.

She had judged all the women by those who'd fled, but now she'd discovered another society. These women were also resolutely waiting for their men, while fighting to save those who had served beside them.

"You have done enough now, and you will only be able to do more if you sleep."

Ellen looked at the woman. There were no beds left in the house and there was no space to rest. If she was to sleep she would have to go back to the room she shared with Paul – *perhaps he would be there, waiting for her.* She'd not even thought of that. "Yes. I will return when I can." Without another word she turned away to fetch her pelisse, leaving Mrs Beard to help the wounded man she'd brought a chamber pot to.

Ellen's heart pounded hard as she hurried through the streets full of men in filthy, bloody uniforms, and prayed with all her strength. But as she entered the room she shared with Paul, she faced an empty space. Desolation hit her. He was not here.

Too tired to stand now she'd thought of sleep, Ellen washed her hands and face. She did not lie on the bed, instead she took up her vigil at the window once more, her feet on the chair as she clutched her knees and rested her head against the back, watching the entrance to the street.

She woke to the sound of someone knocking on the door below the window, her body jolting awake. She stood hurriedly. But it could not be Paul. Paul would not have knocked.

She heard the maid's voice below, and a man's deeper pitch. Outside she saw a horse and two men in the uniform of the 52nd. In an instant she was running from the room, but from the top of the stairs she could only see Paul's Lieutenant Colonel below. The man looked weary, and even though she'd never liked him, compassion burned in her chest as she walked downstairs. "What is it?" He looked up at her. "Where is my husband? Where is Paul?"

She saw the answer in his eyes, but even so he stepped forward and his lips moved. "Captain Harding died on the field."

No! The word was pain in her chest and a roar in head. *No!* She would not believe. She could not…

"No." The word left her mouth on a whisper as darkness crowded in on top of her, stealing her vision.

When Ellen woke she was lying on her bed. The Lieutenant Colonel sat beside her, while the two men dressed in the uniform of Paul's regiment stood across the room with the maid from the lodging house. The room stank of burning feathers. The Lieutenant Colonel held her hand and rubbed the back of it with his other. "Madam…" he said quietly.

Ellen's heart raced as the memory of what he'd said downstairs rushed back and tears filled her eyes. *How can I live without Paul? How?*

"You have no relatives. Am I right?"

Ellen nodded. Paul had always insisted they did not speak of her father.

"Have you money?"

She shook her head. Paul's superior officer must know his wages had remained unpaid for weeks.

"Do you have anywhere to go then?"

Emptiness and loneliness opened a void inside her. There was not even grief – just a space that had been Paul's and now refused to believe he'd gone.

"I think you must come with me then, Mrs Harding."

Ellen looked at him, unable to think. But then her mind filled with the images of the wounded she'd seen over the last few hours. "How did Paul die?"

The Lieutenant Colonel let go of her hand and straightened. "At the end of the battle the 52nd broke the last surge by the French. But in four minutes of gunfire I lost one hundred and fifty men.

Captain Harding was shot. His death was quick. He would not have felt much pain."

The tears which had been trapped within overflowed in rivers. She needed to hold Paul - his strength and warmth, to smell the scent of his cologne. But he was not here. He would never be here now.

"Paul said I am to seek Captain Montgomery's help."

"Captain Montgomery also passed away."

Cold horror chilled Ellen's chest. So many men dead, and – *Paul.* He was alive in her head, saying goodbye to her, kissing her. *How could he never come back?* His face hovered in her mind's eye, youthful and smiling, alive and elemental...

Tears traced pathways of sensation down her cheeks like his fingertips running over her skin.

"Let me take you to my home. Where is your woman? She should pack your things."

"She left" Ellen whispered.

"Then come with me. I shall find you another. But for now..." He looked up at the maid in the room. "Pack Mrs Harding's things. I will take her with me, and send for them later."

Ellen noticed then, he smelt clean. His uniform was fresh; he'd bathed and changed since the battle – washed away any blood.

She shivered.

"Come, Mrs Harding. Let me take you under my protection." He stood and held out a hand.

Ellen rose, but it was in the guise of a ghost. It was not her who moved. She walked downstairs before him as though she was in a dream – no, a nightmare.

She was leaving the place she and Paul had lived for weeks – the only place which might still feel like home, even though he could never come back to it. She was deserting him. In the street, she looked back, longing to refuse to leave, but if she did not go with his Lieutenant Colonel, what would she do?

The Lieutenant Colonel's hands gripped her waist suddenly, and he lifted her up onto his saddle. He had touched her before when they'd waltzed, but now the pressure invaded her senses through the thin layers of her gown and petticoats, uncomfortably bracing her flesh. It was not Paul's touch. She longed for Paul's touch.

The Lieutenant Colonel led the horse through the streets at a walk, as Ellen gripped onto the pommel, her knuckles white, tears flowing down her cheeks.

When they reached the house which she and Paul had visited several times, he lifted her down, his gaze boring into her asking questions he did not speak. When he did not release her waist, she stepped away. Her emotions in turmoil, she turned her back on him, looking at the door.

"Forgive me," he said before stepping about her to lead the way into the house, but he held back at the last moment, encouraging her to enter first. Then he said to the man who stood in a black long-tailed coat at the door, "Send for a maid to escort Mrs Harding to a room. She is to stay."

He led her to the drawing room where she'd waited with Paul a few times before being called in to dinner. Ellen's heart pounded at the memories. She did not believe he was gone. The Lieutenant Colonel spoke, but she did not hear what he said as he moved to pour a drink; she could think of nothing but Paul now.

When the maid finally came, after what seemed like an hour but was probably only minutes, Ellen went willingly, following her upstairs to a room at the rear of the house. There was a sunny sitting room dressed in pink and a separate bedchamber beyond it.

"May I fetch you anything ma'am?"

Ellen turned and looked at the maid, not really seeing her. "No. You may go." Nothing could bring Paul back. There was nothing to help.

When the maid had gone, Ellen walked into the bedchamber, climbed on to the bed, crawled into the middle, curled into a ball, and wept, with her knees hugged tightly to her chest as her heart broke.

~

Sitting up in the bed, Ellen looked out of the window. She'd remained in this room for a day and a night, pain biting in to her heart as she watched the sky change beyond the window, but now the sun had risen again. She should get up, and return to help those who were alive and wounded. That was what Paul would wish of her. She rose from the bed, still clothed. She had neither eaten nor undressed since arriving here.

There was a sharp wrap of a knock on the door of the sitting room. Ellen hurried from the bedchamber into the room beyond it. "You may come." It was not a servant, the knock had not come from the servants' door.

When the door opened, it was the Lieutenant Colonel. He stepped into the room. Instinctively Ellen took a step back.

He lifted his hand, and spoke in a gentle voice. "Mrs Harding, I have come to see how you are. The maid said you have not eaten. I am worried over your health–"

"I am well." She did not say that she had been sick again this morning, it was only because she had not eaten yet. "But I shall return to care for the wounded today, there is a house, Mrs Beard has taken the wounded in, and I… I was helping, I shall return there today…"

He walked towards her. This time Ellen rejected the instinct to back away; it was rude. He had taken her in and given her a place to stay.

When he reached her he took her hand. Ellen recoiled, she could not prevent it, she was too heart-sore for Paul. She did not want the touch of anyone else, but his grip firmed though it was not painful.

"My dear Mrs Harding, you should not leave the house, not yet. I refuse to allow it. You are in shock, and suffering grief. The maid has told me this morning you were unwell. It is not sensible for you to go to help others. For now, you must look after yourself, I insist upon it. I cannot allow you to go. You must stay here, and let me care for you."

What could she say? She had no heart or will to argue. Her spirit just wished to curl up in a ball and be with Paul. How could she live without him? Tears filled her eyes, clouding her vision and then spilled onto her cheeks, rolling downwards in a trickle to drip from her chin. She swiped them away, and nodded.

The Lieutenant Colonel's arm came about her. He led her to a sofa, sitting beside her. "You must not distress yourself, Mrs Harding, I shall protect you now. You may stay with me for as long as you wish, and I shall keep you safe."

Ellen nodded, wiping away more tears. She felt uncomfortable with him, but she had nowhere else to go. She needed somewhere to stay.

"Let me send up some food to tempt you to eat, and I shall buy you some pretty dresses to cheer you."

"I do not need them…"

"But you should have them. You should have beautiful things. I have hired a woman for you. I shall send her to you now so she might help you change. Do you wish me to eat with you? Shall you come down?"

"No." Ellen's answer was vehement. She could not simply sweep Paul away like that and carry on. She looked at the Lieutenant Colonel and said more quietly, realising perhaps she had been disrespectful. "No, thank you, I would rather remain alone…" She left a pause after her words, a pause asking him to leave her now.

He stood, keeping a hold of her hand. She stood too.

He bowed slightly and lifted her fingers to his lips, to kiss the back of them. Then his head lifted and his gaze looked deep into her eyes. "Believe me, Mrs Harding, I shall do my utmost to make you happy."

He gave her a stiff nod, before letting her hand fall, and then he turned away.

Discomfort skimmed up Ellen's spine.

Once the door had shut, she returned to the bedchamber and climbed back up on the bed as tears traced a tingling path down her cheeks.

Chapter Eighteen

"But you have been sick almost every morning, ma'am. When did your last bleed come?"

Three weeks had passed since the Battle of Waterloo. Ellen tried to remember, but she had not been able to think properly since Paul's death.

She looked at the new woman Lieutenant Colonel Hillier had hired to take care of her with a sense of bewilderment. Megan had asked "Are you with child?"

A part of Ellen thought the woman mad.

She could not remember. She had been sick most mornings for the last week of Paul's life too, and before then… Before then… Whenever she thought of Paul, an overwhelming pain absorbed her heart and a burning emptiness opened as a deep chasm in her chest.

It was possibly two months since she'd bled.

"Shall I send for a doctor, ma'am?"

When Lieutenant Colonel Hillier had refused to let her leave his house to help the wounded, it had left her with nothing to think of but Paul and the fact she would never see him again.

She'd cried so many tears there seemed none left within her. Yet she thought the emptiness inside her would never leave.

Ellen looked at the woman finally and nodded.

A child? Paul's...

When the doctor arrived, he pressed her stomach a few times then looked up and nodded. The verdict was swift. "You are indeed with child. Have your breasts felt tender?" Ellen nodded, but she had thought that merely a part of her aching heart, and longing for Paul's touch. "That is all a part of it. I would estimate the child is due in February."

Ellen's fingers covered her stomach as she sat upright, looking at the maid across the room. *A child.*

The man watched her. "And who should I look to for my fee?" Since the battle, with so many men lost, and so much debt dying with them, she'd heard from the maid that no trades accepted credit.

"You must speak to the Lieutenant Colonel," Ellen answered. He had supported her since the battle. He'd bought her new dresses, though she had not asked for them, and sent the best food up to her rooms, though she'd not been in a mood to eat.

"Is the child his?"

Blushing she looked at the doctor, calling him a fool with her eyes.

"Of course not. My husband is... was..." The words stuck in her throat, but she forced them out, hating the sound of them. "A captain in his regiment. He died during the battle."

"And you are living with the Lieutenant Colonel now..." His words carried judgement as though it was wrong for Lieutenant Colonel Hillier to help her.

But he was being kind to her, protecting her...

"Very well." The doctor turned away and Ellen's maid moved to show him out.

A child...

The thought grew like a planted seed in her heart. Her fingers spread over her stomach. Paul was not here but there was another reason to live now. *A child.*

Paul would have loved to become a father... The tears she'd

thought dried up forever, flooded her eyes.

~

A knock struck the sitting room door.

Ellen climbed from the bed.

Lieutenant Colonel Hillier. She knew his knock; it was always the same. The door opened without her calling as she entered the sitting room.

"Ah forgive me, I thought you may be sleeping. I wished to know how you fared. I have paid the physician. He says you are with child." He stared at her, his eyes questioning her as they'd always done.

A shiver spun up Ellen's spine. She ignored it. It was just his way. She was used to it now.

To hide her discomfort, Ellen clasped her hands before her stomach. She was in awe of the news. *Paul's child grew inside her, even though he had gone.* Jubilance, fear, and love overwhelmed her in equal measures.

"You need not fear," Lieutenant Colonel Hillier said in a tight voice. "You may continue to reside with me. I shall keep you, and protect you while you carry the child, and I am willing to look after you once the child is born."

It had never occurred to her that he may not allow her to stay, because if she did not stay where would she go? Yet she ought not to stay forever. She should apply to Paul's family, and her own, as Paul had said.

"Will you dine with me tonight, Mrs Harding, and may I call you Ellen? You may call me Mark, if you wish."

"I will dine with you, yes. But I cannot use your given name. It would be wrong."

He stared at her, his gaze intense and questioning, then turned away. The door shut behind him with a bang as it hit the wooden frame.

He was a difficult man to understand, and yet he was being kind to her, taking her in and protecting her. "*Any of the officers would help you, you may appeal to any of them*" Paul had said when he'd told her what to do before the battle. But he had also told her to look to his father for financial support…

An hour before dinner, a new dress was sent to her rooms. It was a very pale blue, almost the colour of her eyes. The muslin was thin, and very fine, and the white lace that adorned the neck and the hem of the short sleeves, was exquisite. It must have cost a good sum; more than Paul could have afforded.

The maid who delivered it bobbed a curtsy. "Ma'am, Lieutenant Colonel Hillier said he wishes you to wear this gift tonight so you might have something pretty to dine with him." The girl looked at the floorboards, not at Ellen, as a blush heated her skin.

"Say thank you to Lieutenant Colonel Hillier." Ellen replied, bluntly.

She did not feel like dining with him, or even eating. She walked within a nightmare that would not end. Perhaps, in a moment she would wake, and Paul might walk through the door, come up to her, hold her, and tell her all would be well – then kiss her.

She shut her eyes as the door closed, remembering his kiss. Her soul ached for him, desperately.

As her ladies' maid helped her dress for dinner, Ellen was silent, allowing it, not really thinking or focusing, and then she sat before the mirror not at all aware of what the maid did with her hair.

"There, ma'am. The Lieutenant Colonel will be waiting." Megan stepped back admiring her work. Ellen did not even look at the mirror. She turned away, a dark fog surrounding her as she left the room.

It was the first time she had gone beyond the door of her sitting room since coming here. It was odd; everything felt surreal and out of place. She lived with a stranger here – she was a stranger to herself.

Her fingers ran along the oak banister as she walked downstairs.

Two footmen waited in the hall; neither of them looked up at her but merely at the floor near her feet. One opened the door leading into the dining room.

A sharp sudden pain pierced Ellen's breast.

She had entered this room gripping Paul's arm.

The last time she'd sat within it, she'd been sitting beside Paul and he'd talked animatedly with his peers, while she had listened, absorbed in his expression, trying to follow his words and the conversation of the men.

She was sure Lieutenant Colonel Hillier must have seen the tears glimmer in her eyes as she walked in. They distorted her vision.

He stood. "Let me draw a chair for you." He moved to the side, and pulled one out next to him, at the head of the table.

She looked at the seats she had previously occupied with Paul at the lower end of the table as she walked past, her heart aching for him.

"Do sit," Lieutenant Colonel Hillier said, ignoring her distress, if he sensed it.

Ellen bit her lip and swallowed back her tears, shutting her eyes for a moment to dispel them, but as she did so, she saw Paul, smiling at her.

She opened her eyes again, and took the seat Lieutenant Colonel Hillier held. He slid the chair in behind her, as Paul had done on their wedding night.

"The dress looks very beautiful upon you." He sat too.

Ellen looked up and nodded. "Thank you."

"You are a very remarkable woman, but I am sure you are aware of that."

She did not know how to answer.

"Do you like my gift?"

Ellen nodded again, feeling dazed and strange. "Yes, thank you."

"I picked the colour because it is so like your eyes; though I think no man-made colour could match their quality…"

Again, Ellen did not know what to say.

188

He looked up at the butler. "Go ahead then, serve."

A footman came forward to serve her soup, then another stepped forward to fill her glass.

Ellen ate. The oxtail soup was warm, sweetened, and full of flavour. She did not really care, she was not hungry, but she would eat now for the child's sake.

The Lieutenant Colonel gripped her hand. The sensation made her jump. He had been speaking and she'd not heard.

She'd forgotten to wear gloves. How foolish! She thought of the white satin gloves Paul had bought her for the Richmond ball. Where were they? Then she remembered the Lieutenant Colonel saying he'd disposed of the items left behind at her former residence… All Paul's possessions were gone; so many things that would have reminded her of moments with him.

I should be wearing black…

She looked up at Lieutenant Colonel Hillier. "I should be wearing black. I am in mourning." How ridiculous not to even remember something so simple. But then why had he not remembered, why had he bought her a blue dress?

"Would you purchase me blacks?" Her words rang about the silent room. His gaze searched and questioned again.

"Of course."

His fingers became heavier, as they rested on hers. She withdrew her hand.

"Ellen." She had not given him permission to use her given name, and yet she was too tired and hurt too much to care to correct him. "I think much of you. You are a charming woman. I have always thought so. I can be patient. You need not worry. I understand you are grieving for your husband, and I shall allow you to do so…"

Ellen nodded. "Thank you." She wished to return to her rooms, to cry over Paul. There were too many memories of eating with him here crowding into her head.

She did not ask to withdraw though; it would be rude and

wrong, when he was kind enough to have offered her a place to stay, and food and clothing. Instead she remained at the table, picking at her food, and eating what little she was able while he watched her with a gentle smile and talked. She did not listen; her mind was too absorbed with memories of Paul.

~

Ellen sat at a small desk in the sitting room, a quill in her hand.

A week had passed since she'd discovered she was with child, and now, the Lieutenant Colonel had received orders to follow the army to Paris.

Napoleon had given himself up on the 15th July, in the process of trying to escape to America. The 52nd were to follow the Prussian army across France, as were many other regiments, to enforce the peace they'd fought so hard for. *And so many had died for…*

Pain gripped about Ellen's heart as she thought of Paul, remembering the blank sheet of paper she'd faced just after they'd married.

Paul had said, "Write to my father," if he died. But she didn't know what to say. The army had written to tell him Paul had lost his life.

A sharp pain cut into her chest, the one that could still not believe those words.

What to write? *My name is Ellen, you do not really know me, but we did meet last summer, I am your deceased son's wife.* Every word she thought of sounded so much like begging. And she could not bring herself to write the word deceased anyway.

My Lord, she began. The nib of the quill hovered over the paper. *Paul asked me to write to you, and seek your help, should he…* The words halted as a tear dropped on the paper. *I am to move to Paris with his regiment. I thought I should do as he said and let you know, I am with child.*

There was no more to say. *Yours sincerely, Eleanor, your*

daughter-in-law. She'd met Paul's father when he'd come to the house party with Paul but she had no idea if the man thought kindly of her or not. Paul had said little about his father in the months they'd been married, but he'd admitted the distance in his relationship with his family was because he had not kept contact, and not because his father had thought ill of him.

Paul had said their lives were too different.

Ellen understood that now. Her sisters' images crept through her thoughts. Her father's house was another world, they would never be able to imagine this one.

Still Paul had seemed confident the Earl would help.

Having folded and sealed that letter Ellen began another, to her father. *Papa, I do not know if you have heard, but Paul died in the battle of Waterloo.* Again tears ran over and spilled onto the page. *His Lieutenant Colonel is taking me as far as Paris. But I have nothing of my own, no money or items left. Would you send me the money for a passage home? I am with child. Yours affectionately, Eleanor.*

Surely her father would know how hard things were here. Surely he would understand and help.

Once she'd addressed both letters she took them down to the hall. Lieutenant Colonel Hillier had said he would send her letters through the army packets.

He was there. He came from the drawing room as her foot left the bottom step of the stairs.

"Ellen."

"These are the letters I spoke of," she said quietly.

"Take them," he said to a footman, who immediately moved forward to lift them out of her hand.

Lieutenant Colonel Hillier gave Ellen a stiff slight bow, his hands clasped behind his back. She curtsied a little.

Then he straightened and looked up to meet her gaze. "Will you take tea with me?"

It would be impolite to refuse. "Yes."

"Come then." He lifted a hand, encouraging her to join him in the drawing room, while looking at the butler to fulfil the order for tea to be delivered.

When Ellen entered the room his hand momentarily touched her lower back as she passed him. A prickle ran across her skin, but she ignored it.

"Do sit." He lifted a hand, directing her to one of the two soft chairs in the sunshine pouring through the window which looked out onto the garden.

Brushing her dress beneath her to stop the black calico creasing, she did as he said.

He took the seat opposite her. "Your maid said your sickness has eased a little…"

"Yes."

"And do you feel any better in yourself?"

No. She still missed Paul, like there was a burning inflamed hole within her. "I am able to think a little easier now. But I shall always miss my husband."

He was silent, his eyes looking into hers, with unspoken questions. Then he sighed. "Yes, I suppose you shall." He leaned forward and gripped her hand, she wanted to pull it away, but that would be rude. He lifted it. A shiver stirred across her skin as he pressed his warm lips against her glove, for moments.

Why did he not let go? Everything like this he seemed to do for a little too long. Finally he released her hand.

She clasped her hands together in her lap, unable to meet his gaze, but he reached out and touched her chin. "I know you are hurting, Ellen, I understand that, and I shall be here for you."

His hand fell.

"Ah here is our tea." He turned to look at the maid as she carried it in. She was blushing as she set the tray down.

"Will you pour, Ellen?"

She did so. She'd lived in a sheltered safe world in her father's home, and then she'd lived an ever-changing, unsettled life with Paul, but now…. Now she did not know where she stood… What life should be, or could be...

Chapter Nineteen

Paris: four months later

The months since the battle of Waterloo had passed slowly and Ellen had heard nothing from either her father or Paul's.

Paris was just as mad as Brussels had been before the war; flooded with British tourists. They'd flocked to the city as if everyone wished to claim it for themselves, as though they had won the battle.

Ellen had no patience or time for any of them, and of course she had no husband to escort her to events, so she did not attend any of their lavish entertainments, not even the theatre.

She still lived with the Lieutenant Colonel, because she had no money and nowhere else to go.

He'd hired a private carriage for her when the regiment marched to Paris, and paid for her lodgings so she need not live amongst the men.

She supposed the Lieutenant Colonel paid for her keep out of the sum he'd made by obligingly disposing of all Paul's things before she'd been sound enough of mind to even think about what to do with his belongings. Perhaps if she had sold them she could have paid for a passage home.

But some of his things she would have kept.

She missed the dress coat he'd removed and left behind on the last evening most. The one which he'd worn to the Richmonds' ball. It would have held his scent.

Tears came into her eyes; they still did every time she thought of him, and she thought of Paul a dozen times a day. But how could she forget?

She was uncomfortable about Lieutenant Colonel Hillier keeping her, but what other option did she have? Paul had been owed his wages too, so there must be money that was hers by right which he used to keep her.

She looked left and right along the street, waited for a carriage to pass, then crossed. Megan followed.

Ellen had not seen Jennifer, or any of the women she'd met in the last few hours of the battle in Brussels. Unlike in Brussels, Lieutenant Colonel Hillier did not host dinners or entertainments, and at times, Ellen felt guilty because she thought it was in defer-ence to her. But he'd never spoken of dinners, or dances, or even card parties, and she had never asked.

In the evenings she dined with him, but beyond that she saw very little of him. More often than not, once they'd eaten, he went out, and during the day he was out on business.

For weeks he had been gentle with her, forever kissing her hand and offering compliments and comfort, but in the last few weeks, he'd done so less. Now he seemed impatient and angry, but it was not particularly with her; he never said anything that implied his irritability was directed at her. But his conversation at table had become more abrupt and sharp as he watched for her response.

"Megan." Ellen turned and waited for her maid to catch up as they reached the gates of the Tuileries Gardens.

They walked out every day, sometimes twice a day, because sitting in the house became too oppressive, and she would reach a point she wished to escape the silence and the walls about her.

She lived for her child. For Paul's child. She was only eating and breathing for his son or daughter. Between her thoughts of

Paul, her mind filled with images of what his child might look like, and she longed for it to be a boy who would look like him.

She walked a full circle about the gardens, though the shrubberies looked bleak.

It was December. Nearly a year since she'd married Paul. It seemed a lifetime ago. Had she ever been that naïve girl?

She'd been little more than a child herself, so sheltered from the real world.

She spoke to Megan, they frequently talked; she had a better relationship with Megan than she'd ever had with Jennifer. Ellen wondered if Jennifer had managed to return to Ireland safely. She would probably never know.

After an hour, Ellen turned back towards Lieutenant Colonel Hillier's house. She could never call it home. It would never feel like home. Nowhere would ever feel like a home again now Paul was gone.

As she walked towards the door, two men came out. They were two officers from the regiment... Paul's comrades!

She hurried forward, her heart leaping with an odd sense of being close to Paul again. They wore the same uniform he'd worn.

"Captain Smith!" she called out, lifting her hand. "Captain Vickers!"

Captain Smith looked at her first. She was about twenty yards away from them as they stepped onto the pavement. He stared at her for a moment, his eyes widening, but then he turned to Captain Vickers and said something without acknowledging her. Captain Vickers looked over his friend's shoulder at her. His eyes widened, and then his expression twisted with a look of disgust.

They were going to turn away!

Ellen hurried, breaking into a slight run, one hand clasping beneath the bulge of the child in her stomach, the other gripping her skirt to lift her hem. "Wait!" she had no idea what she wished to say to them, but it suddenly seemed so important. They were a link to Paul when she had no other.

They began walking away, their backs to her.

"Wait!" Ellen cried again, hurrying on.

They did not stop, but neither were they walking fast, they merely ignored her cries and her presence.

She caught them up, her fingers gripping Captain Smith's coat at his elbow. "Will you not stop and speak with me? Perhaps—"

"Madam, I have nothing to say to a woman such as you. I admit I was surprised by the news, as I am sure Captain Harding would have been. He would be disgusted. But there is no going back. Good day." He turned away, after looking at her with revulsion in his eyes. So did Captain Vickers. *They are judging me poorly!*

Ellen did not understand.

"Surprised by the news, as I am sure Captain Harding would have been. He would be disgusted…" What did he mean? What news? *"A woman such as you."* A widow?

She stood in the street, lost, as they walked on and then turned the corner.

Ellen turned.

When she walked into the hall of Lieutenant Colonel Hillier's house she took off her bonnet and cloak, then her gloves, passing them all to a footman.

"Is Lieutenant Colonel Hillier home?"

"Yes, ma'am."

"Where?"

"The Lieutenant Colonel is in the drawing room, ma'am."

She went there, leaving Megan behind, as another footman moved to open the door for her. "Lieutenant Colonel, Mrs Harding."

There were empty glasses by the decanters where the men had shared a drink, and a quill, ink, and paper, stood on a desk across the room, where the Lieutenant Colonel stood.

He came towards her, his hands out as if to take hers. "Ellen, this is a charming surprise."

"I have just seen Captain Smith, and Captain Vickers leave—"

He stopped a few feet away from her. "Yes, they were reporting—"

"I do not care why they were here, what I am concerned about it is that they would not speak with me. Why would they not speak with me? They implied I have done something wrong..." Creases of confusion caught in Ellen's brow. *Why?* "What have I done wrong?"

"Ellen..." His pitch became placating as if he talked to a child. He came forwards again and clasped both of her hands. She pulled them free.

"Why would they not speak? What have I done wrong? They said Paul would have been surprised. They said he would be disgusted. Why?" Her last words erupted on a bitter whisper.

"Ellen." His hands came up and cupped her cheeks. "There is no need for such distress. I have said I shall take care of you and I shall. You must not worry about what others think..."

But why would they think anything?

"Ellen." His thumbs brushed over her cheeks, and his gaze grew in depth and warmth. She stepped away. The look was too similar to the one she used to see in Paul's eyes.

"I shall go upstairs."

"You do not wish to join me for tea?" There was a cajoling, pacifying, edge to his words; she did not like the tone.

"No. Thank you. I am tired. It is the pregnancy. I shall go upstairs and rest." With that she bobbed a shallow curtsy and left him.

But before she got to the door he called. "I shall go out then, I think, Ellen, but remember, you are under my care. You should respect that, and respect me!"

She looked back, not knowing how to answer, or what he meant.

He gave her a slight bow. "I think much of you, you know that."

What did he mean? Unwilling to pursue the conversation, she turned away and left him.

Before she even reached her rooms, she heard the front door close behind him.

~

He'd not returned when it came to dinner. Relief crashed over Ellen. She did not wish to see him this evening. Instead she asked Megan to eat with her in her rooms.

They ate speaking quietly and then immediately afterwards Ellen asked Megan to help her undress so she could retire.

Ellen's stomach was large with the child. A prominent bump pronounced her condition. She lay on her side in the bed, longing for her husband who would never come and held the child in her stomach, cradling it, giving it all the love she could no longer give to Paul.

Sometimes sleep was difficult, but thankfully it came quickly.

She woke when it was still dark. There was a noise below, a candlestick, statue or vase, or something else heavy being knocked from a mantle or table. Then a low-pitched bark of orders ran through the house.

Lieutenant Colonel Hillier was back and drunk by the sounds of it. It was not the first time she'd heard him return in such a state, though she had never seen him in his cups. She never went outside her rooms once she'd retired, and certainly not when he was in a mood like this.

She sat up listening as the sound of his ill temper carried upstairs. His footsteps on the wooden struts echoed ominously reaching through the house.

His rooms were to the right of the house and hers to the left. But his footsteps turned in the direction of her rooms.

There was a cold, sharp grip of fear in her stomach as she slid from the bed, in only her nightgown, and hurried from her bedchamber into her sitting room, her bare feet brushing over the cold unyielding floorboards.

The curtains were not drawn, and the room was flooded with silver moonlight.

But before she could reach the door to lock it, the handle turned sharply and it opened inwards.

"Lieutenant Colonel," she spoke in a sharp voice, a voice that said *get out* even if her lips did not. "You have no business in my rooms." Had he made a mistake? Was he too drunk to know where he was? But even as she thought those things her gaze struck his. His eyes were dark and she knew he'd made no mistake.

The fear inside her span out into her nerves, threads unravelling fast into every vein with the beat of her heart. She remembered all the times his stare had made her skin crawl.

"Go to your rooms." Her voice was strong but she could not find the courage to yell at him; this was his house and she was here under his generosity.

"I think not, Ellen." He did not sound so drunk now, not so drunk he was incapable of walking – it sounded the sort of drunk that gave a man confidence and silenced his conscience.

She stepped back, uncertain of the hard intent in his eyes.

"I have a need tonight…" His pitch dropped to almost a whisper, but the bitterness in his tone matched the look in his eyes. "I refuse to pay for a damned whore when I have a woman here. I desire you. I always have. You act as if you do not know, but you must know, and you have taken my protection and offered me nothing in return."

No. The word did not come from her lips; shock had penetrated inside her like the cold of the night outside. She would have backed away further but numbness dropped heavily through her limbs and before she could gather her thoughts his hand lifted and his fingers gripped her hair, pulling it so hard it hurt.

Tears clouded her vision.

"*Please…*" She could not say more. The words would not come and her voice was too quiet as fear strangled her. But the grip on her hair only tightened pulling against her scalp with a searing pain.

He tried to kiss her, but she turned her head.

"Why must you keep thinking of that man? Can you not appreciate all I have done for you?" He tried again to kiss her, but she turned away. She did not want him to kiss her.

"You are too beautiful, Ellen. I have always thought you the most beautiful woman I have ever seen. I have been nice to you, kind to you, and bought you gifts and how am I repaid? By melancholy and pining for a dead man."

No. A sob became tangled with a scream in her throat and no sound erupted at all.

"Kneel to me." It was a barked order, the voice she'd heard several times when she'd watched Paul in the parade ground with his men.

"*Please, do not do this…*" Her voice was a pathetic whimpering plea.

"I said kneel to me! You've had everything you wish, for months! You are under my protection! Do you hear? You owe me. How else will you pay? I want a woman. I want you!" His bitter, hard voice ran through the house echoing into the hall outside the open door. The servants would hear it; she could not bear the embarrassment of them knowing he spoke to her like this. People would judge and accuse her…

"*Please do not…*" she said again, in another quiet plea which sought as much to make him silent as to make him stop.

"Enough of your refusals." The fingers in her hair gripped so tight the pain in her scalp pulled her down, so she could do nothing but give in to it – unless she screamed, or cried out for help. *But to whom, the servants?*

The thought tumbled through her fear, clogging in her chest in a million knots. She had been brought up not to acknowledge servants. Not to share anything personal with them. She had been close to Pippa but Pippa had been like a second mother. She would have called out to Pippa for help, but no one else… *How could she call for a footman and have him find her like this, in her nightgown? And what would he do? He was paid to do as this man asked.* If a footman helped her, he would be dismissed.

"Kneel, damn you!" Her hair was jerked downwards and her knees gave way. Pain pierced like a knife blade as she hit the

201

floorboards hard, putting out a hand to grab the leg of a chair to stop her fall.

The next things that happened seemed to happen so quick she could not recall the detail.

With his free hand, as she overcame the pain of having fallen, he undid the two buttons which secured the flap of his breeches, and in the next the man was filling her mouth as Paul had used to fill the place between her legs.

My God. My God… Like this…

Confusion, horror, and bitter despair reeled through her. She might die. She could not breathe…

The shame…

~

She had prayed for it to end. Prayed to survive…

Now she merely lay on the hard, unyielding floor.

A part of her did not believe what had just happened. She was not certain of anything anymore. The world felt strange.

He had secured his breeches and said, "That is done then, Ellen. Thank you. You will not say no to me again." Then walked away as though he had not just violated her in the cruellest way, using her mouth. As if he had not… done… done… something so *vile*.

She could not get up and go to her bed. She longed to call for Megan, but she was afraid to admit to anyone what had just occurred. How could she have let that happen? Yet the error had not been in the last few moments, in not locking her door, in not having said *no* more firmly and dressing and leaving. The error had been made months ago when she'd accepted his help. *Foolish… Foolish!*

Paul would be turning in his grave so many miles away. His body had been sent home to his family. He would be shouting at her too, for her idiocy in giving away the money he'd left for her to find a pathway home. She should have left with Jennifer.

It was foolish to have thought it was safe to accept anything from this man and think there would be nothing to pay in return.

She held her stomach, protecting their child.

~

Ellen could not look Megan in the eye when she brought her morning chocolate and breakfast, and when Megan offered to return and help her dress, Ellen said, "I am feeling too ill to rise."

"But you have not been sick." Megan swept forward and pressed a hand to Ellen's brow. "You do not feel hot, ma'am…"

No, she was not ill in the physical sense of the word, but she was sick of life and heart-sore. She missed Paul, and she did not wish to rise and keep living today. How could she get up, when she knew what had happened yesterday?

Memories growled at her, like a monster invading her head as Lieutenant Colonel Hillier had violated her mouth; they would not go away.

She sipped her chocolate and felt sick.

She was sick, and Megan rushed to fetch the chamber pot.

"Perhaps you should stay in bed, ma'am."

Ellen nodded and lay back down, turning her face into the pillow to hide her tears.

Megan returned with a luncheon tray at noon, but Ellen refused it.

When Megan came back at four, she stood across the room by the door to the sitting room.

Ellen did not look up.

"Forgive me, ma'am. Lieutenant Colonel Hillier has sent me…"

Ellen shut her eyes as her stomach turned with a need to be sick, even at the mention of his name. She did not wish to hear his name. She did not wish to be here. She did not wish the man anywhere near her.

"I have told the Lieutenant Colonel you are unwell, but he

insists you come down for dinner this evening, ma'am."

Ellen sat up, looking her maid in the eyes for the first time that day, heat burning beneath her skin in a deep blush. "Then you must tell him that I will not."

Megan looked at Ellen for a moment. She knew there was something amiss, Ellen could see it in Megan's eyes, but she said nothing, and nor did Ellen as Megan turned away and left.

A few moments later there was that sharp knock.

Oh my God. Ellen slid out of the bed, and grabbed a wrapper from a chair across the room. She did not wish him in her bedchamber.

"Ellen?" His voice carried the pitch of command, and yet it was also enquiring. "May I come in?"

Her stomach spun. If she ran across the room and locked the door, he would hear.

"I am not dressed."

There was an odd sound, then a cough.

Ellen prayed he would not come in.

"But you are out of bed…" His voice was now coaxing. "You cannot be so unwell. It will do you good to come down to dinner, I think, and I require your company." The last *was* an order.

Tears clouding her vision, Ellen dropped to sit in a chair. She gripped its arms, her fingers clawing into the cloth. She wanted to run. But to where?

"Do you agree to dine with me?"

She said nothing, sobs gathering in her throat.

"Ellen?"

She still did not reply.

"Ellen!"

He would not let her say no, anyway.

"Yes." Her voice was weak.

When Megan returned to help her dress a while later, Ellen did not speak. She could not; if she tried to speak, she would cry. She stood and let her maid do what she would.

Occasionally she caught Megan glancing at her in the mirror. Ellen's skin turning red, she avoided Megan's gaze.

"I am finished, ma'am."

Megan knew something had happened, because when Ellen glanced up, Megan did not smile. She did not want Ellen to go downstairs any more than Ellen wished to go.

As she walked downstairs her heart pounded. She was cold with fear. She looked at the door which led out onto the street, but if she walked through it, what then? Where would she go? Where could she go?

She walked towards the dining room, her feet heavy and hesitant as a footman opened the door for her.

Lieutenant Colonel Hillier stood as she entered, though he did not meet her gaze. He looked at her, but not into her eyes.

She looked at him, directly. Accusing him. Anger flooding her. She hated him, she wished to scream at him, and hit him, and claw her fingernails and scratch him. But what then?

"Come, sit beside me, Ellen." His tone sought to charm as he moved to withdraw a chair.

Ellen could not lift her feet; the floor was like thick mud.

He beckoned her with his fingers. "Come now, no need to be hesitant."

Memories cutting at her soul, she knew there was every reason to be hesitant.

"I have a gift for you." He lifted a small square box from the table.

He had still not looked into her eyes, when every other time it was all he did, and his skin carried a pink tone of embarrassment.

"I am sorry, Ellen. If I upset you, I did not intend to."

She shut her eyes. What he had done could not simply be taken away with an apology.

"Come and sit." His voice changed. When he'd said sorry, he'd sounded remorseful, but now his pitch had slipped into an order.

Looking at the floor, she crossed the room, afraid he would become angry with her before the servants.

When she took the seat, he pushed it in. Loss cut through her as she remembered Paul doing the same on their wedding day.

"Wine?" He beckoned a footman forward as he sat.

Ellen lifted a hand. "No, none thank you, it only makes my morning sickness worse." She wished him to remember she was with child. She wished his guilt to grow and cut deeper.

He reached across and lay the box he held before her. "It is a little present to make amends. Open it, and let us be happy again."

The box was made from a black wood, inlaid with a pattern of pale roses, probably made from rosewood. Ellen lifted the lid. There was a little slip of parchment there. He had written upon it, *To my love.*

A shiver tore through Ellen.

She hated those words. They had been precious to her. Now Lieutenant Colonel Hillier had defiled them.

His hand touched hers. Ellen jumped.

His fingers rested on her forearm. "You know what I think of you now. Take a look."

She lifted the parchment, wanting to crush it in her fingers and throw it on the floor, but the weight of his hand on her arm was like a manacle.

A little brooch, a bluebird, lay on the bed of velvet.

Lieutenant Colonel Hillier stood. "Let me put it on for you."

She stood too; she could not bear for him to stand so close to her.

He merely smiled, as her whole body trembled with fear.

Then he leant to the side and picked up the brooch before slipping one hand into her bodice.

Bile rose in her throat but she swallowed it back, as her skin burned with embarrassment.

The footmen looked on.

"I would not wish to mark your beautiful skin, Ellen." With the back of his fingers on her breast he pierced the muslin cloth with the pin, and secured it. "There."

Then his hand slid away.

Shaking, Ellen retook her seat, as he did too.

"You need not buy me gifts." She whispered through the corner of her mouth once he was seated.

"But I wish too. I wanted to thank you."

She looked up at him, and caught his gaze for the first time. He looked away, the skin on his cheeks scored with a scarlet colour. He *was* embarrassed, and guilt *was* thrashing him.

I am glad. I hope you suffer as you have made me suffer. "I do not want your gifts or gratitude, and I do not want it to happen again. All I want from you is your word that it will not."

He looked up at her, meeting her gaze, and holding it now, though the colour still rose in his skin. "I cannot promise you that. But I will continue to take care of you, and I shall look after you well…"

But for what… What did he expect in return?

Chapter Twenty

"Madam, you should sit up a little more." The midwife helping Ellen was a bulldog. She was physically muscular and from the way she spoke, the woman thought she could merely shout at the child to make it come out.

Her grip rough and firm she pulled Ellen to an almost sitting position.

But Ellen had been in labour for a day and half; she had no more energy. Exhaustion overwhelmed her in a heavy sensation that urged her to lie down and give up.

"Madam!"

Ellen closed her eyes as she collapsed back. She was too tired to fight. Too much had happened to her, too many awful things. What was there to fight for?

"Madam!"

She wished to die. Let it all just be over now.

"Madam!" The last was shouted as her next contraction came.

Ellen gripped the sheet and cried out, longing for the one person who would never come – could never come.

"Paul!" His name came on an agonised cry, not from the pain of labour, but from the pain of her broken heart. It was shattered. She was shattered. "I cannot…"

"You have little choice, ma'am, the child is within you and it wishes to get out." the mulish midwife barked.

Ellen screamed at the woman, opening her eyes and clutching the filthy sheet beneath her, as she glared and yelled out her anger. "Ahhhhh!"

In that instant she hated Paul for dying, and she hated fate for leaving her to survive alone and seek the help of a man who was cruel. Four more times he had used her mouth as Paul had used her body, urging her to be compliant and allow it. Each time he had been drunk, and each time, the day after, he could not look her in the eyes due to his guilt; though he'd send his staff to insist she came down to dine with him.

She would sit at the table feeling the heat of a blush – *unclean* – oh, and hatred, revulsion and anger, roared inside her as she pushed her food about the plate.

She no longer wanted to be in his house eating his food, but where else was there to go, with no money?

She'd asked him once to take her home to England, or at least to pay for a passage home for her. But he would not. He may feel guilty after doing what he'd done, but not enough to give her the means to leave.

Life, fate – was cruel. "Ahhh!" She screamed her pain out into the room.

"Push." the midwife urged her.

Ellen did not wish to push, or try.

"Madam!" The glare she received, when she made no effort at all, condemned her. She would be bullied into bearing this child.

Her eyelids fell again, and behind them hiding in darkness she saw Paul's face. He leaned towards her. "Ellen." She could hear his voice and his fingers touched her face and brushed her hair back. "Ellen, you are strong. You can survive anything. You will survive. You have an inner strength."

His image disappeared and she screwed up her eyes, crushing them tightly closed as her heart poured out its misery. She was not angry with him; she missed him. She missed him so much.

209

She opened her eyes and he was not there. Of course he was not. But his child was inside her, fighting to live.

"Ahhh!" She pushed.

"That's better, madam."

"Harder now."

Ellen's grip firmed on the sheets, as another contraction clasped at her stomach, tightening her muscles in an excruciating hold. She did push, she pushed hard, and she kept pushing, as though pushing might bring sanity back into her life.

"Oh, God!" The blasphemy slipped from her lips as the pressure inside her suddenly burst and was gone and then a child's wail filled the air in the room. She was panting and crying as she looked at the purple being, curled up in the midwife's hands. She lifted the infant as its arms and legs stretched out. The child had come early. It was lean.

"Hold your child while I take care of the afterbirth." The infant was covered in white slime but Ellen took it, and looked down. It was a boy. A son. Paul's son.

Her tears streamed, blurring her vision, as she held the wailing child to her breast.

~

Ellen looked down into the cradle. John was asleep. She rocked it gently for a moment, looking at his perfect face. He was more like her than Paul, and she hated that, she had wished for him to look like Paul, and yet here he was – a small thing to love and hold – draw comfort from.

"John," she said the name quietly, so not to wake him. She had chosen the name because it meant the grace of God. He was here with her by the grace of God, and Paul did not even know he existed, yet even if he did not look like Paul, he was a little piece of Paul on earth. A memory. Something to live for.

She could not resist. Her fingers reached out and touched his little head, feeling the soft patch on it.

He was sucking, as if he was dreaming of suckling milk from her breast.

He was the most precious treasure she'd ever had.

She straightened still watching him for moment. He'd not long been fed. He would sleep a while longer.

She turned and looked at the blank paper which lay on a table across the room. Once again she'd intended to write to her father but could think of no words. Yet she knew she had to get away from Lieutenant Colonel Hillier, and get John away from him too. She did not wish to stay here and the only hope they had of escape was via her father or Paul's. She moved across the room and sat down before the dreaded empty page. Then after a moment picked up the quill.

Papa,

I have a child. Paul's child. A son. I am still in Paris. I am with Lieutenant Colonel Hillier, Paul's superior officer. He has been providing for me, but he cannot do so forever. I wish to come home, with my son, John.

I am asking you if you will either come and fetch us, or send money for me to make my own way. Will you let me return to you now? I need somewhere safe for John to grow up, Papa.

Please tell Mama I love her, and tell Penny, Rebecca and Sylvia also.

At the thought of her sisters Ellen could write no more. They knew nothing of life – of the truth about the world. Tears filled her eyes, but she wiped them away, and said a silent prayer, that she and John would get away from here and home safely, and for her sisters to experience none of the things she had in the last few months.

Then she signed the page, *Eleanor*, not that she used her full name at all anymore. She had gradually, without even realising it, slipped into anonymity. Now, after what had happened over recent months, she did not like to make it known to anyone who she was, that she was a duke's daughter. Although she thought Lieutenant Colonel Hillier knew because he'd posted the letters previously to her father and Paul's.

She wrote a letter to Paul's father now too, telling him she'd given birth to Paul's son. His grandson. Then she sealed both letters and addressed them as she'd done before. But her father's she held to her breast for a moment, willing him to come, before leaving the room and walking downstairs to put the letters for posting in the hall.

None of the footmen were there, and there were four in the house.

It was just past midday, a time when the house was always silent as Lieutenant Colonel Hillier was out undertaking military activity of some sort. It was the first time she'd come downstairs since John had been born, a month ago, and it felt strange to find the place empty. Megan had gone. She'd been dismissed within days of the first time the Lieutenant Colonel had assaulted Ellen. It was another expression of his embarrassment. He did not want a proper ladies' maid to know the truth.

Now one of the general maids had been assigned to help Ellen dress and such.

Ellen returned to the security of her rooms and her son. Once she was there, she pulled up a chair beside his crib and sat, then watched him sleep, love overflowing inside her. It was so wonderful to feel love again.

At about five in the evening, the door to her sitting room suddenly opened without a knock. She rose and turned. John had been asleep for hours and she expected him to wake for a feed at any moment. It was the Lieutenant Colonel. She did not wish his intrusion. But this was his house; what could she say?

"You've spent enough time recovering from childbirth, and enough time in blacks. I expect you to dine with me again tonight, and I expect you to wear a pretty dress and not cover your beauty behind those dull rags." His gaze held hers for a moment, his hand still on the door handle and his foot only one step within the room, but then he pulled back, stepping out and closed the door – as though he'd never been there.

Her heart plummeted.

At the sound of the door closing, John made a little whimpering noise in his cradle.

Ellen turned, bent, and lifted him to her chest; holding him secure as love swelled and rocked inside her, like the surge of the sea when they'd sailed to Ostend.

She pressed a gentle kiss on his temple then whispered over his skin as she cradled him in one arm and began releasing the buttons of her bodice. "I love you…"

She almost expected the tiny living soul in her arms to say it back.

She moved the baby to her breast and felt him clasp and suck as she sat again.

Once John was fed and sleeping once more, having sung to him for a little while, rocking him gently, Ellen called the maid to help her dress. She wore a pale pink dress, made of very fine muslin. She did not mind giving up her blacks. Now she had John, it was time to leave her mourning for Paul behind.

Her fingers shook as she went downstairs. She did not wish to speak with Lieutenant Colonel Hillier.

As she entered the dining room, she saw a box on the table.

It rested in the middle of her place setting.

Terror cut through her.

"I bought a new gift for you." the Lieutenant Colonel said as she sat, and a footman pushed her chair under.

It sat in a box before her, a silent threat.

"Open it."

She did not wish to; she knew it meant he wanted a gift in return.

"Go ahead, Ellen." His words became snappy, and his tone the one he'd use on a parade ground.

213

He was in a beseeching mood – a dangerous mood.

She opened it, because there was nothing else to do.

Inside the box rested a string of pearls.

He stood.

She did not.

She remained seated, facing the table; her legs would not have held her up. Her hands shook. She slipped them beneath the table.

As he leaned across her, his breath touched her neck, making the small hairs on her skin rise as they had done even the first time Paul had introduced her to the Lieutenant Colonel. She wished she could run. But to where, and what about John? How would they survive without Lieutenant Colonel Hillier's shelter and his food?

He slipped the pearls about her neck, his fingers brushing her skin as he secured it.

She shivered.

It felt as if he had secured a collar about her neck, a collar with a chain upon it.

"There, they look perfect against you skin, and your hair, Ellen." He sat.

Ellen said nothing, unable to look at him.

"Are you not going to thank me?" His pitch had changed from the tone he used when he believed himself to be expressing love, to the one that forced.

Ellen looked at him, her eyes accusing. *I hate you.*

He held her gaze, his look becoming harder. "I said, say thank you."

"I do not need them or want them," Ellen answered quietly, hoping the footmen would not hear.

"You will be grateful for them." His pitch lifted in defiance.

Damn. Damn… The coarse words she'd learned among Paul's men spun through her head. She wished to throw them all at Lieutenant Colonel Hillier… "Thank you," her answer was whispered, while the words in her head were shouted. *I hate you.*

He looked away and bid the butler, "Serve the meal."

No matter her fear, when dinner was served, her stomach growled at the prospect of a proper meal; she'd been eating only leftovers, cold meat and cheeses in her room.

Her plate was filled by a footman, as another poured her wine, and then she ate, listening to the Lieutenant Colonel speak without replying in anything more than words of a single syllable, "yes," "so," desperate to finish the meal and leave.

He drank constantly, taking a gulp of his wine between nearly every sentence. By the point her glass was empty his had been replenished thrice.

Ellen held her hand up, covering her glass when a footman sought to refill it.

"Let the man pour." Lieutenant Colonel Hillier barked.

Ellen looked at him, discomfort unravelling in her nerves. "I do not wish for more wine, thank you."

"You are living in my home, if I say have more wine, you will have more wine."

Embarrassment and anger prickled up Ellen's spine, and she moved her hand, she could not bear the servants hearing his rudeness.

Looking down at the remains of her dinner, she was no longer hungry. She moved her knife and fork together and left them on the plate. Her hands fell into her lap, as her gaze rested on her full untouched glass of wine.

"Well, drink it as it has been poured for you."

The man was obnoxious. She looked up and saw that he'd drained another glass and held it up to be refilled. Her stomach tumbled over, unease closing in on her as if the walls of the room were moving forwards.

"Drink," he ordered. With the servants in the room to watch, she did, uncomfortable to even live within her skin. She wished to get out of this house.

Sipping only a tiny little taste of wine she watched him smile, as if pleased. He talked again, between mouthfuls, as Ellen continued sipping her wine and watched him, saying nothing now.

The plates were taken away and dessert presented – a grand statement of meringue and orange jelly. The sweetness was oddly bitter in Ellen's mouth, as across the table she saw Lieutenant Colonel Hillier's glass refreshed again. He was edgy, and irritable, and she was afraid of doing or saying something which would... *No*, she could not think of that nor endure it, not now John was upstairs sleeping in his crib.

But he had bought her a gift and she knew what that meant.

The pearls lay heavily about her neck.

They ate the last course in silence, as the footmen stood back and watched, and while Ellen occasionally took tiny sips of her wine to prevent the Lieutenant Colonel's anger, he took great gulps and then waved a man forward to refill his glass.

Ellen longed for home, and yet what was home? Somewhere she felt safe. It had been her father's house for most of her life, and then it had been with Paul. And now? Now there was nowhere.

When she set her spoon and fork down on the plate, he took another large swig of wine.

He was fortifying himself – building up courage.

Either that or he simply wished to be in his cups within the hour.

Ellen shut her eyes, searching for ideas – how to escape...

Once he had finished his dessert he let his cutlery drop sharply on the plate with a metallic clink against the porcelain, then looked at the butler. "Clear this."

Immediately, the footman moved, taking away their empty plates, and the remnants of the meal. Ellen leaned back counting down minutes in her head to the moment it may not seem too early to rise and leave the man to his port, and when she went up to her rooms she would lock the door.

The footmen moved about her, and then finally walked from the room in a line. Ellen swallowed and stood. "I shall leave you?"

"No." The answer was sharp. Looking from her to the butler, Lieutenant Colonel Hillier said, "Leave and shut the door."

Ellen froze as her heart kicked into a rhythm of panic.

"Sit." It was an order.

She did so as the door shut, too afraid to react before the butler, while internally she longed to run.

Too much of her life had been spent learning to show nothing of her emotions amidst servants and strangers. She had received constant warnings from her father to always appear serene. She did not feel serene – terror ripped through her middle.

Lieutenant Colonel Hillier stood and crossed the room to his decanters, then poured his own port.

Ellen's heart thumped, the sound pounding in her ears as well as pulsing through her blood.

She looked at the door, longing to run.

But to where?

He did not speak.

What am I to do?

He turned and looked at her.

Fear chilled the blood in Ellen's veins. It was a look of avarice – want.

"You know I love you, Ellen. I always have, and I have tried to make you love me, but I believe you will never let the ghost of Captain Harding rest. He seems to hover over us. Well I am bored with it. My patience has run dry. I have given you much, and you have given me very little in return."

Her stomach tumbled over, bile rising in her throat.

He came towards her and stood over her, his fingers pressing on her shoulder to keep her seated when she would have stood. She looked up at him, only because there was nowhere else to look. His fingers swept a lock of her hair back behind her ear, then moved beneath her chin and embraced it. "Such a pretty face. Do you even realise how beautiful you are. I was envious of Captain Harding on the first day he introduced you. You are the grand prize, Ellen…"

She was just a woman, like any other.

Or perhaps *not* like any other – after the things he'd done to her.

"Do you not think you owe me more?" He said the words in a very low, quiet, voice, as if he was afraid of saying them.

More what?

He set his glass down on the pristine, starched white tablecloth beside her, then he bent.

As she realised he intended kissing her, she turned her head away.

His lips brushed her cheek.

"Not good enough, Ellen." His hands braced her face, holding her head so she could not turn, as he had done before when he did that unspeakable thing. "I have waited while you mourned, but you have had long enough. Now I want to be kissed." His lips pressed against hers, hard and firm.

It was not with love… It was not love… It was nothing like Paul's kiss.

When he would have pushed his tongue into her mouth, she bit her lips and pulled back against his grip.

He freed her and straightened, staring down at her. For a moment he just stared.

She remembered all those times he'd watched her when Paul had been alive. Had he been thinking of this then? Had he been planning this from the moment Paul had died when he'd arrived to collect her, smelling freshly bathed? He'd paraded her through the streets on his horse.

"You know, Ellen, you have a choice. You can be my mistress and I shall continue to keep you. Or you may take your son and go and walk the streets, and perhaps become the mistress of a hundred different men to earn enough to feed and keep your son…"

She looked to the ceiling and prayed for help.

What can I do?

"Well?"

She did not speak. What was there to say? He could not really expect her to choose to be his mistress…

"It is your choice whether or not you stay. But if you stay with me now, Ellen. I expect you to be compliant. Do you understand?"

No, she did not.

"You must do all that I wish…"

A stone dropped from her stomach to the soles of her feet as she sat and stared at him again. She had a child who was only six weeks old upstairs. A child who needed a roof and a cot. She needed food to be able to feed him, and it was still winter; it was icily cold beyond the door.

Her heart beat harder. *What was she to do - get up and walk away? Walk where?*

"Shall we try this again, Ellen?" He did not even wait for her answer. He knew her answer could only be acceptance. What other choice did she have? His fingers gripped either side of her face, and tilted it upwards as he bent again. "Open your mouth." His words were spoken over her lips, hot and scented of wine. She did, and his tongue slid into her mouth, making her feel sick with hatred and dread. Her body shivered with disgust.

He broke the kiss and rose. "I said you must be compliant, Ellen. I also meant you must participate."

No.

Tears burned in her eyes as he bent again and her arms hung limp, as his tongue pressed into her mouth. She moved her own tongue, not in a caress, she felt too sick, but just in answer… *Oh God.*

How has my life come to this?

His hand slid and touched her breast, then ran lower.

~

Ellen lay curled in a ball on the sofa in the downstairs drawing room, in the dark. She had not found the strength to rise. She had no courage.

She was an adulteress now, too. He had a wife in England.

219

The Commandments she had been forced to read more than a thousand times the day she'd eloped with Paul, ran through her head. *Thou shalt not commit adultery…*

But it had not been her choice.

Yet her first sin had been her choice.

Was this payment for that? *Honour thy father and mother.*

What could she do?

How could she have let it happen and done nothing?

How could she leave without money or possessions?

What am I to do?

Tears had run down her cheeks the whole time Lieutenant Colonel Hillier had touched her, and when he'd done what Paul had done, she'd sobbed aloud until he told her to be quiet. Then she'd bitten her lip and wept silently again. She was unclean now. Filthy. She itched inside and she wished to scrub within her body.

"Ma'am… Forgive me, ma'am." Ellen sat up instantly and looked towards the door, which had been left ajar but now stood open. The housemaid who'd become her own maid stood there. "The little boy is crying for you…"

Ellen stood and wiped away her tears, looking down, hiding the marks on her face as she swallowed. "I am coming…" She hoped the maid would go but she did not. Instead she came further into the room.

"Ma'am, if you do not wish for another child. I can show you things you may do to help. There are no guarantees, but…"

Ellen stared at her, a fire flaring beneath her skin to think this woman knew what had happened. But then perhaps it had happened to her too.

"Do you wish me to tell you?"

"Yes…" The word was whispered. *But now I need to go to my son.*

Ellen hurried out of the room, rushing past her to escape the sense of shame.

"But I shall come then, ma'am, because if you are to do something to prevent it, you must do so now."

The maid hurried up the stairs behind, Ellen.

Chapter Twenty One

Ellen knelt on the floor beside her son. John sat upright, playing with some wooden animals which the maid had bought him from a carver in the market.

Paris was still busy, flooded with hundreds of tourists, and people came to the city to make money from them – people whose property and land had been spoiled by war, as her own life had been. But her life was barren in a different way.

After the battle of Waterloo she'd seen some of the physical wounds stitched.

John was the stitches holding her together. She lived only for these moments of quiet peace, when they played together and she could pretend the rest of her life was not a tangled, jagged wreck.

"Ball, now." John looked across the room, at the ball which they'd been playing with earlier, then turned onto one knee and set off for it at a fast crawl. He stirred her heart whatever he did. She had never thought it possible to love anything or anyone so utterly.

When he returned with it he held it up towards her. "Throw, Mama."

She caught him up into her arms, without taking the ball from him, instead tipping him backwards. Then she blew a loud kiss on his neck, which she knew would tickle. He laughed. It was the most beautiful sound, like water running over rocks in a stream, and a wave washing over pebbles on the seashore.

"Mama, throw." He lifted the ball again once he stopped laughing. He had a stubborn streak, and a strength of will like his father's. She brushed back his black hair and looked into eyes the colour of her own.

"I love you…" she whispered and kissed his brow, before taking the ball from his hand, and tossing it upwards. He looked up and laughed again. Her heart ached.

"Mama." When it landed, he crawled off to collect it and bring it back for her to throw again.

She heard the knocker strike the door downstairs. It hit hard, the sound running through the walls of the house.

"John," she called in a low voice, urging him back to her. Lieutenant Colonel Hillier was not at home. If it was someone calling for him, they would be turned away. But even so, her instinctive reaction was always to keep John close.

Lieutenant Colonel Hillier was too unpredictable, especially when he'd been drinking. She was never sure when he would expect things from her, or what, or when he would be aggressive, or when he would be unbearably gentle, as if he truly thought it was love he showed her.

Whatever he did to her only made her feel sick. She did not wish him to touch her at all.

Footsteps echoed on the stairs, and then came along the hall, before someone knocked on the door to her personal sitting room.

"Ma'am." It was one of the footmen.

"Yes."

"There is a gentleman below; he wishes to see the woman living here."

Ellen looked up and stared at the closed door. *The woman living here…* Was that all she was, a nameless being? A body used for the gratification of Lieutenant Colonel Hillier and nothing else. She stood, almost in a trance. Then John turned, with the ball in his hand, holding it up triumphantly. "Mama!"

223

She had a name.

"Come, John," she bent and whispered, and once she'd lifted him to her hip, she stroked a black curl off his brow. He was a strikingly handsome child. Her child. She wondered what Paul would have thought of him.

Taking the ball from his hand, she bent and picked up one of his wooden horses instead. "Here, carry this and we shall go and see who is calling." He immediately started chewing on his poor horse. He had six teeth so far. She checked them every day to see if a new one had come.

When she opened the door the footman stepped back. "Ma'am."

"Do you know who it is?"

"No, ma'am."

"Are they wearing livery or a soldier's uniform?"

"No, ma'am."

She frowned. "Is there a carriage outside?"

"Yes, ma'am."

Instead of leaving her sitting room she turned around, still carrying John, whose legs clung either side of her hip as she balanced his weight on her hand.

There was a glossy black carriage outside the house and the coachman still sat on the box, waiting in the street below. A footman in non-descript black livery held the horses' heads, as another waited near the carriage door.

It would not be a servant bearing some message from Lieutenant Colonel Hillier then. It was someone of standing.

But why would they ask to see her?

She saw no coat of arms on the doors of the carriage.

"Horsees." John, pointed down into the street with his wooden toy.

She looked at him, "Yes, darling, horses."

"Ma'am, what shall I say?"

Ellen looked back at the footman. "Nothing. I will come down. Where is the visitor?"

"In the drawing room."

"I'll show myself in to see him. You may go." The man turned and walked away as Ellen looked at John, her heart thumping. What was this now?

"I suppose we should go and see who our mysterious guest is then, John. What do you think?"

He smiled his lovely open-hearted smile. His affection for her shone in his eyes, even though he was too young to know what love meant, or to say it aloud, she knew he loved her as she loved him. "I love you…" she said it again, so he might learn, and then pressed another kiss on his temple before leaving the room, walking swiftly.

Her heart raced as she descended the stairs looking at the closed doors leading into the drawing room. The footman had not waited in the hall, but returned to the servants' quarters, so it was silent, and there was no sound from within the room.

She looked at her son, who was busy entertaining himself with his wooden horse, his gaze transfixed upon it as he trotted it over her arm.

She took a breath, her heart pounding out the beat of the marching drum, and then turned the handle with the hand which was not balancing John's weight and pushed the door open. She stepped in, looking up.

Ellen collapsed back against the door, and her fingers gripped John's leg over tightly, causing him to squeal.

"Papa…"

He turned to face her. As soon as she'd seen the straight posture and black hair, she'd known it was him.

His intent silver gaze studied her for a moment only, but then fell to John, and stopped, staring as a moment ago she'd watched John stare at his toy horse.

She could not explain the muddle of overwhelming joy, fear and intense embarrassment. She could not remember who she had been the last time she'd faced him in a room. Two years ago when she'd run away from home to marry Paul, she'd been little more than a child. Had it only been two years? So much had happened to her. But her time in hell was over now. "You came…"

"Let me take the child." He reached out. Pain tore her apart-relief. He had come for them, to take them home to safety. Tears brimmed in her eyes and poured over as the ache in her heart and her throat became too much. She wiped them away. He would not wish to endure emotion. He would think it weak.

"Oh, Papa, I am–" she let him take John, and smiled as he interrupted.

"I do not expect your gratitude. I am taking him home…"

He continued talking, but Ellen struggled to hear. There was a woman in the room with him. She stepped forward to take John.

Ellen's brow creased in confusion.

"Taking who home?" Her voice sounded pathetic. "I don't understand, Papa, have you come for us, as I asked?" She looked into his eyes and saw no love or emotion for his child, as she felt love and emotion for John.

"I have come to fetch my grandson. I am…" Again his words just seemed to get lost in the room.

"Papa?"

As the woman carried John away, her father spoke, his voice dropping. "Stop calling me that. I am no longer that to you."

She didn't understand.

"I will have nothing to do with a soiled woman. You are an insult now."

Still not understanding, Ellen whispered in return, "I am your daughter."

"Not now. You are a whore and nothing beyond it. You are dead to me. But the child is my heir…"

Oh my God. The truth crashed in on her, as though he'd slapped her face with it. He was taking John away, but not her. She turned and rushed from the room. The woman was already in the street, about to lift John up into the carriage. Ellen reached for her son.

Thank God the woman did not fight her.

Tears clouded Ellen's vision and wet her cheeks as she pressed her head to John's, holding him close and tight, even though he hated to be coddled and was now complaining bitterly. "Nothing is wrong, my darling, you are safe," she whispered to his ear, rocking him gently and taking him back into the house. The woman followed.

Her father stood in the hall.

"You cannot… I will not let you take him." Ellen pressed John's forehead to her shoulder as he wailed, gripping his precious toy horse.

"And you think you have a choice? Would you bring him up here in a house of sin?"

Pain cut deep into Ellen's heart with a knife thrust.

"This is not a place for a child. I can give him a decent life, education, and I can protect him from *this*." His hand swung out as disgust crossed his face.

She clung harder to John.

"Have sense. The woman is a nursemaid, she can feed the child at her breast while I take him back to England, and there he shall have the house and grounds to grow up in, and be secure. He may learn to manage what will be his one day." He looked at her harder. "A duke cannot have a mother who has sold her body. I will not leave him with a whore."

"I did not… I am not…"

He pulled out a rolled parchment from an inside pocket of his coat. "I've had this document drawn up, confirming you relinquish any right to the boy–"

"What?"

"You must have nothing to do with him, else he will be damaged by your sin."

There was a crushing emptiness inside her.

"Have sense. Think of the child…"

She cradled John's head, as he fidgeted and fought to be free.

More tears slipped from her eyes into his soft hair, making it damp. How could she let him go?

Think of the child… A duke cannot have a mother who has sold her body… in a house of sin. I can give him a decent life, education, and protect him from this…

If she kept John, how would she hide what she'd become? How could she keep him safe here? What would happen when he was older? And it was true; where would she find the money for education?

She held him still, whispering into his ear. "Mama loves you. Mama loves you so much…"

But if she really loved him then she would do the best thing for him, and her father was right – the best thing for John was to let him go.

New tears flooding her eyes, she nodded at her father. She couldn't bring herself to say the word *yes*.

Hate burned in her heart, tearing at her soul, as the woman moved forward.

Unable to speak for the pain in her throat Ellen let the woman take John, and turned to accept the parchment from her father's hand. She took it to a small desk across the room, and found a quill and ink. Her father came and stood behind her as she signed her name. Mrs Eleanor Harding. She did not even remember who that woman was.

She blotted her signature and moved aside, leaving the quill in the inkwell for him. He signed the paper too. Then called the nursemaid forward to make her mark.

Ellen took John back, and balancing him at her waist, looked into his blue eyes. She brushed his hair back from his brow as his gaze met hers. "You are to be good," she whispered. "And you are to always remember how much I love you. I am not letting you go because I do not, but because I do…" Her quiet words stirred locks of his hair as her voice broke and she whispered to him. "You will grow up to be clever and wise, John."

His fingers lifted and touched her lips, then the tears on her cheeks. He did not understand.

She swallowed back more tears, though more still leaked from her eyes.

"Take the child." Her father barked.

The nursemaid moved closer. Ellen's heart broke, shattering into tiny pieces. She let the woman lift John from her arms, swearing to herself that this would not be the end; that one day she would have him back.

"You are at least still sensible," her father stated coldly.

She wished to slap him for his insensitivity, but she did not. This was merely another emotion to be buried deep and trapped somewhere it could never be let out again.

"That is resolved then."

Ellen's tears ran even more freely. Then she begged in a quiet voice. "Will you not take me with you too? I do not... I am afraid here..."

He only stared at her, with his cold inhuman look. Then he turned away. "Take the boy to the carriage."

He left the room after the nursemaid who carried John.

Ellen followed; walking through the hall and out into the street. "Let me hold him one last time?" Her voice was quiet but desperate.

He at least did not deny her, but waved a hand for the woman to allow it.

Ellen held John as tightly as it was possible to do, and smelt the sweet scent of his hair. Then her fingers ran over his face as he looked at her with large eyes, not understanding. "I will miss you. I love you."

"Mama..." was all he said as the nursemaid reached to take him back.

Her father did not even look at her as he climbed into the carriage after the maid, leaving Ellen standing alone in the street.

A footman closed the door, then climbed up onto the back of the coach.

The pain in her heart tore at her, unbearable and vicious. It was lacerating. The carriage pulled away. She'd thought when Paul had died, she'd felt as empty and heart sore as it was possible to feel, but now...

Her fingers clasping either elbow, she stood and watched until the carriage disappeared about the corner of the street. She swore to herself, "I will have you back, John, I will ensure you always know how much I love you, and I will have you back..."

Author Note

The truth in the story. The 52nd had been posted to America, after the end of The Peninsular War, and having spent the summer in Britain, sailed as far as Cork in January 1815. They were stranded there waiting for the weather to improve for weeks.

When word came that Napoleon had escaped Elba, they were ordered to Ostend and then to Brussels.

I was extremely surprised when I learned the sheer volume of men who fought in the battle of Waterloo, over two hundred thousand men took part and twelve thousand were killed.

As for the 52nd ...

They had been brought around to take the last of the French Imperial Guard, who were making a final surge on the Allied army. There was a fierce firefight, that only lasted for four minutes, but during that brief moment, right at the end of the battle, one hundred and fifty men from the 52nd (Oxfordshire) Regiment of Foot died.

We will remember them

*

To find out what happens to Ellen after this, read *The Illicit Love of a Courtesan* and turn over for a sneak peek at Chapter One...

The Illicit Love of a Courtesan

'Pure, unadulterated romance.' BestChickLit.com

'The romance pulls at the heartstrings.' 4.5* RT Book Reviews

'Romantic, sensual and heartbreaking.' bookworm2bookworm

Chapter One

Perfectly positioned to view one of the *ton*'s fairest sons, Ellen's eyes were drawn from Lord Gainsborough's playing cards to the man seated across the table—Lord Edward Marlow, the second born son of the tenth Earl of Barrington. He was newly in town and therefore a novelty, an enigma. Every mistress and courtesan in the room had been watching him all evening and she was no exception.

Lord Edward's long, manicured fingers moved, poising above his cards. Ellen openly stared, the low light in the room and its stale hazy air, thick with tobacco smoke, hiding her scrutiny from the watching crowd.

His hair was dark brown and gentle curls tumbled from his crown, licking his forehead and the high collar of his black, tailed evening coat, Brutus style. In the candlelight thrown by the chandelier above, his hair glistened with a variety of rich, roasted coffee bean shades.

His head lifted and she indulged her eyes with his severe yet perfect, profile. He exuded authority. The man was sleek strength and sophistication. The muscle of his jaw tight, his lips rose as if to smile, but hesitated as though some thought stopped him, and she saw doubt or indecision pass across his expression. Then his eyelids lifted and his dark, intense gaze clashed with hers, a pale blue, more like slate-grey.

Embarrassed and a little flustered, Ellen's appraisal fell to his hands.

His fingers teased out a card and threw it to the table while she felt his gaze burn into her.

Desire stirring, she pictured the pleasure those fingers could give a woman and the air in the room was suddenly hot and thick, despite the cool winter night outside.

Ellen lifted her open fan and fluttered it gently to cool her skin as her gaze drifted back to his face. He was still watching her. One dark eyebrow rose and his broad lips smiled. Her gaze hovering on his, she mirrored his smile, her heart pounding as though she was already coupling with him. She imagined his mouth on hers and a hot blush touched her skin. The sweeps of her fan increasing, her imagination drifted on towards indecency—impossibility—picturing tangled limbs and warm flesh.

Light caught the jet-black pools in his eyes, as though he saw the pictures forming in her thoughts and his captivating smile twisted with implied agreement. It turned his features from handsome to utterly devastating.

A hot flush spread like a caress down her throat to her breasts and lower, racing across her skin.

"I shall raise you a hundred, Marlow. Will you match me?" Lord Gainsborough's brusque challenge sliced through the silent communication she shared with Lord Edward.

His gaze tore away, his blank expression cutting her, apparently dismissing their flirtation. Instead it focused upon Lord Gainsborough.

Ellen stood behind Lord Gainsborough and slightly to his side, in her protector's shadow, oppressed. Oppression was Lord Gainsborough's pleasure and Lord Gainsborough's pleasure was her life. Her gaze fell to the seam at the centre of the back of his black evening coat. The pressure of his bloated body strained it. Excess was another of his passions.

235

Revulsion stirred. She despised the man—her protector. Yet preference was irrelevant. She was tied to him, trapped by him. He had blackmailed her into obedience five years ago and now here she stood, her soul and conscience dead while her body lived on, fulfilling his dissolute desires. She was empty, a vessel, deaf to the voice of morality and blind to shame.

Laughter hovered behind her closed lips, ringing in her thoughts, a sound of silent madness.

Lord Gainsborough liked flaunting his pretty vessel—his precious trophy. Sometimes he let others touch, taunting them with what they couldn't have. Wickedly she wondered how he would react if she let someone of Lord Edward's ilk touch her. He'd be furious.

Hiding her self-deprecating smile behind her fan, Ellen glanced over its top at the gorgeous man across the table. Was it very wrong for her sinful body to want a man like that? How would it feel? How would it feel to be free from her so-called protector for an hour or two and play his games with a man of her choice? Choice was a holy grail; a cup fallen woman longed to drink from. And she would love defying Lord Gainsborough.

As though pulled by an invisible cord winding between them, Lord Edward's gaze lifted to her while he contemplated Lord Gainsborough's call. His eyes widened, darkening, perhaps reading hers, and what appeared to be amusement twitched his lips before he looked back at his cards.

Ellen snapped her fan shut and lowered it to her waist, turning her attention to the game. Only Lord Gainsborough and the younger Lord Edward were left in play. The others sitting about the table simply watched, and behind them stood a crowd three deep. The dense ring of silent observers were men in the formal black evening dress Brummell had made popular, with the occasional female, mistress or courtesan, draped upon their arms. They were men enjoying the hedonistic lifestyle of the sleazy gentlemen's club, or gaming-hell as it was more commonly known. Gaming-hells, like this one, provided the thrill these men craved from high stakes games, with women and wine to increase the rush.

For Gainsborough, she knew this place fuelled something else—his desire to be envied. He brought her here to show her off. Lord Gainsborough wore her as women wore their jewels. She was an adornment—his precious, beautiful, trophy. He'd not even dislike Lord Edward's attention—he'd relish it. Yet if Gainsborough knew she was enticing Lord Edward, she would pay a price.

"I will meet your hundred, Gainsborough, and raise you ten."

"Are you sure you have it, boy?" Lord Gainsborough's tone rang with condescension, ridiculing Lord Edward. It fell flat. Lord Edward was younger, but he was in his prime. She would place him at his peak, mid-twenties at the least.

Receiving no answer, shifting in his seat, her protector pulled at the cuffs of his evening coat, while the eyes of their crowd turned to Lord Edward.

"Now your brother is back, Marlow, surely you have lost your portion. Should I request security for your funds?"

That barb seemed to hit a mark. Suddenly leaning back in his chair, Lord Edward's eyes narrowed, his nonchalant air shattering as anger flashed in their blue-black depths. For all his beauty and youth he lacked nothing in masculine strength. Ellen sensed ruthlessness in the look he threw back at Lord Gainsborough.

"Play the game, Gainsborough. I've no desire for conversation."

"But you are able to honour your debts? I need not wait for you to tug your brother's purse strings for payment?"

Ellen watched Lord Edward's grip tighten on his cards while his other hand reached for his glass. A slowly indrawn breath and he appeared back in control.

Everyone had heard the talk. He'd been running his brother's estates since the age of eighteen, while his brother, the eleventh Earl, wasted both time and money abroad. Now his brother was back, potentially to bleed dry the estates which were prospering under Lord Edward's careful hand.

Lord Edward had arrived in London a week ago, angry and bitter, from the reports of the gossipmongers in the *ton*, and his behaviour this evening certainly concurred with the tale. His mask of serenity had slipped, revealing the man beneath the façade. He appeared out of sorts with the world, playing hard and deep, drinking heavily—and this from a man known for his dislike of vice.

His gaze lifted, meeting hers, anger and mockery in the look, as once more he caught her contemplating him. The determination in his eyes seemed to challenge her to speak. To what, agree with Gainsborough? Does he think I would condemn him? I am in no place to cast judgement.

Again his gaze ripped away from hers. "I have enough of my own blunt, Gainsborough," he said, looking at his cards. "I have no need to beg from my brother."

The nuance in his voice made her feel as though the words were said for her.

"I'm glad to hear it. Then I will raise you another two hundred guineas."

Lord Edward's narrowed eyes lifted suddenly to look at her protector.

He didn't have it, she was certain of that. He could not afford the stakes but would stupidly bury himself in debt because of some bizarre falling out with his brother, or stubborn male pride.

Unwilling to play audience to his downfall, she lowered her gaze and saw Lord Gainsborough's cards had changed. The ten had become an ace, and the eight exchanged with a king. Disgust twisted Ellen's stomach. Gainsborough would win by deceit and Lord Edward would be neatly leashed with the debt a whip in Lord Gainsborough's hand. Her protector had no decent, honest bones in his body. He manipulated people. That was Gainsborough's art; he used, broke and discarded people like puppets. She prayed daily he would cut her strings and cast her off—set her free—even though she had nowhere else to go. But he never seemed to tire of the power she gave him. Yet she need not watch him secure another victim in his sadistic sway.

Her heart pumping hard, looking up, she found Lord Edward's eyes on her again. An odd feeling assailed her, a sense that he saw into her thoughts. His assessment was no longer admiring, nor mocking or angry, instead his gaze intently studied hers, searching for something.

She darted her gaze down and up, trying to direct his attention to Lord Gainsborough's cards with her eyes while simultaneously flicking open her fan and then fluttering it beneath her chin to distract attention from their silent communication.

Lord Edward's brow furrowed. She could see he didn't understand.

Widening her eyes, she once again looked to Lord Gainsborough's cards, then snapped her fan shut and tapped the tip against the long sleeve of her satin glove.

Smiling, or rather smirking, Lord Edward looked down at his cards.

Ellen glanced about their audience but she saw no one watching her.

"I will meet your stake, Gainsborough, and double it to see your hand. Show me your cards." With that Lord Edward tossed two jacks and two eights onto the green felt and then Lord Gainsborough laid a royal flush down in opposition to the pairs. Lord Gainsborough's hand won. An exclamation rang from the gathered crowd, voicing congratulations for Gainsborough. Then comments of consolation followed, as Lord Edward's shoulder was slapped.

Ellen held her breath, her gaze fixed on the table, her heart pounding. She was too afraid to look up in case Lord Gainsborough identified her collusion when, if, the accusation came.

It did. "You are a damned cheat, Gainsborough! Take off your coat!" From Lord Edward's voice she could tell he was standing, facing them across the table.

239

Ellen stepped back as Lord Gainsborough rose, his bulk lifting from the chair. He was old enough to be her father and looked older still after years of debauchery, broken veins marring his fallen cheeks and bulbous nose. But despite his age and weight he could still move quickly when he wished. Tonight he did not wish, he stood slowly, making no effort to do Lord Edward's bidding.

"Don't be ridiculous, boy. I am a Viscount. I have no need to cheat." Gainsborough's voice welled with ridicule. He knew this game. Act the aggrieved. Turn the accusation back upon the accuser. Be above reproach, and you are. She had watched him play it numerous times.

"Yet still, I ask you to remove your coat, my Lord, and prove your innocence, if it is so." Lord Edward's eyes searched their audience then and settled on a man similar to him in age. "Find Madam, have her bring her brutes and we will sort this out." The other man instantly disappeared obeying the request.

"You are talking nonsense, Marlow. I refuse to be challenged like some damned guttersnipe! Come, my dear, we're leaving." Painfully gripping Ellen's arm Lord Gainsborough turned her away. "My man of business will contact you, Marlow. Then you will settle your debt." As Gainsborough thrust the words sideward over his shoulder, his grip steered her into the parting crowd.

"You played me false, Gainsborough! You'll wait until it's proven!" Lord Edward's voice resonated throughout the room, a barked order carrying no deference for Lord Gainsborough's seniority in age and status.

Irate voices rose, supporting Lord Edward, "Yes, Gainsborough!"

"Take off your coat!"

"Prove it!"

The crowd grew, closing the avenue before Ellen. Lord Gainsborough's hand fell from her arm as he turned back. She knew he was starting to realise he was not going to win so easily this time.

A swell of satisfaction stirred in Ellen's chest. Revenge would be another sin to add to her list of many, but it tasted sweet, even if the victory was minor and he'd no knowledge of her part.

The crowd about them parted again for the gaming-hell's tall, slender, aged and highly painted female proprietor to forge a path towards them. Ellen was aware of two of Madam's burly doormen moving behind her.

"Lord Gainsborough? What is this accusation? My house is honest. Please, if you have done nothing wrong, you shall not mind removing your coat."

Gainsborough took a breath and then snorted, scoffing at the crowd, apparently casting them all fools. But he was cornered, he could do nothing but concede.

Slipping the buttons of his double-breasted evening coat free, he looked at Ellen, growling, "Woman, help me!" before turning his back to her and holding out one arm. "Tug the sleeve loose." He threw her a warning look over his shoulder as he spoke. She understood it exactly. He expected her to hide the cards.

Afraid. Her heart thumped. Gripping his cuff in fingers and thumb, Ellen felt the cards hidden within his sleeve, but she refused to help him. She loosened his cuff from his hand then let go and lifted hers to ease the coat from his shoulders. The cards fell to the floor and she gasped to make it appear accidental, but the sound was lost amidst the outburst of the watching crowd. They shouted in shock and disgust, a burst of masculine irritation.

This would cost her. Their battlefield had revised and her involvement was too visible, but she was not letting Lord Gainsborough crush her first assault.

Gainsborough's anger and accusation struck her as he looked back, and she stepped back, afraid he would strike her physically, her heart pulsing as panic turned her stomach to ice.

"As I told you," The statement of vindication turned Gainsborough's attention to Lord Edward, "the winnings are mine, Gainsborough. The question is what should I request in compensation for not handing you to a magistrate?" Lord Edward's steel like gaze passed from Lord Gainsborough to her and a wicked smile played on his lips. Her heart missed a beat. What was he doing?

His gaze passed back to Lord Gainsborough. "Give me the woman in consolation."

"For an hour, no more," Lord Gainsborough barked.

Ellen blushed. They were bartering over her as they would over horseflesh. Another piece of her died. Men had taken her self-respect as well as her body. They were arguing over the vessel, not her, not the living, breathing, feeling woman within it.

"Two hours and you may keep your stake beyond what is on the table."

Ellen opened her mouth to protest and closed it again. What good would it do? They did not care for her. Her eyelids falling over the moisture in her eyes, she drew a breath. She'd helped Lord Edward—he was hurting her. The cost of her involvement had just tripled.

"You agree?" Lord Edward prompted.

"I agree," Lord Gainsborough snarled.

Because there was no other choice, Ellen thought, not willingly. Her manipulator had met his match, and she'd given Lord Edward the means to make this manoeuvre. Even her satisfaction in seeing Lord Gainsborough beaten at his own game was hollow. It was earned at her expense. She was a fool.

"Madam, we need a room," Lord Edward ordered, soiling the images Ellen had appreciated earlier. This is hell, not heaven. I want choice not coercion.

The air escaped her lungs and Ellen opened her eyes.

He stood barely a foot away, facing her, watching her intently.

He was taller than he'd seemed when seated, a good seven to ten inches taller than her. He towered over her. His appearance was no longer impressive, but imposing.

She'd thought him authoritative before, now she knew him to be overwhelmingly commanding. Fear grasped her more tightly.

"Please follow me, Lord Edward." Madam Marietta beckoned

with her fingers.

Without speaking, he lifted his arm, a look of steel daring her to refuse to accept it. Compelled by his will alone, Ellen laid her fingers on his coat sleeve. The gentle weight of his other hand covered them, as though fearing she would run he urged her to stay. The impression it conjured up in her head was a knight in shining armour, like the heroes in the fairy tales she'd read as a girl.

But this was no act of chivalry.

He was no saviour of a lady's virtue.

He had just bartered with another man for the use of her body! He was no rescuer come to release her from Gainsborough's evil grip. I should not long to lean on his strength.

Yet, the strength beneath her fingers and the assurance implied in the hand resting on her own sent warmth running into her blood. It suggested security—constancy. Like the scent of fresh bread stirring hunger, his touch set alive silly speculating notions in her head—dreams—desires for a happy-ever-after that could never be.

Silent, Ellen found herself guided in Madam's wake. She knew instinctively all eyes were on her back and she felt Lord Gainsborough's burn between her shoulder-blades, imagining them narrow with anger and calculating revenge. Her courage failing her, Lord Edward's aura of undaunted power kept her walking as they crossed two rooms in which Madam's customers played at tables. The attention they drew apparently did not disturb him. But when they reached the hall as if sensing her fear, his arm fell away from beneath her hand and instead his fingers gently but firmly gripped hers.

"I would rather not go upstairs, Madam. Have you a private parlour we could use down here?" While he spoke his fingers squeezed Ellen's, as though offering the comfort and reassurance her spirit craved.

The temperate strength gripping her hand unsettled her, setting speculation whispering through her head again. He is not my rescuer.

Marietta hesitated, looked aloft, and then clearly thinking quickly, she held forth a hand encouraging them to follow her around the foot of the stairs and along a narrow hallway. There she opened a door. "This is my own sitting-room. No one will disturb you here, my Lord. Is there anything I may bring you?"

When they entered the room, Lord Edward let Ellen's fingers go and she took the opportunity to move away.

Crossing the room, she trailed her satin clad fingers over the chair-backs as she passed them until she reached the far side.

"A decanter of port and two glasses, Madam, nothing else…" Ellen looked back, answering his pause and met his gaze. "Unless you are hungry or have another preference?"

She shook her head before finding her voice. "No, my Lord, thank you, I am in need of nothing." *What a lie, I am in need of everything.*

She turned away and ran her fingers over a polished mahogany writing desk which stood against the wall. The room was different to the public areas. It was decorated in tasteful greens not the gaudy gold and reds which adorned the gambling rooms, and, she also knew, dressed the bedchambers above. There were two winged armchairs and a chaise-lounge, all upholstered in moss green velvet which matched the closed curtains. In the grate at the centre of the hearth, a low fire burned and on the floor before it a Persian rug covered the boards. The walls were dressed with painted patterns of green ivy.

The door clicked shut. Ellen turned back swiftly and her fingers gripped the rim of the desk behind her as her gaze reached across the room to meet Lord Edward's again. Marietta had gone and he stood watching Ellen, assessing her as he'd done in the card room while she'd watched him. Then he held out his hand reminding her of a man approaching a nervous colt. Did he not realise she was used to being payment in kind? He need hardly fear she wouldn't give him what he wanted, she was no debutante. *I am a thrice damned courtesan.* There was no need for courtship or kind words. She knew what he wanted. He didn't even have to ask.

His mouth suddenly lifted to a smile, tilting at one side. "Why did you tell me?"

It took her a moment to register that he spoke of Gainsborough's little trick. Why did she? Because she'd seen something in his eyes she'd warmed to, or just because he was handsome and she was drawn by his looks, or possibly only because it gave her opportunity to rebel? It could be any of those things, but she knew herself too well. The person she'd once been, the stranger surviving deep inside her heart of ice, couldn't see another human being brought down to her level. He hadn't had the money. She couldn't see him trapped, even if he was a man.

Her misguided generosity had led her here. She was trapped. Caught in the hands of another man who'd sate his lust for her body—the woman within it was irrelevant. He wanted to use it but he'd use her too.

Her eyes caught her reflection in the mirror hanging above the fireplace at his back. Her beauty was incomparable. She was not blind to it. She'd been told it dozens of times. It lay in the starkly pale blue of her eyes, the dark sweep of ebony hair across porcelain coloured skin. God had made her perfect in face and figure. The look of a Goddess, her husband, Paul, had once said. Then compliments had pleased her. Now beauty cursed her.

A sound escaped his throat, drawing her attention back to him. She didn't know if it was a prompt, but she responded anyway. "It was obvious you could not afford the stake, my Lord. I am surprised you took the bet."

He dismissed her words with a wave of his hand as a tap sounded on the door. "Enter!" His voice carried considerable confidence for a man she'd classified no greater in age than his mid-twenties, but then he'd probably lived his whole life with the proverbial silver spoon in his mouth.

"Put it there." He pointed to a small table as a footman brought in a tray bearing the decanter and glasses he'd ordered.

"Thank you."

The words of gratitude surprised her as the servant left and closed the door.

Lord Edward's gaze crossed to her again. "You will take a drink?"

She nodded. She'd need the fortitude that strong liquor brought to see this through.

Turning away, he answered her earlier statement, "I'm not in such dire straits as rumour would have it. I care not if I win or lose, as proven by my letting your friend keep his money." His shoulders lifted in a shrug as he spoke, before pouring the port from the decanter.

When he faced her again he had a glass in each hand and, walking towards her, he held one out.

She took it, looking at the ruby coloured liquid. "Then why play, my Lord?"

"Because I find myself at a loose end. I need diversion. Please, sit, Miss... What is your name?"

He asked as though he'd only just realised he didn't know it.

"Ellen, Lord Edward." Her voice sounded cold even to her, and formal.

"Sit then, Ellen. Let us get to know one another."

Perching on the edge of an armchair she felt like a mouse before a cat, waiting for the moment he would pounce.

He sat in the chair facing her and leaned back, his legs splayed slightly, drawing her attention to the physical strength in his muscular thighs.

The instinctive awareness which had ailed her earlier returned. She was attracted to him, despite all else. The room suddenly felt hot, she looked up blushingly to meet his gaze. The light in his eyes implied he saw her susceptibility, but he did not speak of it. "Your age, Ellen?"

"Women do not speak of their age, my Lord," she snapped, angered by his ability to move her and apparently remain unmoved.

He smiled, a heart stopping expression. It set hers skipping against her ribs.

Am I really so shallow I will simply succumb to his looks?

"I am four and twenty, if it makes you feel better to know my own," he answered, his tone relaxed. "There, it's not so hard to say one's age."

"I cannot see why you care to know it." She could remove a year, two, even claim to be younger than him, she could pass for three and twenty, but she was unwilling to lie. Her life had been so full of sin, adding another lie, no matter how small, felt suddenly intolerable.

He said nothing, waiting for her reply.

"I am eight and twenty, my Lord. Older than yourself, and now you have embarrassed me."

"It matters not. We are adults, Ellen, age makes little difference."

"Then why ask?" she bit back, annoyed by his languorous tone. He disturbed her, she felt hot and uncomfortable, afraid—yet not afraid. Her heart thumped; a hammer ringing upon an anvil in her ears.

"Because I cannot understand what you are doing with a man like Gainsborough. He must be twice your age. You cannot persuade me it is his looks or character which draw you."

Spurred, anger flashed through her. Who was he to judge her? He'd bartered over her body. How could he accuse her of poor choice? Surely it was obvious why she was with Lord Gainsborough; she had no choice. But she would not admit it. Not to him or anyone. She would not face that humiliation. Instead she played the part of a woman who chose to be a man's chattel.

"Because he was the highest bidder, my Lord, what other reason would you think?" Deliberately she edged her voice with a sultry cutting pitch. The role of harlot was now instinctive. She would act it for Gainsborough too once this was done, to placate his damaged pride.

"Are you telling me I cannot afford you, Ellen?" He was amused by her; she heard it in his voice. She imagined him laughing at her, inwardly.

Lord, the self-confidence of the man was infuriating.

"Your words, my Lord." She took a sip of port from the glass in her hand.

"Yes, my words." he repeated, his pitch sobering. He drained his glass, set it aside and stood. "But I do not need to pay, do I, Ellen?"

A dart of longing pain stretched through her core, confirming his words. No man had stirred this reaction in her since Paul. He was right. Her body craved his.

"Come." He stepped towards her and leaned down. Mesmerised by him, she watched his movement, while uncertainty and fear warred with attraction.

His long, beautiful fingers wrapped about the bowl of her glass and lifted it from her hand.

Unwilling to look up, unable to meet his gaze, she heard the click of the base as it was placed on the table.

His fingers then closed around hers and encouraged her to her feet.

She was silent as he lifted the string of her fan from her wrist, stripped off her gloves and put them down beside her half empty glass of port. Then he moved closer and one hand pressed against the small of her back while the other curved beneath her chin, lifting her face.

"Ellen?"

She met his gaze, hearing a question and a statement in that single utterance of her name and somehow knew he wouldn't force her, as others had done before. He was asking permission and offering admiration, she saw it in his eyes.

"You have such beauty. I swear I've never seen the like." His gaze holding hers, his curled fingers trailed upwards, the tender, gentle touch following the line of her jaw and sweeping up across her brow, before brushing down her nose. Then his thumb rested on her mouth, running over her lips.

"Do you wish for this too?" he whispered.

There was no need to ask what he meant, her body sang with longing for his, her skin was already hot and sensitised by the flush of desire. The pressure of his palm at her back pulled her lower body hip to hip with his, making the level of his arousal blatant as the outline of his erection pressed against her stomach.

He'd said he wanted diversion.

She needed him for release. If only for an hour or two, she could escape.

Her lips brushing the pad of his thumb, she formed the single word of agreement, surrender, her arms lifting to his shoulders. "Yes." No, for the first time since Paul, this was not surrender, this was choice.

The rhythm of her heartbeat lurched to an even greater pace, her gaze locked with his, captured by the invisible link she felt woven taut between them.

His hands fell, resting on her hips in a gentle brace, just for a moment.

His touch was like an expression of awe, not domination. His hands skimmed upwards across her ribs and then reaching the soft flesh of her breasts, his palms and fingers clenched her through the thin material of her gown. Time stopped, suddenly suspended as his gaze dropped to her lips and he lowered his head.

When their lips met, the rush of desire through her veins was overwhelming. Instinctively her fingers slipped upwards delving into his soft hair, clasping it. His tongue slid into her mouth and he tasted delicious. He drugged her senses, taking her away somewhere else, somewhere outside of her sordid, soiled self. His crooked thumb dipped into the low neck of her gown and brushed across her breast, stroking her casually as his mouth ravished hers. A pleasant spasm ran from her breast, spiralling down through her body to her stomach and into her womb. Her body already ached for fulfilment.

Feeling brazen to the core and every bit the wanton whore life had made her, her tongue passed across his lips, into the warmth of his mouth and her fingers fell to his shoulders, splaying and running downwards. They slid over the taut muscles beneath his evening clothes, revelling in his athletic physique and descended to his breeches.

An erotic, pain filled sound resonated from his chest and reached her mouth as heat. But abruptly his fingers left her breast, grasped her hand and removed it as he broke their kiss. Yet his eyes were still dark with longing as they met hers. She knew her look mirrored his.

The timbre of his voice thick with desire, he said, "I would like that, Ellen, but it is not what I want tonight, not yet. Let me lead. I want to see you gain your pleasure first."

He wished to give her pleasure? The ice about her heart cracked and warmth seeped into her blood. This was more than lust, much more, it was longing beyond a physical need. She'd given herself to men for years, she knew what pleased them. None of them had cared for what pleased her. Pleasure during sex—was it still possible? If it had been like that with Paul, she'd forgotten.

His head bowed and his lips brushed her neck while his gentle fingers slipped the straps of her gown from her shoulders then followed the neckline of her dress, slackening the material and drawing it down. With his head lowered his hair caressed her skin as his fingers lifted her breasts free, then one taut peak was absorbed in the warmth of his mouth. It sent a tremor across her skin and pain and pleasure reaching inside her.

He did not just want her body, he wanted her soul. It had only ever been Paul's. But with Edward Marlow she wasn't sure she could keep it safe. When Gainsborough touched her—when she touched him—she detached her mind. He took her body, but only her body. This man would claim everything.

He lifted away from her again and began plucking pins from her hair, watching the dark curls fall to her naked shoulders and over her breasts.

"If someone comes in?" Ellen heard her breathless words.

"No one will." His voice was deep. He sounded as lost in lust as her. His hands rested on her shoulders and turned her to reach the back fastenings of her dress. The small ivory buttons slipped free one by one, and he kissed her exposed skin.

"You're so beautiful." The whisper brushed her neck as her dress fell in to a pool at her feet. Then his fingers swept her hair across her shoulders before tugging at the lacing of her light corset.

When her corset fell away too, he began stripping off her chemise, lifting it over her head and baring her breasts before throwing it aside. Then his hands reached about her and gripped together, drawing her back against him as he kissed her neck.

"You are nature's finest art."

Her head tilted back, savouring his caresses and his hand slid down over her stomach and then slipped under her cotton underwear. No one had ever caressed her with such tenderness. She ached for him—he made her feel—every nerve in her body was humming for his touch—it was a rising floodtide inside her. It was torment, unbearable. It stole her awareness of everything but him. She wanted to cry out, to protest and scream. She did not. He did not stop. Oh, she was afraid of it, of this unfamiliar feeling.

There was an explosion of pleasure. It rushed through her blood, a flood, racing, ripping her apart, an unearthed power she hadn't known existed tearing into her limbs and leaving them weak. She felt him take her weight as she nearly fell and her fingers gripped his forearms. His lips brushed the skin behind her ear and he did not cease.

"Not again, please." Her words were breathless. She was afraid of the torrent that might flow now the dam was breached, afraid of losing control. He was still a stranger. It was too hard to trust.

His answer was to turn her and kiss her. She willingly returned it, her hands gripping fists full of his hair, as the tide of his passion swept her away again and he leaned her back a little so the chair's seat pressed against her calves until she fell back. She knew it was

251

by design when he knelt before her and smiled and then his gaze dropped and he began loosening the ribbon securing her drawers. He slid them off, leaving her naked—exposed—while he was still fully clothed.

His warm breath brushed her breast. His eyes were glazed and his pupils wide dark onyx pools as his gaze swept over her body.

Awareness of the room, of him, refilled her. "This is not fair." She hesitated, unfamiliar with desire. "I want to touch you."

Amusement and compliance shining in his eyes, he released the knot of his cravat while she pushed his coat from his shoulders.

Once he was stripped of neckcloth, coat and waistcoat, she tugged his shirt from his waistband and lifted it off over his head before throwing it aside. Then she reached for the buttons of his breeches but his hands stopped her.

"Not yet."

Why? What else could come?

Lean muscular contours rippled across his torso, shadowed by a dusting of dark hair across his chest which narrowed to a line delving into his waistband. Instinctively she licked her lips, only to be disturbed from her admiration by a sound of humour in the back of his throat.

"Careful, you'll make me think you've not known pleasure like this." His voice was low and husky, laden with lust and unexpected humour.

His hands gripped her hips and drew them forward, tumbling her backwards, and his head bent to kiss her stomach. Her muscle tightened, caught by surprise, but she was equally overwhelmed by a feeling of tenderness—care. It pierced her disordered thoughts. It was in his touch. She knew if she asked him to stop, even now, he would.

Moisture rushed into her eyes. This man is kind and gentle. Longing swelled inside her, body and soul. Desire and hope.

But he is not my rescuer. She had to push the thought away and shield herself behind denial. Her heart could not be involved in this. It was a physical hunger. He knows the art of sex better than other men I've known, that is all.

His fingers slid down her thighs and up again. "Relax, Ellen," he whispered, looking up and smiling.

She closed her eyes, took a breath and tried to, but she felt so nervous and uncertain. When his lips touched her, her fingernails dug into his flesh.

She'd thought herself incapable of embarrassment after a lifetime of humiliation, yet this intimate caress made her blush. No one else, not even Paul, had kissed her there.

She clung to him, hanging on as he urged her back into the pool of sensual delight. He knew more than Paul had done, Paul had made her happy, but never like this.

This time when the flood swelled, smashing aside her sanity, Edward did not let her escape but pushed her over another wave. It was then he freed the buttons of his breeches and filled her.

An exclamation of satisfaction left her lips.

His slate-blue-eyes looked into hers and his closed lips smiled as he pressed into her again. He smiled more and she gripped the arms of the chair.

Well, she had wanted escape. He was certainly giving her that.

The sweet sensations transported her beyond the room, body and soul, and she clung to him, watching him through a haze of lust.

He was so beautiful, hard, masculine, yet gentle.

She loved this man, she had known him only moments but still she knew she loved him. He'd possessed her body and her heart.

He released her hips and held her hands, weaving their fingers together.

How could this? How could anyone stand such..? Light exploded within her.

The man was a God, an athlete, his strength, his stamina, his gallantry all spoke of it. There was no doubt.

"You are…" She stopped, hardly knowing what she said, and

then her fingernails digging into his flesh she fell over the edge of reality into an abyss of sensation far below.

A virile cry escaped his throat, erupting from deep in his chest and he hastily withdrew.

When she felt the warmth on her stomach, she was plummeted back to reality and felt cheated, insulted. She was still a whore whom he would not want to bear his child. He was no hero, just another man. For a moment she hated him, even though he'd only really shown forethought and kindness. He'd reduced the possibility of a child. What good would a bastard child bring? No good, except a memory of this one night of release and him.

Ellen felt cold, thrown from a warm hearth in to snow, soiled again, naïve and foolish. She'd given herself completely, crying out. Anyone in the hall outside might have heard her. She hadn't just let him use her, she'd let him pluck and strum her sensual strings. He had played her like an instrument for his amusement. She'd spent years under the influence of men and still she had not learnt this lesson. Men took. He simply had a greater skill and different tastes.

Yet the delicious feelings he'd stirred up inside her still ran through her blood, overwhelming her tangled senses. Without looking at him, she accepted the handkerchief he pulled from his coat and held towards her. Then she wiped her stomach, expecting him to reach for his clothes and make himself ready to leave. Instead he did something which surprised her. He handed over her glass.

"Drink, it will steady your nerves."

She sipped the ruby liquid and as its warmth slid down her throat, she dared herself, lifted her gaze and looked at him.

His fingers slotted the buttons of his breeches into place and then he bent over and picked up her undergarments. Seeing her watching, he smiled. There was no hint in it that he intended to simply walk away, no rake's art, nor aversion. He looked embarrassed too. She could see his pulse flickering at the base of his throat.

Drinking down the remainder of the port in one swallow, she waited. She wanted a word from him, an acknowledgement, something. Something to confirm his life had been changed by this, by their private interlude. She wanted it to not be her imagination.

But what could change?

Nothing.

He did not have the money to free her from Gainsborough.

She could not escape.

Just because he was beautiful and gentle and she'd engaged her heart in this, it did not mean he returned her feelings. The man was in his physical prime, he could have any woman he wanted. *It doesn't make him my hero.*

She had to stop this ridiculous hope from rising to lessen the pain when he walked away.

Her stubborn heart clenched in her chest. He'd been kind. He was being kind now.

How pathetic she'd become, craving so much for kindness she would love a man after little more than an hour, simply because he'd thrown her crumbs of it.

She accepted her undergarments from his hand and rose, pulling them on while he donned his shirt and tucked it in.

"My corset?" She couldn't tie it alone with the lacing at her back. "Would you send for Madam?"

"I'll lace it." He smiled, a masculine blush darkening the skin across the bones of his cheeks and took the garment from her hand. She turned.

Her fingers pressing it to her ribs, his threaded the laces at her back.

The gentle tug as he worked each lace, the pressure of her corset as he pulled it tight, the brush of his fingers as he tied it off—sent warmth racing through the heightened senses of her skin.

Daft, foolish woman to make so much of this. His skill with the lacing of a corset was testament to the level of his past experience.

He bent and picked up her dress. "Lift your arms, Ellen." And so, she was dressed.

While his fingers worked the tiny buttons at her back into place, her senses reeled and her head told her heart over and over again, this was no more than sex.

When he returned to the task of his own attire he faced the mirror to retie his neckcloth.

Ellen blushed, remembering those fingers, now adeptly crafting a fashionable knot, playing master to her body's whim moments before.

He smiled at her in the mirror.

She caught sight of her disordered hair and her heart kicked in fear.

Panic locking the air in her lungs, she knelt and began picking up her scattered hairpins. She couldn't leave the room looking like this.

In a moment he was on one knee beside her, helping her. He must have sensed her concern for he caught one of her hands and held it still. "There's no need to worry, Ellen."

For you perhaps, but not for me, for me there is every need. She pulled her hand free and continued the task, but tried to make light of her fear. "Not if you can dress a woman's hair."

"I can make a fair go of it." His voice was jovial in response.

All pins recovered, they rose, her eyes meeting his. She took a breath. "Then do your best, my Lord, please."

His hand cupped hers and looking down he tipped the pins she held into his other palm. She shivered, remembering his touch; the things he'd done. In answer his eyes lifted, and she saw an unspoken question visible, pondering her skittish start.

"Edward, at least, Ellen," he admonished while one hand pressed her shoulder, turning her to the mirror. She looked at his reflection as he took a single lock of ebony hair in his fingers. Then, their sixth sense speaking, his gaze met hers in the glass. He smiled before looking away and concentrating on the task.

256

His touch was soothing, light and tender. Her body bathed in it, like rain on dry ground, her heart soaking it up.

When the job was finished their gazes collided in the mirror once more, desire burning clearly, like fire, in his. But the echo of it was in hers as she looked at her reflection too. "When can we meet, Ellen?" The question was whispered.

She shook her head in denial then tore her gaze from his, turning to retrieve her discarded fan and gloves. There could be no repetition. Gainsborough would not allow it.

Lord Edward will not help me. He cannot.

His grip caught her elbow and turned her back. "Do not deny me."

Stiffening her spine, Ellen lifted her chin. *I have to.*

As though he sensed the change in her, his hand slipped away before she spoke.

"My Lord, there can be nothing more, I thought that was clear."

Such cold, unemotional words. She set her face and eyes to match them, locking him out of her heart.

Did she imagine the sudden look of pain in his eyes? This was just sex for him, surely. He felt nothing. He would walk away unchanged. My heart is wounded. Not his. She couldn't escape Gainsborough. Dreams were not reality. Succumbing to Edward tonight had been enough risk. She did not dare repeat it. But she did not want him to know fear held her back. Nor did she wish him to pity her. "Your agreement was with Lord Gainsborough. I am his, not yours, my Lord, Edward."

The look in his eyes hardening, it was not pity she saw but disgust.

"I must go."

He moved, forming a wall between her and the door.

She met his gaze and waited, without answering the accusations lying there. This was who she was. He'd known that. He could not change it, and he could hardly judge her.

His lips a tight line, he bowed his head and stepped aside. But before she had time to reach for the doorknob his fingers caught hers.

"Tell me your full name? At least tell me that." His deep pitch was so full of emotion the ice she'd begun re-laying about her heart cracked, flooding her body with warmth. Warmth she longed to hold on to.

"Ellen Harding." Her married name, but even that she did not normally reveal.

Withdrawing her fingers from his, she made a final plea. "Please, do not acknowledge me again if I see you, my Lord. There can be no communication beyond tonight." But something dreadful pierced her chest as she spoke, and perhaps it showed in her eyes because his lips fell to hers, the kiss deep and fulfilling, belittling her denial. And she knew he knew it, but she could not unsay those words, she had no choice but to walk away. *He cannot save me, no one can. I'm already lost.*

Setting her palms on his chest she pushed him away, turned from his grip and grasped the doorknob, refusing to look back.

Masculine conversation spilled from the adjoining rooms and filled the high ceilinged space as she crossed the hall, broken by the occasional trill of a woman's laughter rising above the lower tones. She kept walking, ignoring the sound of a door slamming behind her, and the heavy tread of quick masculine strides hitting the floorboards.

Crossing into the first room she saw Lord Gainsborough seated at another card table by the far wall. He was waiting, watching. He rose. The men about him turned to follow his look, rising too. Her heart racing she took the few steps to where he stood.

Ribald jests and jeers greeted her from the male audience who were oblivious to the reality of his little welcome scene.

Refusing to cower she met Lord Gainsborough's glare of accusation.

She'd angered him, yes, but she could see he was equally enthralled to think another man had taken her but yards from where he sat. She knew his sadistic lusts must have thrilled at it, while his need for control revolted.

A round of laughter rang from another room. The men about them turned back to their game. Gainsborough's hand lifted.

As she heard the front door slam shut she felt the first strike across her face. The world about her tilted, time shifting to a slower pace as her vision hazed.

"Good God, Gainsborough, no need for that!"

"My God, man!"

A dozen calls of outrage echoed in her head. Reaching out blindly to stop her fall, she felt Lord Gainsborough's painful grip catch her and haul her back, holding firm.

"Mind your own damn business!" his bellow rang. "Out of my way!